W0114002

the Fangirl Project

ALSO BY BETH REEKLES

BETH REEKLES

the Fangirl Project

Delacorte Romance

Delacorte Romance
An imprint of Random House Children's Books
A division of Penguin Random House LLC
1745 Broadway, New York, NY 10019
penguinrandomhouse.com
GetUnderlined.com

Text copyright © 2025 by Beth Reeks
Cover art copyright © 2025 by Art of Nora
Greek geometric border by Omeris/stock.adobe.com, scribble by babayuka/stock.adobe.com,
checkmark by alex83m/stock.adobe.com, drawn hearts by Kebon doodle/stock.adobe
.com, cross out by Yanka/stock.adobe.com, paper texture by weedezign/stock.adobe
.com, dragon doodle by kronalux/stock.adobe.com, Scottish castle doodles by Mutiah
/stock.adobe.com, book doodles by setory/stock.adobe.com, tree doodles by veekicl/stock
.adobe.com, hand-drawn beetle by Ekaterina/stock.adobe.com, deer skull doodle by
Limolida Studio/stock.adobe.com, sword and knight doodle by kronalux/stock.adobe
.com, sketched knight armor by fafarumba/stock.adobe.com, stack of books doodle by
Zen20/stock.adobe.com, and drawn fairy-tale castle by Luka/stock.adobe.com
Emojis used under license for Shutterstock.com

Penguin Random House values and supports copyright. Copyright fuels creativity,
encourages diverse voices, promotes free speech, and creates a vibrant culture. Thank you
for buying an authorized edition of this book and for complying with copyright laws by
not reproducing, scanning, or distributing any part of it in any form without permission.
You are supporting writers and allowing Penguin Random House to continue to publish
books for every reader. Please note that no part of this book may be used or reproduced in
any manner for the purpose of training artificial intelligence technologies or systems.

Delacorte Romance and the colophon are trademarks
of Penguin Random House LLC.

Editor: Kelsey Horton
Cover Designers: Ray Shappell and Torborg Davern
Interior Designer: Megan Shortt
Production Editor: Colleen Fellingham
Managing Editor: Tamar Schwartz
Production Manager: Tim Terhune

Library of Congress Cataloging-in-Publication Data is available upon request.
ISBN 979-8-217-03149-8 (trade pbk.) — ISBN 979-8-217-03150-4 (ebook)

Originally published in the United Kingdom as *Do You Ship It?* by Penguin Books,
a division of Penguin Random House UK, London, in 2025.

The text of this book is set in 11-point Adobe Garamond Pro.

Manufactured in the United States of America
1st Printing

The authorized representative in the EU for product safety and compliance is Penguin
Random House Ireland, Morrison Chambers, 32 Nassau Street, Dublin D02 YH68,
Ireland, https://eu-contact.penguin.ie.

Random House Children's Books supports the First Amendment
and celebrates the right to read.

For my fellow weird kids and fandom nerds

Your ticket to the Worlds Beyond fantasy con today . . .
See you there, CERYS!

I skip through the email, looking for the QR code, but not before my eyes widen at the reminder that "weapons, even makeshift and nonthreatening, will not be allowed into the convention center."

"What am I getting myself into?" I mutter.

A glance around makes me even less sure that I've made the right decision to come along: there are streams of people walking past with armfuls of posters ready to get signed, wearing questionable wigs and fake elf ears, in T-shirts that look like less-cool versions of the *Stranger Things* Hellfire Club. Some of them are even completely dressed up, like they're going to a Halloween costume contest. A guy strides by me in brown armor made of papier-mâché, with antlers the size of my *arm* sticking out of his head.

I take a deep breath. *This is all just a means to an end,* I tell myself, *and it's going to be totally worth it.* I just have to walk up, scan my ticket, and go find Jake.

I've hardly seen my best friend Jake since he moved away at the start of summer and started going to Colleg Carreg for the last two years of school to study A Levels, instead of going to St. David's sixth form with me in Cardiff. I can just *feel* him slipping further and further away. Every time we've made plans to hang out over the past few weeks, the rest of the old school gang ended up joining us, which would normally be fine, except . . .

Except I haven't been able to shake the full-blown crush I developed on Jake months ago, and it's true what they say: absence really *does* make the heart grow fonder. And how am I supposed to initiate a romantic move on him if he's only ever going to see me in *that* context? I'll be stuck in the best friend zone for life.

And, like, what's the alternative? Tell him I have a massive crush on him and I think we'd be great together, risk total rejection, and lose the best person in my life for good because I've made it too awkward between us?

Yeah, right.

No, I have to find a better way. I have to *show him* we're perfect for each other.

Hence, The Fangirl Project.

Hence, I'm now at some random industrial estate, in front of an old warehouse turned convention hall, surrounded by strangers in cosplay and ready to spend all afternoon pretending I'm totally excited to be here.

There's a huge banner stretched across the front of the warehouse. WELCOME, TRAVELERS! it declares. TO THE WORLDS BEYOND FANTASY CON, FOR FANS OF *OF WRATH AND RUNE*!

Why couldn't Jake have at least picked something, I don't know, more mainstream to be a die-hard fanboy over? I probably could've gotten on board with *Lord of the Rings*, I've seen the memes about it and even that weird Isengard song video. And I've seen all the new Marvel films with Jake, even if I don't actually know what he's talking about when he goes on about the different "phases."

But no, he had to go and pick *Of Wrath and Rune* to be his favorite thing. A niche, low-budget TV show with a cult following and *eight* books—eight!—that aren't even a finished series yet. I have some idea what it's about, mainly secondhand knowledge from Jake talking nonstop about it when I have managed to see him lately: It's a high-fantasy adventure, with fauns, some Robin Hood–type characters called the Rascals, and an evil wizard or something.

I figure I have enough surface-level knowledge to not make a complete fool of myself today, and then I'll try to watch the TV show. It'll be like homework. All part of my ultimate mission to become Jake's dream girl and give us something new to bond over so he'll finally realize it.

Speak of the devil—my phone buzzes with a text asking if I'm here yet. I wonder if he knows I'm stalling out here, thinking about him? (Although, to be fair, I am *usually* thinking about him.)

His text only serves to remind me how quiet our message thread has become; when I open it, I can see back to texts I sent four days ago, agreeing to come to the convention. My reply sounds bright and breezy, thankfully—I'd been internally screaming when he invited me after I mentioned oh-so-casually how I was thinking of giving his favorite new series a go, seeing what all the fuss was about. I even swapped my usual Saturday shift at work so I could be here.

As I slowly make my way to the ticket scanners, I scroll a little farther back, seeing too many half-made plans that fell through. Usually because he was busy with soccer, or his family. But one name in particular keeps glaring up at me from the screen: *Max*. They made fast friends after Jake moved, and ever since it's Max this and Max that, and . . .

I can't help but feel like I'm being replaced. Like Jake's forgetting about me.

I shove the phone into my pocket, jaw clenched in determination. I have to change that. I have to get things back to how they were. And, if possible, make them better.

All right, I think, striding toward the doors. *Showtime!*

I'm not really sure what I was expecting from a convention, but I'm immediately overwhelmed. The noise of people chatting and someone speaking over a microphone is amplified by the high, corrugated metal ceilings into a cacophony that makes me feel like I've accidentally wandered into a nightclub. It's way busier than I was expecting, with people clustered in huge groups to get things signed or have their photo taken with someone, and spilling out of a curtained-off section where I figure there must be a panel going on.

There are loads of stalls selling merch, too. Not just *Of Wrath and Rune* things, but general fantasy junk. There's a huge display of crossbows and swords, which I think is pretty rich, given the so-called rule against having weapons in the convention hall.

This, I decide quickly, is so not my thing. Jake tried to get me to play Dungeons & Dragons with him and his older brother, Thomas, a couple of times, and I just could never get into it. I don't care about elves and sorcerers and trolls and faeries, and I *really* don't want to spend my whole Saturday hanging out with people who do.

It's not too late to turn around and get the bus home. I could just say I wasn't feeling well. There's got to be a better way to get Jake's attention than all of *this,* right?

Also, it turns out it's not everyone in their costumes and fan-made T-shirts that looks weird in here: It's me.

In the cute blue sundress and brown sandals I picked out especially to impress Jake, I stick out like a sore thumb.

I'm buffeted across the back of the head and the blow trips me forward. Looking over my shoulder, I see a woman in a giant set of painted cardboard wings, one now slightly askew. She straightens it, not seeming to notice our collision. Her friends are busy laughing about something, and then shout in unison, *"For glory and destiny! For wrath! For ruin!"*

I fix my ponytail, heart thudding hard.

I don't know what I was thinking—I don't belong here! Everyone can see it, and I bet they're all thinking it. My throat feels tight and my mouth bone-dry, a familiar, creeping dread that I'm intruding and not wanted. Except, this time, it's not people in the schoolyard at break time, or my parents shouting at each other at home, and there's no Jake to rescue and reassure me. It's—

"Cerys! You made it!"

I turn in the direction of my best friend's voice, immediately breathing a little easier for hearing it, and find Jake striding through a gap in the crowds and right toward me. My heart does a little somersault. I know I only saw him two weeks ago just before school started, but I drink in the sight of him, some paranoid little part of me trying to work out if he's already turned into someone else.

But he looks just the same as always: short sandy-blond hair styled in that way that looks effortless but I know takes him a solid twenty minutes every morning; tall, lanky frame and bright blue eyes that crinkle behind his glasses; and that huge, loving smile that makes you feel like the center of the whole universe, it's so big.

Have I changed? Will he notice all the extra freckles on my skin brought out by a late burst of summer sun, the extra care I put into styling my pale blond hair today? The fact that I'm wearing my good bra (the one that actually gives me some cleavage)?

Jake envelops me in a bear hug, crushing me against him, which, in turn, serves as a crushing reminder that *my* crush is very much unrequited. This definitely isn't how you hug a girl you see as a romantic prospect; I've seen enough rom-coms to know. His hand is meant to linger on the small of my back, at *least*.

He draws away, and I see he's wearing one of those T-shirts like most everyone else. It's a deep forest green, with a large circular emblem that looks sort of ancient-Roman-inspired, and sharp, blocky text is splashed across it, reading BE YE A RASCAL, ROACH?

Note to self: look up "roach," confirm if it's a character name or a literal cockroach.

Actually, the T-shirt doesn't look *so* bad . . . It's a flattering cut on Jake, and the shimmer of the circle thing is really pretty. I should get one, if I'm going to be part of this.

Am I going to be part of this? I'm still not sure.

"I'm so glad you're here! You missed the panel about the special effects, which sucks because I think you'd have loved that. And OMG, I totally beat the rush for getting a photo with the guy who plays Daxys, and he was *so* awesome. Why do they say never meet your heroes? I swear, it was *the* coolest three minutes of my life," Jake is gushing, and I realize I haven't even said hello yet, but that's so normal that I relax even more. What's "hello" in the face of five years of friendship?

We only got friendly because we were in the same class when we first started "big school"; what if he's only stayed friends with me because it was convenient? What if we're the sort of people who drift apart the second they're not forced to spend time in the same building five days a week? Or he makes all new friends—like *Max*—and I get pushed out? I actually don't know what I'd do without Jake in my life.

He's my only constant; I can't lose him.

"So?" he says now, waving his hands out, his smile growing even wider. There's a flush in his cheeks; he's so clearly in his element. "I know you're a total newbie to the fandom, but is this the most awesome thing you've ever seen, or what?"

"Er . . ."

Oh God, come on, Cerys, think! There's got to be something good you can say! But the more I look around, the more overwhelmed I feel—everything about it is making my brain scream that this is a place packed with people with a shared passion that borders on obsessive, and my total apathy is not the vibe.

"It's . . . huge!" I say at last. "There's so many people here!"

Neither statement is probably the enthused awe that Jake is hoping for, but his eyes still brighten. "Right? It's, like, a total coup. I can't believe it's basically on our doorstep! Apparently one of the showrunners is kind of local—well, she's from Pontypool, so close enough—and once they got her on board . . ."

"So cool," I agree. I swing my ponytail over my shoulder to twirl a piece of hair around my finger, trying to rearrange my pose into something that says "flirty." Jake's trusty denim jacket is hooked carelessly through the strap of his backpack, and I'm already formulating a romantic plan for later. While Jake might be the master of all knowledge when it comes to *Of Wrath and Rune,* my encyclopedic strength lies in every rom-com movie trick since the eighties. He'd lend it to me if I asked, but that's not the point. I need to get him to *notice* I'm cold, and offer it to me.

But he's too busy checking his phone to be distracted by my hair-flicking or my jacket-burgling plan and just says absently, "The panel with the cast starts in about forty minutes, so we'll have to get in line soon if we want to get seats. And OMG, Cer!" Jake grabs both my shoulders in excitement. "I forgot the best part. You've got to meet him. Where's—?"

The next part all seems to happen in horrible slow motion, like

I've gotten stuck in an actual nightmare. A cluster of convention-goers parts almost cinematically as a figure all in black strides through the middle of them, eyes focused and forward. He's wearing leather armguards, a long, heavy cloak with more pieces of armor accented around the shoulders, and some intimidating-looking piece of what I can only describe as a harness-slash-holster over his torso. The old-fashioned linen shirt he has on is loose around the neck to show off a necklace on a rope chain, and his long white-blond wig is tucked back behind a pair of pointed ears.

"Here he is!" Jake lets go of me to grab this stranger by the arm, and says the very words I've been dreading ever since he told me he was going to a different school than me.

"Cerys," he tells me, beaming. "This is my new best friend, Max."

When Jake and his family were packing up their old house at the beginning of summer, I tried to stay out of their way, I really did.

But one morning there were boxes and suitcases being packed up at *my* house, too, so I snatched up a roll of brown tape and left for Jake's. I was smiling when he opened the door, and waved the tape in his face, saying, "Honorary member of the Team Wandsworth house move, reporting for duty!"

Jake took one look at my red-rimmed eyes and pulled me into a hug. When he let me go, it was to grab his shoes from the rack next to the door. He called over his shoulder to his mom that we were going out.

"Won't you get in trouble? I thought you had to help . . ."

He shook his head. "Nah, they'll be fine for a few hours. Come on."

We ended up walking along the canal for a while. As usual,

Jake chatted a mile a minute about anything and everything. I was pretty crap company. I kept fidgeting with the tape, turning it around and around and picking at the end.

Eventually we got to one of the locks, and Jake clambered along the thick wooden beam to sit, his legs dangling. The NO CLIMB- ING sign glared at me from the opposite side of the bank, but Jake beamed at me, so I followed him.

I'd been harboring a crush on Jake for a little while, but when he put his hand on mine, I couldn't even think about how this was A Huge Deal and whether I should lean my head on his shoulder or turn in for a kiss. I just gulped down a shaky breath.

"Your dad's moving out, then?" he said.

"Yeah. I know I've been saying I wish they'd just get on with it, and I can't wait to have some peace and quiet once they're not living in the same house and constantly arguing, but . . . I don't know, it's just *weird*."

"Weird doesn't have to be a bad thing."

"I know. I know, but . . ." Tears started welling up, and I didn't have it in me to blink them away. Jake patted his pockets for tissues he definitely didn't have, then scooted closer and tucked me into his side instead. "Everything's changing, you know? Dad's moving out, we're heading into sixth form, *you're* leaving—"

"Hey, I'm not going anywhere, Cer. Well—all right, techni- cally I'm going *somewhere*, but that doesn't change anything. Not between us! We're still best friends, aren't we? We'll always have each other. Geography's got nothing to do with how much I love ya."

He said it so casually, and it wasn't like it was the first time either of us had ever said "Love ya!" But it *was* the first time I realized I wanted it to mean something more. It was the first time I had this pang in my chest like, *I want you to be* in *love with me, though.*

Which, obviously, I didn't say out loud, because I didn't want to ruin such a nice moment. He was reaffirming how much I meant to him, and I really, *really* needed to hear that from someone right then.

So we just sat on the canal lock, legs swinging, leaning into each other. We talked about all the things we'd do this summer, when we'd see each other after he moved, what films we'd see in the cinema . . .

And I thought: *This is him. This is the boy I'm going to fall in love with.*

Faced with Jake and his *new best friend* in the convention hall, I have two immediate choices.

1. Run sobbing to the nearest bathroom because I thought it was just going to be the two of us, and my plan to be Jake's number-one fandom friend and then his girlfriend has been ruined by the fact he's already *found* a fandom friend, and end up alienating both of them with my reaction; or

2. Be super chill and act super nice to Max, thus infiltrating their new friendship so I can swiftly undermine

him and remind Jake that *I* am his best friend, not this interloper he barely knows.

It's not that difficult to decide.

Which is why I give Max the very best smile I can muster and say, "Wow, great wig! That's such a cool, um, *cosplay*."

A word I know thanks to Jake, and which I can't believe I've actually just had to use in real life. I'm reeling—too busy trying to take it all in to care if they think I'm staring.

Can you blame me, though? This guy is dressed up like—like—well, I don't know what, because I haven't actually seen the show, but he's in armor and a cloak and wearing *elf ears*. He doesn't even have a backpack with him; did he get on the bus looking like this? Actually go out in public and leave the house wearing that stuff?

I genuinely can't fathom it. The mental image is so outlandish to me, it's pure static in my brain. And, oh God, is Jake going to start dressing up in cosplay too now? Am *I* going to have to, if I want to fit in and be part of all this?

The skin on the back of my neck prickles and I'm aware of a pair of eyes boring into me. I find Max looking at me, taking in my sundress and obvious lack of "I'm an *Of Wrath and Rune* fan!" accessories, and he actually *smirks*.

Like *I'm* the one dressed up like an idiot.

"He looks totally badass!" Jake crows, slinging an arm around Max and giving him the same affectionate shake he's given me a hundred times. I feel a stab of jealousy.

Jake is oblivious.

He runs a hand over one of the pieces of shoulder armor Max is wearing, studying it closely. "Damn, I just cannot get over how awesome these are. You look like a real fighter; it's so freaking cool. I *wish* I could pull that off."

Max's face relaxes a little as he tosses Jake a smile. "I told you I'd help you with a Daxys cosplay, if you wanted."

Feeling cut out already, I clear my throat. Jake startles slightly, but his grin is focused full force on me once more within a split second, and it's so easy to smile back at him.

"Max, this is Cerys, the girl I told you about."

I balk. Is that it? Five years of being best friends, of sharing in-jokes and cutting class together and swapping homework to help each other out, and the grand sum of my introduction is *the girl I told you about*?

Unless . . . unless Jake's already told him *so much* about me, I need no introduction? Maybe he's gushed about me nonstop to all his new pals and I'm "the girl Jake has a crush on," or at least "the girl Jake doesn't realize yet that he has a crush on, but he won't shut up talking about her and it's obvious to everyone."

Yeah. Yeah, that's it. It's got to be.

This is the classic friends-to-lovers story; I know how it goes. It's like in *The Duff*—he's my Robbie Amell and just needs to see me in a new light, that's all! I force myself to relax, to pay attention as Jake carries on talking, now waving a hand in Max's direction, his arm still slung around his shoulders.

"Cerys—this is Max. He's at my new school. Remember, I've told you about that guy in my physics class, I met him at soccer earlier this summer when I switched teams after the move? This is him! And get this—he's a *huge OWAR* fan, too! Talk about serendipity, huh?"

"Really?" I say dryly, and let my eyes skirt over the cosplay again. I can't help it. Even his pants aren't, like, just normal pants. Where do boys even *get* leather pants? "I'd never have guessed."

"And you're the newbie," Max says. His voice is lower than I was expecting. Slower. He sounds *bored,* which is a very nice way to treat his new friend's best friend. He clearly did not choose to take the high road, like I have. What an ass.

But if this is the kind of guy Jake wants to be friends with—if this is what he bonds with people over, the sort of thing he loves . . . it just drives home the genius of my plan: get into the fandom to spend time with him.

I'm not about to let Max steal my friend. I'm not going to be *usurped* by some guy who wears arm guards and a blond wig out in public. Especially not one who has the audacity to somehow still be smirking at me. Is he trying to go for the world record, or am I *that* much of a joke to him?

I must be staring (*glaring*) at him too much, because he adds, "So Jake was telling me you're pretty new to the fandom?"

If that's his attempt at an olive branch, it's a fail. He only succeeds in sounding snarky.

I need to get ahold of myself. I can't stoop to this guy's level and be as judgmental as him. I need to prove myself to Jake, not risk this distance between us widening more than it already has. I paste on a smile, shrug my shoulders back, and shift my weight to one hip in a more visibly relaxed posture—pointedly mirroring Jake's body language.

"Yes. Yeah! Well, sort of. I've heard plenty about *OWAR* from this guy here." I giggle, giving Jake a playful shove. *See, look at me, using the lingo, calling it "OWAR"!* Jake laughs, too, and winks at me. My stomach flutters with butterflies.

"I've been trying to get Cer into it for ages, man—and she finally caved! Couldn't resist the ol' Jake Wandsworth charm, huh?"

"Oh, don't you know it." I give him another little push, right on the bicep. Between that and the eye contact, it's a total Moment. Then, to really drive home my commitment to this thing (and to Jake), I tell Max, "I don't know why I put it off so long, it looks so interesting. I bought all the books last week. Jake thinks I should start with the show, then read the books, but it's always better the other way around, right?"

"Hmm, it depends. The books are pretty dense, especially the first one. Things don't really get going until book three. I think the show's probably more accessible if you're not huge on fantasy . . . Kind of like with *Game of Thrones,* you know?"

"Oh, for sure." I nod, despite the grand sum of my knowledge being that some guy called Ned Stark dies in, like, the first episode, and people really love Pedro Pascal's character.

I may be way in over my head here.

"Cerys is more of a romance gal. You know, *She's the Man, To All the Boys* . . . I gotta say, she talked me into watching that one, but that series was *so good.* But yeah, you're not usually that into fantasy stuff, are you?" Jake adds, turning to me.

O ye of little faith.

"That changes today!"

Max is giving me another very mean, very unimpressed look, but manages to say, "Well, *OWAR*'s got something for everybody. You'll be a Silversmith shipper before you know it."

My smile freezes. "Um, right. Sure."

Shipper? What, like, rooting for a fictional couple? It's not a romance show, is it? Jake would've told me if it was.

Jake, though, is laughing, turned away from me once more. "As if. I keep telling you, man, those two are not endgame. Everybody's wasting their time with them. Cerys will agree, I bet, just you wait and see. Now come on, I am *not* missing this panel."

He grabs each of us by the arm, propelling us toward the mass of people near the curtained-off section. The previous panel is over, and people are flocking out while we join the entrance line.

Jake hops on his toes, grinning from ear to ear, and it's so adorable that my heart gives a longing little squeeze. His excitement is so infectious that even though I have zero attachment to this show, I'm suddenly looking forward to hearing people talk about it.

Max ends up standing behind me, which is ideal because it means I might be able to not-really-but-actually cut him out of conversation to have a little one-on-one hang time with Jake, as planned.

I'm trying to think up the best topic of conversation—not school, and not how practice with his new soccer team is going, but maybe something about the gang from our old school, something only the two of us can talk about—when Max clears his throat, suddenly standing just a little too close.

"You know, if you really want to get involved in the fandom, Cerys, there's a Discord channel that's great. They're pretty welcoming to newcomers."

Maybe you could take a page out of their book, I think, glancing over my shoulder at him.

"I'll get Jake to send you a link," he tells me.

"Sure," I say warily, not even sure what Discord is, and not willing to admit that and face yet more judgment. But Max must hear it plain as day in my voice, because he rolls his eyes.

"It's a chat room forum thing. There's an app. You can be anonymous, if you want, though most of us have shared first names and stuff."

"Anonymous?"

Max gives me an odd look. "Well, yeah. You just pick a screen name. Most of the ones in this Discord are *OWAR*-related. Like . . . puns of character names, or about the Rascals. But since you're not familiar with it all, you could just throw together a couple of words like magic, mythic, legend . . . or elves, goblins, witches. Stuff like that. Anyway, this one's all local people. Lots of Cardiff Uni students too. They've organized meetups before, but I've always missed them."

"And they just . . . talk about *OWAR*? Online?"

"Yeah. Fan theories, character analyses, swapping fanfic links, sharing cosplay pics, that kind of thing." He shrugs, so nonchalant he can't even meet my eyes, like this is so basic and my question is so stupid. It sets my hackles up, but I can't tell if that's because of the odd dedication that it must require from the chat room members, or Max's cold attitude.

But I guess it might help me understand more about this series Jake loves so much, so I say, "Cool. Count me in."

Max grunts, a noise that might be annoyance or might be a bored "okay." Either way, it's perfectly clear *he* doesn't want to waste any more of his time with a newbie like me, so I turn back around and plunge into gossiping with *my* best friend about our mutual friends and some school drama, doing my best to salvage this day out with Jake.

The convention isn't so bad, I guess. I don't get most of what the panels are talking about, but sometimes there's a good joke or something interesting about the creative process that piques my attention. And apart from Max, nobody seems to be giving me judgy looks anymore. It makes me wonder if they ever really were, or if that was all in my head.

Plus, at the end of the afternoon Jake buys me a Roach T-shirt like the one he's wearing and presents it to me proudly. "To officially induct you into the cult!" he jokes, and I put it on immediately.

(I do take it off as soon as I'm on the bus home, but he doesn't need to know that.)

And then, that evening, among a string of texts as the two of us chat utter nonsense about anything and everything and it feels like I've got my best friend back, he drops me a link to the Discord channel and says, Maybe see you in the chat sometime!

This is *it*.

I'm going to be the biggest *OWAR* fangirl he's ever seen.

OWAR Discord #324
#general

@mythicwitch
Hi everybody! Newbie to the OWAR fandom here! I'm
Cerys. Any takes on whether to start with the books or
the show?

@wizeguy
sup Cerys! Welcome to the Discord! And, books.

@fauningforhim
Don't listen to him, Mythic. The TV show is best if
you're just starting! Take it from me—I only just got into
OWAR last year, now a die-hard fan!

@silversmithhh
Hmm, depends . . . If you're a Twilight/Court of Thorns
and Roses girlie, definitely start with the show. If you're
a Homer's Iliad or Les Mis fan, the books are a cinch

@fauningforhim
looooool mood

@silversmithhh
(In case it wasn't obvious, **@mythicwitch**, start with
the show. Always.)

Private chat with @runicrascal

@runicrascal
Hello newbie! Fancy seeing you here

Glad you accepted the invite!

And, yeah, start with the TV show

@mythicwitch
I'm getting that vibe, haha! And also, nobody thought to mention these books have maps in them? What? Literally, what world have I entered? (They are kinda pretty, though. Like, why do I sort of want to get a poster of one for my wall?)

@runicrascal
Oof, the maps are what got you? DEFINITELY start with the TV show in that case

We don't want you bolting before you've left the gate, huh?

@mythicwitch
Almost! I'm here for the long haul though ;)

@runicrascal
Welcome to the fandom, Cerys!

THE FANGIRL PROJECT

Become an "OWAR" fangirl to convince Jake I am his dream girl and we are actually a match made in heaven:

1. buy the books ✓
2. watch the ~~show~~
3. remember to call it "OWAR" like a real fan ✓
4. go to a convention (cringe) ✓
5. . . . cosplay??!?? (something CUTE!!! that Jake can't resist)
6. DO NOT badmouth OWAR in front of Jake
7. who/what is "Roach"??? Find out!
8. wear the new T-shirt Jake bought me next time I see him!
9. join this fan-forum-chat thing on Discord (whatever that is?) and talk to Jake in it to prove that I really AM all in and therefore the love of his life ✓♡♡

Despite the fact that this is my third week at St. David's already, that first-day dread hasn't budged even a little. My heart hammers and my palms are slick with sweat at the idea of walking into a space where I know almost nobody, have a more flexible timetable, and am suddenly treated more like an adult than a child, when I really don't feel very grown-up at all. It all feels too intense, too *free*, and I miss my smaller, more contained world of my old school, where the dynamics were fixed and I didn't have to stumble blindly into a whole new, unknown environment.

I thought, after the first couple of days, I'd get used to it and the dust would settle. I thought I'd have new friends, but all I've managed to do is make small talk with some people I sit by in classes, and busy myself with some coursework or notes during my breaks.

There are a couple of sixth form schools in the area, so our group from school inevitably split up a little when it came to studying A Levels before uni, but I stayed signed up for St. David's even after Jake moved. I told myself that I liked the idea of a fresh start, even if it meant not being with my old group from school day to day, but deep down I know it's because St. David's has a better reputation for art.

Art was always my favorite subject when I was younger, but I'm not naive enough to want to pursue it further—it's just an easy A to go alongside my English, history, and media classes. A career in art hardly worked out for my dad, and I've seen firsthand the kind of fights and resentment such an unstable choice can cause.

I am starting to regret giving in to the pull of the impressive student art shows and great facilities, though, because the reality is that aside from a few people I didn't know very well at my old school, I'm stuck somewhere I don't have any friends at all.

In my head, I know I'm not the only one in this situation. Everyone in my classes has come from different schools, and we've obviously got similar interests if we're studying the same things, but it's like I missed some vital memo on that first day. Cliques began to form, groups banded together, and I'm left on the outskirts, trying to fit in.

I stand in front of my bed now, debating between a pastel yellow top and a lilac shirt, like my life depends on it.

It sort of does.

At my old school, I never had to worry too much about fitting in. Our friend group was established very quickly at twelve years old, bonds forged by trivial things like sharing the same bus stop or being in the same homeroom, and it never really changed much.

And I always had Jake.

So I never really felt like I was missing out on something better when I'd see the cool girls at school. But everything is different now—and I'd be lying if I said I'd never been at least a *little* in awe of them.

Girls like Evie Price. Pretty and smiley and polished, not the kind of Regina George "cool" that involves snide put-downs and catty smirks.

Evie was never really my friend at my old school, but I've seen her around St. David's and she's in my art class. She's got in with a group of girls who are always giggling and gossiping together, linking arms in the corridors and swapping sticks of cream blush and coursework notes.

Everything always looks so effortless and easy for girls like them. Not just when it comes to things like boys and clothes, but . . . *all* of it. Friendships, homework, liquid eyeliner, sports, music . . .

I bet their home lives are a lot less stressful, too.

I bet it's all so much easier, when you're above it.

God, I would love to be one of *those* girls if I could, and now feels like the perfect time to reinvent myself. And why can't I? It's just . . . refining how I present myself, until I believe it, too.

I open Instagram and see Evie's new group—they've already uploaded Stories with their outfits of the day, causing me to promptly scrap both the yellow and lilac tops and pick out a tan turtleneck instead. It's too warm for it, really, and I'm sweating as soon as I put it on, my hair a static mess of flyaways, but according to these girls' social media it's pumpkin spice latte season, global warming be damned.

I swap my sneakers for a chunky pair of boots, and grab a jacket on my way out. Step one: complete.

Getting in with the girls at school isn't that much different from immersing myself in the *OWAR* fandom for Jake. A few small changes here and there, and voilà, everything will fall into place exactly the way it should.

As I make my way downstairs, I hear Mom shouting in the kitchen, "I *told* you I had a meeting to dial into this morning before we speak to the lawyers—"

And Dad snaps, "What, and I'm supposed to starve just because you're in a meeting? I'm only here because *you* needed a lift into town while your car's in the garage. So much for doing you a favor! Why can't you just wear your bloody headphones?"

"Because they can hear that stupid blender of yours down the street!" Mom yells back. "As if some *headphones* would make a difference—"

I hesitate at the bottom of the stairs, hand gripping the banister so tight it hurts. I'm holding my breath, too, and hear the thudding of my own pulse hard and loud in my ears while Mom and Dad carry on bickering. There's a clatter of Mom gathering up her stuff and then Dad saying, "Well, what's the point in that? I'm done, I'm already leaving—"

She hisses back, "*Yes,* you are," with such venom that I flinch.

I nab my keys off the hook by the door, and slip out in silence.

There's a Costa coffee shop on the way to school, if I get off the bus a stop early, and this morning I do. It's part of The Fangirl Project.

Well. The *Other* Fangirl Project. Not to be confused with *The*

Fangirl Project of becoming a fangirl to get Jake to fall in love with me. This one is less monumental and life-changing, but it's still important. I refuse to get stuck being some weird loner girl on the outskirts for the rest of the school year—or worse still, for the *entire* rest of high school—so it's time to change things up.

I've learned—mainly through a few overheard conversations, but partly through social media posts—that Evie's group go to Costa every morning on their way to class. I'm too embarrassed to ask outright if I can sit with them at lunchtime or something, but we can totally strike up conversation on more neutral territory, I'm sure of it. It'll be like a rom-com meet-cute, only with less romance and hopefully no spilling an entire coffee over someone's white shirt.

I run the risk of being late for my media class, but when I get there and see some of the girls chatting near the end of the counter, most of them with cups in hand already, I know I'm making the right decision. After all, what's five minutes and a disappointed look from a teacher compared to two entire years of loneliness?

Evie isn't there, though, and she was going to be my way in. Even if we weren't friends at our old school, we were friendly enough. What am I going to do now? I feel too far in to bail.

My palms are clammy and my chest feels tight, but there's no Jake to save me now, with all his exuberance and openness and charm so I can follow his lead. I'm going to have to do this for myself.

Hell, if I can go to an *OWAR* convention, I can do this—right?

I join the queue, trying to look casual even though my eyes dart in their direction every few seconds. I'm sure they must be able to hear my heart thundering from all the way over there, and I fight to keep from readjusting my stance to appear my most cool and carefree, while feeling anything but.

Finally, though, I get a bite.

One of the girls glances my way as she talks, and we make eye contact.

Even though that was always my intention, I flush, feeling caught out.

She lifts a hand to wave, and smiles. "Hey! Carys, right?"

"Um." I clear my throat, but say, "It's Cerys, actually," and hope it doesn't sound like I'm shouting across the café.

She pulls a face, somehow looking embarrassed but unbothered at the same time. Her name is Daphne—"like *Bridgerton*! And I'm, like, perpetually late to stuff, so my mom's always yelling at me to *make haste,* lol!" as I heard her proclaim in our media class at the beginning of term—but she has a look more reminiscent of a Love Islander than a Regency-era duchess.

Today, she's in an oversized cream sweater and khaki leggings, and her hair is slicked back in a neat bun. The other girls have done their hair the same way. I pat down the flyaways that I never quite got under control around my own ponytail. She's even got the knack of outlining her lips with lip liner to make them appear bigger, which I tried copying a few days ago and had to scrub off immediately. While she looks glamorous, I felt like a clown.

I've practically got a mental file on all of the group from seeing them around campus (and from stalking on social media). Daphne is very much into the clean-girl aesthetic; she's willowy, with long black hair and pale skin that's flawless, thanks, she claims, to her very well-documented-on-Instagram nine-step Korean skin care routine. There's Nikita, a curvy brunette who reposts a lot of snarky, sarcastic memes, is a die-hard *Married at First Sight* fan, and tends to wear a pop of color with her beige-and-black-toned outfits; today, it's a high-necked green sweater. Yesterday, it was a pair of red boots.

Evie, of course, I already know, but I looked her up on socials all the same. Blond and petite, but with a far curvier figure than I have, in a way that makes her look dainty instead of flat or boxy. She's very into beauty influencers and fashion hauls, and alters her style often. Lately, she seems to have taken Daphne's and Nikita's lead, like I have.

And then there's Chloe, who has the exact opposite of a resting bitch face. She does a lot of show jumping and horseback riding, and is usually clad in thick leggings and tall, worn boots, even if her glasses are Versace. Her dark hair is often braided, and it must take her hours to get the styles looking so intricate and neat. Quite honestly, I don't know where they all find the time to put so much effort into how they look, every day before school. It's sort of awe-inspiring.

"Cerys," Daphne corrects herself, still smiling at me. "Right! I'm sorry. We have media studies together, right? Cute sweater, by the way."

Nikita adds, "*Love* the shoes. I'm obsessed. Are they thrifted?"

"Oh, um . . . sort of. They were my mom's."

"Vintage! Ugh, I wish my mom had taste like that."

Chloe jokes, "I wish *my* mom didn't have such hideously big feet, so I could actually borrow her shoes!"

"Oh nooo," Daphne says. "Not boat feet!"

"Never mind *boats,* they're like cruise liners." Chloe gives a melodramatic eye roll that makes everyone laugh, and then it's my turn to order from the barista. I try not to glance their way for approval, but order a pumpkin spice latte. I've only had one once before; Jake hates them, and I still remember him choking and sputtering after trying mine, how he claimed he could still taste it a week later.

The girls carry on chattering without me, resuming their conversation, but I'm pleased when they wait for me to get my drink before Nikita says to me, "Ready to go?" and I get to join them for the walk to campus.

I sit by Daphne and a couple of her friends in media studies, and afterward, even though I'm the first to history and take my usual seat, Nikita comes to sit next to me when she arrives, and then I end up going to lunch with her to join the others. Evie smiles brightly when she sees me there, waving me over enthusiastically as if we've never been anything *but* close. It feels genuine, and I let myself be swept into the fold, trying not to give away how much I could cry with relief at how easy and straightforward this turned out to be.

I'm sweating inside my turtleneck and boots, and I don't know how they all look so cool and unbothered in their own sweaters and layers, but it's so worth it to be included.

I *knew* I just had to find a way in.

If only things were this easy with Jake.

On Wednesday afternoon, I'm sitting in art class. It technically started fifteen minutes ago, although our teacher has yet to show
up. Some people have carried on working on their projects—we're
spending this term compiling a portfolio of one study in five different mediums—but most people are scrolling on their phones or
chatting with friends.

I feel like I made a huge mistake in opening my sketchbook
to carry on with my work; Evie is perched on a table on the other
side of the room, her legs swinging as she chats with a couple of
people. I should have gone over and joined in. Is it too late now?
Probably. I don't want to intrude, and it's not as if Evie invited me,
is it? (Should she have? Was I supposed to assume a sort of standing
invitation? Will she be more annoyed at me for barging in?)

It feels like when I go into the breakroom at the H&M I work
at in town, and some of my older colleagues are talking about university courses or childcare or a hundred other things I can't relate

to, and I get stuck on the fringes, too intimidated to try joining in. Too in my head to make a decision.

I stay put.

The piece I'm working on isn't even any *good*. We've been given the broad theme of "nature" to work within, and my still life of a single rose in a vase is bland and lifeless and so basic that, while technically decent, I wonder why I spent so many hours wrestling with the lighting when it's so wholly uninspiring.

I am wholly uninspired.

Art used to make me feel . . . *something,* at least. Now it's like I'm just . . . ticking a box. Like it's the easy A I told my parents it would be. It's certainly not the hobby it once was, all those evenings I'd rush home from school to pull out the paints and canvas from under my bed. It was a fun class at school and I had really encouraging teachers, but then it became something to desperately distract me from the latest round of bickering that was going on downstairs between my parents. At least I've realized I'd be wasting my time to think it could be a career; Dad had to give up being an artist when I was little, and he's become really resentful about it these days. I'm glad I'm learning from his mistakes before it ruins my life, too.

I flip the page away from my crappy rose, landing instead on a half-done sketch from last night. My pencil moves lightly over the drawing, falling into the habit of refining lines and expanding on the outline of the image, adding detail and suggestions of shadow to tend to later. It's just something to keep my hands busy, since I've committed to not joining Evie in her conversation.

The edge of my left palm is smudged gray as my pencil moves

across the page, solidifying the lines of a stag's skull and adorning the antlers in vines that will melt back into the forest behind it. It's only as that part of the vision takes hold in my mind that I realize what I'm drawing.

It's a scene from *Of Wrath and Rune*. I finally watched the first two episodes last night, and while they were very slow and very strange, there was this part where one of the forest creatures emerged from the woods. I think it was this antlered character I saw that guy dressed up as at the convention, and while the episode droned on I ended up down a Wikipedia rabbit hole, learning that because of the low budget most of the special effects like that were done with makeup and clever artistry rather than relying too heavily on CGI.

I ended up rewinding that episode to watch it again properly, feeling a little flutter of excitement when the weird stag-man appeared as if from nowhere in the tree line, thinking of all the agonizing artistic detail that must have gone into making that so seamless.

He's coming to life now, on my page, little by little.

As I realize this, I almost drop my pencil, recoiling in my chair, breath catching and eyes darting side to side like someone's going to suddenly notice. Objectively, I suppose there's nothing wrong with fanart, but this is . . . *weird*. Isn't it? Jake told me that *OWAR* notoriously has a *very* dedicated fan base; I'm not sure I'm ready for everyone to think of me as one of those obsessive nerds just yet.

But I would like Jake to think it, so I slip my phone out of my bag and grab a photo, trying to be as discreet as I can.

I'm going to be really mad if the stag-guy dies by episode 3 after I've dedicated my art project to him, I type out, exaggerating the truth only . . . mildly. (I mean, it's *an* art project . . . of a sort.) Of course I'd updated Jake as soon as I'd started watching, and he wanted all my reactions live-texted to him, but I think he'll appreciate this a lot.

See? OWAR is totally on my mind, I'm already a huge fan! Now ask me on a date already!

Maybe if I make some fanart, I won't have to read the books?

Jake doesn't reply instantly, which is fair because he's probably in class himself at the moment, but I see I have a couple of Discord messages from him that I missed. The app is buried away in a folder so nobody would see it if they looked at my phone, but I feel a little thrill at seeing a few messages from @runicrascal a little while ago.

@runicrascal
So here's the thing with season 1—it's slow. Like, real slow. This is all worldbuilding, laying groundwork for character arcs and trying to introduce you to the dynamics of the kingdom and how the magick systems work and who's who and why you're rooting for them

s1 is literally the entire first two books. Which are awesome, but . . . also very slow. But if you can make it through this, you'll probably be attached enough to the characters to enjoy the extra content in the first two books! Which is kind of a bonus?

Don't give up on it just yet, though. You won't even meet some of the fan faves until about episode 3 or 4!

I reread the messages three times over and realize I'm beaming at the screen. Jake played it so cool over text last night when I was watching the first two episodes, but it's clearly been on his mind today, too—*I've* clearly been on his mind, if he messaged me two hours ago about all this.

Maybe he wants to keep our text thread for everyday chatter, and put all the *OWAR* gushing in Discord? We used to exclusively send memes via Instagram DM, so I'm used to holding different conversations with him in different apps.

Even though I just sent him my art-project-in-progress over text, I put the photo into the Discord chat, too. This time, I write,

> **@mythicwitch**
> Drawing fanart = fangirl status solidified?

Half an hour later, he replies.

> **@runicrascal**
> WHOA! Is that Téiglin?? He looks amazing!
>
> Hardcore, newbie. Already getting attached enough to characters with only three minutes of screen time that you're making fanart . . .
>
> Don't worry, him emerging from the forest in ep1 to nurse a messenger stag beetle back to life gets to everyone
>
> **@mythicwitch**
> "Only" three minutes? NO SPOILERS. If my adorable dead forest stag hybrid guy dies, I will riot.

@runicrascal
My lips are sealed. (But, you're good. Téiglin's pretty beloved, and you don't get that far by dying as soon as you show up onscreen. Also you do realize he's not dead???)

@mythicwitch
His head is literally a skull?

@runicrascal
Oooh I cannot wait for you to find out about the masked cult of forest creatures

@mythicwitch
I honestly can't tell if that's a joke or not

@runicrascal
No spoilers, remember?

As I'm trying to formulate a reply—and trying to decide if I *really* want to get invested in a show where there are characters wearing animal skeleton masks as part of a cult, even if I'm just pretending—my phone buzzes again, and this time Jake has replied to the photo I texted him.

Jake

Sick! He looks amazing! Told you that you'd love the special effects, didn't I? It's almost like I know you too well or something x

My heart skips a beat, my smile so wide I cover my mouth with a hand before someone sees.

Because he does; he knows me *so* well, just like I know him so well. I don't know how he doesn't see it—how perfect we are for each other, that we're not just best friends, but meant to be. Jake's never really had a girlfriend, though, or dated anyone, so I'll just have to work a little harder to make him recognize the signs that I am interested, that I do have feelings for him.

I've never dated, either, but that's more to do with a general lack of interest from boys at school. So maybe *I'm* missing some signs, too.

His messages are all his usual friendly, teasing self, though, so it's hard to work out if he's flirting and this is the sort of back-and-forth banter I see all the time in a good rom-com, or just Jake being Jake.

Maybe I can ask Daphne or Nikita, I think, but I don't really want them to mention anything to Evie. There's a chance that if *she* knows, it might make its way to Jake or our old group from school via mutual friends, and I don't think I could bear that embarrassment. Maybe in a couple of weeks? I might know the girls well enough by then to swear them to secrecy and get their advice.

In the meantime, I'll just have to carry on with The Fangirl Project and try to arrange another opportunity to hang out with Jake. This time, hopefully, it'll *actually* be one-on-one—with no old school friends being an inadvertent buffer between us, and certainly no Max to lurk like a sullen third wheel.

Near the end of class, I get up to wash my hands at the paint-splattered sink in the corner, scrubbing off all the pencil that shines on the edge of my palm and has left gray smudges on my fingertips. When I turn back around, there's a girl standing over my desk, looking closely at the sketchbook I left wide open.

I recognize the girl. Anissa O'Shea. She went to my old school. She was sort of a loner; I'd always see her tucked out of the way on the field in the summer with a book, or in the corner of the cafeteria during rainy lunchtimes with her headphones in, her long hair falling in a curtain over her face. She never came out anywhere and never talked much to anyone, and had a reputation as . . . well, kind of a weird kid. Generally as someone people kept their distance from, for no apparent reason other than *she* kept her distance from the rest of us. I don't know that I've ever had a conversation with her beyond a group project for geography. I don't know her well at all.

But I *do* know that I don't like the way she's studying my drawing.

The bell sounds, and there's mass motion across the classroom as everyone begins to pack away their stuff or stand up from their seats. I run through them all to slam my sketchbook shut.

"Hey," says Anissa. "Is that—"

"Cerys!" Evie shouts from the doorway. "Are you coming or what?"

I bundle my stuff into my arms and sling my bag over my shoulder. I mutter a quick "Sorry" to Anissa and run after Evie, who's already chatting at me a mile a minute, recounting some funny story she was just told by another classmate.

I'm sure I can feel Anissa's eyes burning into the back of my neck, but I don't dare turn around to find out.

On Friday evening, Mom knocks lightly on my bedroom door. I quickly close my sketchbook and slip off my headphones.

"I was thinking of ordering some takeout," she says, smiling at me. "How about a girly movie night and Chinese?"

I grin. "Yes please. That sounds perfect."

We haven't done that in *ages*. Dad used to watch the movies with us, too, even if he'd grumble through half of them and secretly enjoy them, but it's always been my and Mom's thing, really. She's a sucker for a good romance.

I guess that's why she hasn't suggested watching any for months now. A bitter, drawn-out divorce must make Julia Roberts going after her best friend at his wedding tricky to swallow.

Maybe since Dad moved out a couple of months ago and they've both gotten some space, they're finally getting over themselves? It sounds brutal even as I think it, but it's true. *Everything* recently has been about the failure of their marriage, the counseling that didn't work, that endless back and forth with divorce lawyers, the fights that culminated in *flipping a coin* to see who'd move out and who'd stay in the house with me. The very least they needed was space from each other—I'm just glad it seems to be working.

"What're you working on?" Mom asks, nodding at my sketchbook. I wish I'd shoved it farther out of the way and made it look like I'd just been scrolling TikTok or something instead.

"Just something for school. Coursework."

Which it is, sort of. It's another sketch of Téiglin the stag creature, this one a rough outline for the version I want to do on canvas with acrylics, a little more abstract and less precise. It fits in with the nature theme, and it's certainly more technical than a rose in a vase and would get me a better grade—or at least that's what I'm telling myself. Not because I'm *enjoying* it, or intrigued enough by *OWAR* that it's inspired me . . .

"Can I have a look?"

I tug the sketchbook a little way off the desk, like I'll hug it to my body if she comes too close. "It's not ready yet."

Mom clicks her tongue and laughs, used to me not showing my schoolwork. She jokes that it's because I'm a perfectionist like her, and I let her go on thinking it. The truth is, in the past couple of years it's been more a case of not wanting to show off my artwork, because it usually leads to a fight with her and Dad and then they end up at each other's throats.

Dad was an artist, when they met. He would do wedding photography, and he liked painting in his spare time. He even sold a few pieces, and had been looking into a gallery exhibition, but ultimately he gave it all up for a more stable job working for a marketing agency. I'm not exactly sure what his job is these days, but I know it's more corporate and a lot less creative. Lately, he's blamed Mom for "stifling" him and forcing him to give up his passion, although I haven't seen him pick up a paintbrush in forever.

I found all his old art supplies in the garage when I was little. Half-dried-out tubes of acrylic paint and stiff paintbrushes and a stack of unused canvases.

Mom threw them out when she found out I was using them, although I *had* just spilled a big blob of scarlet paint on my cream bedroom carpet. Dad bought me a new set of supplies, but these days I'm pretty sure it was in retaliation, and less about supporting my new hobby.

I hated feeling responsible for their fights, even in a small way. Whenever I think too hard about it, I end up with more questions than I honestly want the answers to; but I know my pull toward art is tangled up in a lot of messy emotions for both my parents, so I've learned that it's easier to bury it away, rather than thrust it in front of their faces.

So I appreciate Mom asking and showing some interest, but I wish she wouldn't. There are a lot of things I don't bother sharing with my parents these days; a rough sketch of a woodland scene is the very least of it.

Mom goes back downstairs to order the food, and when the doorbell rings with our delivery I pack up my stuff to go join her. We lay everything out on the coffee table and load up our plates, resting them on our laps to eat while our movie of choice plays on the TV. Tonight, Mom's chosen *Notting Hill*.

She asks me how school's going, and I tell her it's fine. She asks if I've made any new friends, and I say sort of.

"There's some girls in a few of my classes I've been eating lunch with" is about all I offer up, not really feeling like getting into it now. Once upon a time I probably would've agonized with her over every exchange, every Instagram like and in-joke, but this is probably the most we've really talked in a while. It's a nice change; that distance from Dad and the divorce stuff must really be helping.

Adults are always saying teenagers are a law unto themselves and don't talk to their parents, but it's really the other way around. My parents are both so wrapped up in their own lives—and their ongoing divorce—that I'm just . . . *there*. I guess I'm old enough to look after myself now, though, so maybe this is what it's like for everybody my age? Maybe this is just their way of treating me like a grown-up, like the teachers at school who don't need us to ask permission to go to the bathroom during class anymore.

"Haven't you got any plans with them this weekend?" Mom asks me.

"No . . . not yet."

"Well, you can always invite them over here, if you like? Order in some pizzas or something."

It's all I can do not to laugh in her face, and instead I choke down my food, spraying a little egg fried rice out on to my plate as I cough. I cover my mouth with my hand and Mom hands me my glass of water.

In what world could she *ever* think I'd want to invite people over here? *I* don't even want to be here sometimes.

But I just say, "Maybe. I'll see. It's early days, so we're not really that sort of friends yet."

"And what about Jake? How's he been?"

"Yeah, he's fine. He's busy tonight with the soccer guys."

They've gone to someone's house to play Xbox. I bet Max is there, since he's on Jake's team. I grit my teeth just thinking of his smug, judgmental face from the convention last weekend. The fact he's probably there tonight feels like a point for him, a loss for me.

Which is silly, I know. We're not *competing* for Jake's friendship, but . . .

We are.

We're absolutely competing for it, even if Max doesn't realize that yet.

Mom senses there's something I'm not saying, because she lowers the volume a bit on the movie and pierces me with a worried look over the top of her thick-framed glasses. Her eyes aren't the deep mossy green mine are, but ringed with a hazel that makes them look gilded. "Are the two of you not talking very much anymore? You've hardly mentioned him recently, even after you saw him in town on the weekend."

"Oh my God, Mom—"

"It's really normal for that to happen, Cerys, you know. Especially at your age. Going off to different schools, then universities, living all around the country, growing up . . . Lots of friendships just fizzle out. Life gets very busy."

"That's *not* what's happening," I snap, a little too sharply. She raises a blond eyebrow. "There's just not a lot to say, that's all. We still text loads. And I might see him Sunday, actually."

I've asked if he's free, if he wants to hang out and watch a couple more episodes of *OWAR* with me, but of course he hasn't replied yet; he's busy with the boys. I messaged in the Discord, too, about how I need some more Téiglin content for my art projects, but Jake hasn't replied there, either.

There's a hollow, raw feeling in my chest, and it doesn't go away even after Mom pulls a blanket over both our legs so we can snuggle into the sofa with our food comas for the rest of the film.

My phone finally pings a little while later—a text from Jake.

Jake

Agh I'm over with the grandparents on Sunday! Nan's doing a roast, and it's Gin's last weekend home before she's back to uni. Maybe in the week, after school? I'll get some snacks! x

The kiss makes my heart flutter more than any single letter in a text message has any right to. I try telling myself that sometimes Jake sends a kiss when he's being extra-nice, or even an "xo" if he's being snarky and goofing around to make me laugh, but it doesn't dampen that giddy feeling, or the way my brain immediately starts planning an outfit for our not-quite-date after school to watch *OWAR*. Maybe I should watch the episodes in advance, so I can think of smart things to ask him and he can show off his knowledge of the show?

Mom and I watch another film—*Four Weddings and a Funeral*, as Mom decides she's on a Hugh Grant kick tonight—and by then it's late enough that she sends me off to bed.

"Your dad's coming over for dinner tomorrow, by the way," she says when I'm almost out of the room—launching the grenade she's apparently had her thumb on for the past few hours. I grit my teeth, wondering if that's what this whole "film and takeout" night was about.

Not about just spending time together, after all.

"Oh. Right. So, um . . ." Is this her way of telling me to make myself scarce? I don't know how to ask that. "Do you have more stuff to go over together, for the lawyers?"

Mom gives me such a look of exaggerated shock, then laughs. "No, you silly thing, he's just coming over for dinner! We *are* still a family. We thought it would be nice."

NICE? I want to scream. Nice? Dinner? With *both of them*? I can't remember the last time that was *nice*. Tense, maybe, and full of long stretches of silence broken only by one of them asking me to "pass the salt."

"We discussed it in couples' counseling this week," Mom adds, which is the grenade exploding. My stomach drops away.

"I thought you stopped going to those sessions?" I manage, my voice sounding at least halfway normal.

"No! No, we started them back up a little while ago. They're helping lots!"

Are they? Shit. I don't want them to get help, I want them to *get the divorce they've been on the verge of for years!* I can't cope with walking on eggshells around them both for another two years until I can leave for uni. They've tried this before—all the back and forth of "learning to communicate" and "doing the work," and it never actually helps.

It's not that I don't want to see my dad more—I miss him a lot since he moved out, even if he's still been around plenty. I just hope

to God this isn't some latest attempt at any kind of real reconcil-
iation.

I'm almost about to make up some excuse to get out of it, but
I've already admitted to having no plans this weekend, so I'm stuck
saying, "Great, that'll . . . be nice, yeah," before making a hasty
escape up to bed, already emotionally drained at the mere thought
of tomorrow's so-called family dinner.

As I tuck myself into bed and check my phone, there's a Discord notification, and my mood instantly lifts.

> **@runicrascal**
> Just wait for episode 4. It's a DOOZY.
>
> Assuming your Friday night plans were more exciting
> than watching your new favorite obsession, Of Wrath
> and Rune. Hope you had a good one 😊
>
> **@mythicwitch**
> V exciting, thank you. The kind of plans involving Hugh
> Grant and Julia Roberts and a bookshop.
>
> . . . wait, what happens in episode 4? DOES he die?

I'm unduly attached to this stag-skull character. I can't tell if
that's just because he's a perfect subject for my art coursework, or
if it's the banter with @runicrascal spurring me on. It's kind of fun,
if only for the excuse to chat with Jake.

> **@runicrascal**
> Notting Hill? A classic choice.
>
> **@mythicwitch**
> You know it!

@runicrascal
And about ep4 . . . that would be telling. I thought we said no spoilers?

@mythicwitch
I'm starting to see where you got the "rascal" part of your username, Runic.

@runicrascal
:D

I am a bundle of nervous energy on Wednesday in media class. It's my last class of the day, so I'll go straight from here to the bus to Jake's house for some episodes of *Of Wrath and Rune*. I decided not to watch them in advance, which suddenly feels like a bad idea. I don't want to make an idiot of myself in front of him, not when it's something he loves so much.

It really has come to something, when "making an idiot of myself" is not fully understanding one of three magic systems ("magick," apparently, if the Discord is anything to go by) and not going out in public wearing a wig and elf ears.

But these are the lengths we go to for love; and romance *is* all about grand gestures.

Daphne notices I'm all worked up, because in the middle of class she nudges me in the side and whispers, "What's got into you? It's like you downed a can of Red Bull! You haven't stopped jiggling once."

"I . . . I sort of have a . . . a date tonight," I blurt, too fraught and excited to think up a white lie. Daphne gasps, eyes brightening, and I get a surge of panic, remembering too late about how I didn't want this getting back to Evie and possibly then to Jake. "Sort of. Not really. Maybe?"

"You don't know if it's a date?"

I shake my head.

"Well, did he ask you? Is he taking you out somewhere?"

"It's . . . um, I don't know. He's a friend, so it's a little complicated. I'm just going to his house to hang out."

Daphne's mouth widens into a grin, and I relax to see her instantly sharing in my excitement. "Are his parents going to be there?"

I shrug. "I think they might still be at work? I'm not sure."

"If they're not, it's *definitely* a date."

"Right. And if they are?"

She ponders this for a minute. I know from her social media that she had a boyfriend for two years, and then she's mentioned a guy she dated over the summer, so Daphne is definitely more worldly when it comes to this sort of thing than I am. I'll take any advice she wants to give.

"I think it still *could* be . . . but maybe don't make *too* much of a move—let him come to you. You don't want to be like Cher in *Clueless* and fall off the bed just trying to flip your hair!"

The two of us giggle, and our teacher shushes us and throws a warning look our way. We return to our notes for a few minutes in silence before I risk whispering, "I love that movie."

"Me too! It's one of my favorites. I love those old rom-coms."

I feel a little lighter, more confident, to hear it. At least a shared love of a movie genre is some good ground to bond over, if all else fails.

I add, "Seriously, though, I haven't even *thought* about if we go up to his room . . ."

Which is true; I hadn't. I've been in Jake's room plenty of times before when we've hung out, but I haven't seen his bedroom in the new house. When we hung out this summer, it was mainly in his garden or the "orangery" (which seems just like any old sunroom, if you ask me) or in town. And if this *is* more of a date—if it's part of us growing closer and taking our friendship to a different level . . .

Well, that changes things.

"Definitely let him make the first move," Daphne tells me, more authoritatively now. "Especially since we don't know if it's really a date yet. You don't want to make it awkward. But you just have to make sure you're *open,* you know?"

I'm so alarmed by the way she says it that all I can do is blurt, "What, like . . . ?" and part my legs wide under the table, pulling a horrified face. I'm not going there to try to have sex with him! I haven't even *kissed* him! She can't honestly be suggesting . . . ?

Daphne squeals with laughter so suddenly that she snorts when she tries to smother the sound and ends up gasping for breath. A tear escapes her eye and she swipes it away. I sit there and watch, confused and embarrassed, feeling like I've just made a complete fool of myself—that she won't want to bother with me if I don't know how to act in a guy's bedroom on a maybe-date.

"Daphne," barks our teacher. "If you cannot control yourself, I will have to ask you to leave my classroom. I expect better from my students."

"Sorry, sir," she wheezes, her pale cheeks flushed an almost iridescent shade of pink. She refuses to look at me for several minutes, until she's sure she won't laugh again. She ends up hissing out of the side of her mouth, "Cerys, you kill me. You're hilarious. *Obviously* that's not what I meant, but—" She throws her hand up in front of her face to block me out, even as her shoulders shake with barely contained laughter.

Oh thank God. She doesn't think I'm a boring old prude! She just thought I was making a joke.

She thinks I'm *hilarious*!

I warm with pride, bottling it up to remember the next time I'm not sure if I fit in with this new group of friends, and only once the bell rings and we're out of class does Daphne carry on our conversation. She follows me to the bathroom, where I hoist my bag up on to the sinks to rummage through for the makeup I brought with me. I want to glam myself up a little in case it *is* more of a date, and to send the right sort of signals to Jake, but obviously I can't go overboard when we are, really, just hanging out to watch TV.

My hands brush over the T-shirt bundled up in my bag. Forest green, with a shimmery pattern and slogan printed on it. I thought the fandom T-shirt Jake gifted me would be perfect to wear tonight. He'd think it was a joke before he thought it was try-hard, but I'm *really* hoping it'll drive home my dedication to this—to *him*.

But Daphne is right there, and—

"Ooh, is that what you're wearing?"

She's pulling it out of my bag before I can protest, and my cheeks burn. Her face creases in confusion as she studies the BE YE

A RASCAL, ROACH? motif, and I'm so mortified I want the ground to swallow me whole.

"Er," she says, and I feel our tenuous friendship slipping away.

I blurt, "My friend—this guy, tonight—bought it for me. It's, like, a gag gift, you know? Some weird in-joke . . ."

She gasps, enthralled. "*He* got it for you? Oh my gosh, you *have* to wear it! And the color is *so* perfect with your eyes." She holds it up against me, grinning. "It really makes them pop! I bet he totally knew that when he bought it, too. *So* cute!"

She pushes me toward a toilet stall to go change, and I do, fussing with how the T-shirt sits as I emerge. Daphne helps direct me to tuck it in just so, giving my straight frame at least the illusion of a more defined waist. The boxy fit makes my chest look even flatter than usual, but I bite my tongue before humiliating myself further and asking Daphne if she thinks I should stuff my bra. (Are we still doing that?)

As I bundle my sweater into my bag and go back to touching up my makeup, Daphne's already chattering away again.

"You have to just put out the right vibes, let him know you're available and interested, that's all! Not—" Daphne throws her legs wide and fans her long, elegant fingers around her crotch and throws in a few thrusts for good measure, making me laugh this time. "You know, angle your body toward him, draw attention to your mouth or your hair, mirror his body language, try keeping your hand there for him to hold but *not* so it looks like that's what you're aiming for, if he isn't going to."

"Got it," I say, a little relieved when these are all the sort of tips I've already accumulated from years of watching rom-coms.

It's nothing new, outlandish, or extreme. To hear more-experienced Daphne back up my fictional education is reassuring, too.

"Can I do your lips for you?" she asks.

"Do you—d'you mind?"

Excited, she nods and plonks her own bag down, rummaging through for lip liner and a thick, sticky gloss to paint my lips with.

Surely if *anything* is going to solidify a friendship, it's this? Gossiping about maybe-dates, doing each other's makeup. And Daphne's makeup always looks so good.

I can't wait for Jake to see my new and improved look.

"There! OMG, you look *stunning*!" Daphne pops the lip gloss applicator back into the tube and I turn toward the mirror, bursting to see the transformation, how she'll have accentuated my lips and made me look irresistible and . . .

Oh.

Hmm.

I must stare a beat too long, because I swear Daphne's face falls a little in the reflection of the mirror. I say quickly, "I love it! Thank you! This is perfect!"

I'm not sure "perfect" is really the word, though . . . My mouth definitely looks bigger and poutier than normal, but it also looks more like I got stung by a bee and it got infected than the dramatic, pretty look it is on Daphne. She hasn't done anything different or wrong as far as I can tell, but the color doesn't seem quite right for my freckled skin and fair hair, and I'm forced to admit that my features just can't carry off this kind of look.

I finish applying some fresh blush and highlighter to my cheeks, and then I'm ready to go, promising Daphne that I'll text her as soon as I'm home later to let her know how everything went, and promising a second, in-person debrief at Costa tomorrow on the way to school.

I glance at my reflection in the bus window and lift my chin. I can be the kind of girl who carries this look; I can be bold and pretty and confident like them.

And, well, if nothing else—it'll definitely draw Jake's attention and hopefully, finally, get me a kiss.

When I step off the bus outside Jake's house, my palms are sweating and I can't stop fidgeting with my clothes. I'm questioning everything and I hate it.

I haven't *always* been like this around Jake. Up until a few months ago, I rarely thought twice about what I was wearing when I saw him; sometimes I might hope he'd notice and I'd feel pleased whenever he said I looked nice, but I never picked an outfit with him in mind.

Then again, I'd never had to actively *work* to make sure he didn't forget me or let our friendship slip by the wayside. As one of the few genuinely good-looking, decent guys in our class, he was always someone I'd harbored a small crush on, but it wasn't until he turned down another girl and asked if I wanted to go to prom with him instead that I realized my feelings for Jake ran a *lot* deeper than just cherishing our friendship. I started daydreaming about how we'd be hanging out, and so easily, so naturally, he'd turn to me and we'd be kissing . . .

I *did* hold out hope for a movie-worthy moment at prom. I wanted to be Rachel Chu arriving at Araminta's lavish wedding with all the aunties stunned speechless in *Crazy Rich Asians,* Laney in her red dress in *She's All That.* We were all sharing a limo as a group, but I got ready at Jake's house. His big sister, Ginny, was home, so she'd offered to help with my hair and makeup, and I had visions of walking down the stairs and Jake catching his breath, unable to take his eyes off me . . .

The exaggerated wolf whistle I got wasn't quite what I'd hoped for.

I wish he hadn't had to move, or go to this new school. It's almost an hour on the bus to get to his new house now, not just a fifteen-minute walk down over the canal. Before summer, we used to hang out almost every day. Mom's comment about growing up and growing apart suddenly resurfaces in my brain, but I refuse to acknowledge it, instead shoving it deep, deep down.

The big driveway is empty; Ginny's not home, and Jake's parents are still at work.

According to Daphne's logic, this is *definitely* more like a date.

It's good news, but my stomach ties itself into such knots I think I might be sick. Why does it suddenly feel like everything hinges on how this evening goes? We're just hanging out, like we've done a thousand times before. I won't be trying to make any moves, like holding his hand or leaning over to kiss his cheek, so it won't ruin our friendship, but if it's *not* a date—

If it *is* a date—

As I walk down the garden path to Jake's front door, I force myself to concentrate on my breathing, which feels too loud and a little ragged. I try to regulate it, but it's hard now that I'm actively thinking about it. Not too shallow, not too heavy. *For God's sake, breathe like a normal human, Cerys!*

Before I can lift a hand to knock on the door, it swings open.

And there's Jake, beaming at me, a fingerprint smudge on his glasses, the white shirt he has to wear for his uniform looking a little disheveled; the sleeves are falling down where he folded them up in his usual carefree manner. He stands barefoot on the door-mat, and I'm already grinning back, wondering excitedly, *Was he standing there waiting for me?*

"Hey there, newbie! The sensor went off on the Ring camera," he says, reading my mind in that way he does. My cheeks heat, and I try to will the blush away, not sure I'm very successful at it. Then he looks at my lips, and my stomach flips and I inhale sharply as Jake says . . . "You're, er, trying something new? That's a different look for you."

I bite my lower lip, just barely. It feels sticky. "Do you like it?"

Jake's not looking at my mouth anymore, though, he's looking just at me, with one eyebrow twisted upward. "Do *you* like it?"

I'm deflated, I'm crushed, I'm . . . actually honestly reassured that it's not just me who thinks this is not really *me*. I laugh shakily. "One of the girls did it for me. I love it on her, but . . ."

"Maybe a different . . . color?"

"Maybe," I agree, and we lock eyes for a moment before we both laugh; it makes me feel lighter, everything feeling normal between us again.

See, Mom? We aren't drifting apart. We're solid as ever.

"T-shirt looks great, though!" he tells me with a wink that

buoys me enough to strike a little pose, hip jutted out and hand fanning down the length of my torso.

"Fandom's a good look on me, huh?"

"And to think—we're only just getting started." His tone is cheeky, borderline flirty, and I'm too giddy to think up a good response.

"Come in, we were just making a snack. You want anything?"

"Sure," I say, and it comes out too breathless. *Crap! Breathe, Cerys, don't be weird!* "Yeah, I'd . . . Wait, did you say 'we'? But I thought . . ."

I look again at the driveway in front of the garages, which is empty.

Jake, though, points carelessly over my other shoulder, where there's a small and slightly battered black Ford parked at a crooked angle on the pavement. He's already moving inside, assuming I'm following, as he says, "Yeah, Max is here. Our physics lesson got canceled, so we came back here to try to catch up on the classwork. Explain to me how the teacher gets sick, but it's on *us* to make up for that? Is St. David's like that, too?"

My mouth opens, but I can't respond.

Max is here.

Why is Max here?

This is meant to be *our* time, *our* hangout.

What on earth made Jake think I wanted his new friend around? He's not *my* friend.

I shouldn't have been so nice to him at the convention. I've obviously given Jake the wrong impression and made him think that Max and I are cool.

I am already mentally crafting a text to Daphne. *This is absolutely, categorically, NOT a date.*

I'm also mentally adding another step to The Fangirl Project—*GET. RID. OF. MAX.* It feels more imperative than ever. I underscore it about sixteen times in my head.

Jake, as ever, reads into my silence, and looks back at me from where he's halfway down the hall to the kitchen, and I'm standing frozen in the doorway. His eyebrows pinch together, and his mouth turns downward.

"You don't mind that Max is here, right? I thought it'd be chill. He'll enjoy rewatching a couple of episodes of *OWAR* . . ."

"No!" It bursts out of me too fast and too shrill. How do people do this? How do they keep their cool around a boy they like, when there's a massive wrench thrown into the works by the name of Max? I try again. "No, that's—it's totally chill, yeah."

Jake relaxes, grinning at me once more. His hair is all askew, like he's had his hand tangled in it on one side while he studies, and I'd love to reach over and smooth it out. I settle for taking my shoes off instead, lining them up neatly on the shoe rack in the entryway to distract my hands.

"D'you wanna go on up? We're just hanging out in my room."

"Oh! Um . . . I thought . . ." Is Max not also downstairs? Am I going to have to hang out with Max *one-on-one*? In a *BEDROOM*? This is so not how this evening was supposed to go. I swallow the lump in my throat. "Are you sure you don't want some help with the snacks? I can make some cups of tea, maybe, or—"

Jake wanders toward the kitchen and waves a dismissive hand over his shoulder that feels like a slap in the face. "Nah, don't be silly, you go kick your feet up. I'll follow you in a minute. Cheese and pickle?"

"Ooh, go on then," I reply, trying to be normal, and he fakes a gag before disappearing into the kitchen to make his go-to after-school snack: a grilled cheese sandwich.

I dither in the hall for the count of three before I make my way upstairs, taking them slowly. I can't avoid the inevitable, but every second shaved off hanging out with Max counts.

Jake's new house is bigger than his old one, considerably. It doesn't make sense to me—I thought most parents downsized when their kids left home, and Jake will be off to uni in two years like Ginny is—but I look in awe at the sleek architecture of the massive landing window and the reading nook his mom has created in a little annex between bedrooms, making the expansive white space cozy and homey. Most of the doors are closed, except for one wide open and showing a bathroom with a walk-in shower, and another cracked open that must be Jake's room. There's music playing inside, low enough to be background noise to a conversation.

A floorboard creaks beneath my foot as I step closer, which I don't doubt Max will have heard, so I suck in a breath and step inside.

Jake's room is . . . more or less exactly the same. The configuration is all different, but the furniture and colors and posters and clutter haven't changed: the blue and gray bedsheets, a navy feature wall behind his bed, his desk overtaken by a gaming setup and a couple of books stacked neatly. There's a new addition to his dorky collection of posters—an *OWAR* one, signed in silver Sharpie by several cast members he met at the convention recently. It's got pride of place behind the TV.

The only thing out of place is *him.*

My eyes snag on Max after a quick scan of the room, and linger.

He looks surprisingly . . . well, *normal,* actually. He's sitting in Jake's low, curved gaming chair, wearing a white school shirt like Jake, although his is still tucked in and the sleeves are rolled up more neatly and firmly, in no danger of flapping loose. He's concentrating on a textbook in his lap, a highlighter in hand and a pen pinched between his teeth, brow furrowed in concentration.

Once again, all I can do is *stare at him.*

He's got dark hair. Thick and almost jet-black, worn half up in a loose bun, the rest long enough to brush his chin. Even without the weird armor things to bulk them out, his shoulders are broad.

He glances up, eyes locking on mine intensely, and he doesn't say so much as a hello. He notices my lipstick, staring unashamedly just as much as I am at him. His gaze flicks to my T-shirt then, and one of his eyebrows twitches upward as if in disdain. *He* clearly thinks it's a try-hard move.

I blurt out, "I would never have recognized you without the wig and the ears."

It's true. If I'd walked past him in the street, I'm not sure I would've known it was him.

"And here I thought you'd show up in full cosplay for an *OWAR* marathon," he quips, and even though his tone is light, it's laced with just enough sarcasm that it feels like a dig. For a moment, I think maybe he can even see right through me, and knows why I'm *really* here. "I'm kind of let down, newbie. You call this commitment to the fandom?"

I hate him.

I actually, properly, hate him.

I drop my school bag and perch on the edge of Jake's bed, which is about as far away from Max as I can get. I tuck one knee up and lean on my hand. It's a pose lots of the movie heroines do, and I can only hope I look as confident and effortless as them. I do *not* need Max knowing he's gotten under my skin, or Jake thinking I hate his new friend.

So I will be his friend, too. I will be nice to him, and I will be polite, and I will *not lose my cool* and lose Jake in the process. I can't. And if that means putting up with this judgmental jerk, so be it.

"Oh, Max," I tell him. "You have *no* idea how committed I am."

8

I am in Jake's bedroom, sitting on his bed, alone with a boy.

I feel like the universe is laughing at me.

Max clears his throat and goes back to his textbook, and while I'm a little put out that he thinks algebraic equations for projectiles are more interesting than talking to me, I'm also relieved. He clearly doesn't like me very much, either, which suits me just fine.

Still, as the silence stretches on and the only sounds in the room are the quiet indie-rock playlist on Jake's speaker and the scratch of Max's highlighter, I feel almost claustrophobic. His indifference grates on me, prickles along my skin, and my leg bounces agitatedly against the side of the bed.

How long can it possibly take to make some grilled cheese? Has Jake suddenly turned into Gordon Ramsay, attempting a full gourmet experience?

Unable to bear the silence any longer, I fumble for the only thread of conversation I can think of—which, somehow, is *Of Wrath and Rune.*

"I started reading the books, you know."

Max glances up, not quite lifting his head from the textbook. "Did you get very far?"

I flush, although I should've expected that question. "No."

I've been carrying the first book around in my bag for the past week, waiting for the perfect moment when I'll suddenly pick it back up and make it beyond the fifth page. I've studied the map a few times on the bus, though. It's actually quite pretty.

Max laughs, a low, scoffing sort of sound that makes me bristle. "Many more intrepid adventurers before you have failed in this nigh impossible quest."

I don't know if it's a quote from the series, or if he sincerely talks like that. I'm not really sure which is more cringey.

"Well," I say, thinking about my chat with Jake in the Discord, and hoping it'll make me sound like I know what I'm talking about to show Max up. "Once I've watched a few more episodes and really get to know the characters, the books will be a fun way to learn more about them."

His mouth cracks in what I *think* might just be a smile, and I feel a flare of triumph.

Maybe this fandom isn't really for me, and I'm only trying to get into it for Jake's sake, but I refuse to let Max feel any kind of superiority just because he's a "true" fan and I'm not. He's not smarter than me for having read these doorstop novels, and he's not better than me for liking this series.

Finally there's the tromping sound of Jake's feet heavy on the stairs, and I let out a sigh of relief. My best friend enters the room carrying a tray laden with steaming mugs of tea and plates of grilled cheese, holding a giant bag of Doritos between his teeth.

"Give us a hand!" he mumbles. Laughing, I hop off the bed to help him out. Max sets aside his textbook and pens to come grab his portion of the snacks.

When he reaches for the green mug that says JUST DANDY with a bright yellow dandelion painted beneath, I practically slap his hand out of the way.

"That's *my* mug."

It's technically Jake's, but I got it for him one Christmas as part of some in-joke I barely even remember now and I've used it every time I've been over his house. Even his parents will grab it for me if they make tea when I visit.

"Oh," Max says awkwardly, looking at Jake. "My bad, I . . ."

I look at Jake, ready to share a laugh about that forgotten joke, but he looks away from me quickly and cringes. "Sorry, Cer, that's on me—I've been using it for Max, he's sort of . . . commandeered it."

Now the two of *them* share a look, and chuckle.

Max explains, "I fell on my face at soccer the first time Jake played with us—I *literally* ate dirt, except I mostly got a mouthful of dandelion. One of the big ones you blow on, you know? I was spitting the fluff out for days, I swear."

"Any time he coughs, we're all like, 'Make a wish!'" Jake adds, and the two of them crack up again. Jake pushes Max in the shoulder playfully, making a show of pretending to find some more dandelion fluff in his long hair and blowing it away.

It's like a knife in the chest, carving a jagged space out where my friendship with Jake belongs. I cast about for our own story, but it dances at the edge of my memory. Something about Jake making fun of a teacher who used some outdated slang? Which teacher was that? Was it even Jake who started it?

"Yours is this one," Jake tells me, now that they've both stopped laughing. He prompts me to take one of Ginny's mugs. It has a cartoon pug on it giving the middle finger, which is about how I feel right now. "Max doesn't take sugar in his, so . . ."

So there's no swapping, and I've been downgraded, ousted.

I pick the mug up and force a smile. "That's okay! Thanks, Jake."

"You guys take your grilled cheese the same, though. Ugh! With pickle! Grim." He fake-gags again, and I'd find it funny, except having something in common with Max stings. Like it's *another* thing he's taken from me, and I know it's ridiculous but I have the sudden urge to find a new favorite type of grilled cheese, just to separate us.

It's just not *fair*. I've known Jake for five years. Max has barely known him for five minutes!

I take my plate with a mumbled "Cheers," and return to my perch on the edge of Jake's bed. He sets his stuff on the nightstand before flopping down, sitting up against the headboard with his legs stretched out in front of him.

Should I go sit next to him? Does it even matter now, with Max-the-third-wheel here?

I stay put.

Jake turns the TV on, finding the streaming service with *Of Wrath and Rune* and calling up episode three. After his comment in the Discord about not meeting some fan-favorite characters until around this point in the show, I'd kind of wanted to share that experience with him.

I hope we still get to have that. I hope Max doesn't spoil it.

I also suddenly hope that Téiglin the stag-guy doesn't die. I'm not sure I'm prepared for that, and I don't need Max scorning me if I dare to sniffle about it.

As soon as the title sequence starts up, though, both boys are consumed by the show, and it's like I'm not even there. The theme music is heavy on the strings—Jake sings that part, and Max joins in with the trumpets later, both of them bopping along in place to the bad graphics on the screen rolling through different scenes and overlaid with the cast.

It's hard to concentrate on the show when I'm so conscious of my every reaction and whether Jake is watching. Worse, whether *Max* is watching, and judging me for being too disinterested or too fake or not getting something.

My right leg starts to get pins and needles where I've tucked it underneath me, and I'm hyperaware of how every time I shift on the bed to try to get more comfortable, *I am on Jake's bed, and Jake is right there.* I've also got Daphne's voice in my head saying that I don't want to do a Cher from *Clueless,* so I'm too scared to move much at all, terrified I'll somehow slip and fall right onto the floor.

So I end up staying still, suffering through my numb leg and a plot-heavy show with cheaply done CGI sets of fantasy cities and intense conversations full of subtext between characters whose names I can't quite remember.

Every so often one of the boys will say something like "Oh man, remember this?" or "The costume department's come *so* far, dude." And sometimes, Jake will give me a gentle poke in the hip with his foot and say, "Watch this, Cer. This scene is *so good*. Did you notice the stag beetle in the background?"

My mind drifts as we watch. I'm paying more attention to the makeup and set design than what characters are saying, or thinking about the map in the front of the book and trying to pair it up with whatever land is onscreen now.

Finally, though, something nabs my attention.

The scene is in a bedroom—a "bedchamber," really, with a huge four-poster draped in velvet hangings, and a vanity with an ornate gold mirror—and a pointy-eared woman who just snuck in through her window sighs when she sees a (normal-eared) man in leather standing there, arms folded. He looks distinctly unimpressed.

I glance at Max, biting the inside of my cheek, wondering if he recognizes that kind of judgy look.

So far in the story, all I've learned is that she's a noblewoman who sneaks off to . . . fight? Adventure? *Quest?* Generally get in trouble, and do it with a righteous attitude, leading a double life as a demure lady by day.

The elvish woman hisses, *"Devon, if you say a word—"*

"My lady, you cannot keep . . ." He trails off as she steps into the lamplight, holding her arm awkwardly. There's blood shining red on her fingers, and he moves closer. I'm leaning forward on Jake's bed, the scene sucking me in.

"You're hurt."

"It's nothing."

"Who—"

"You told me once not to tell you anything that would risk your position in my father's guard, that you owe him too much to betray his trust; I would advise you now—do not ask questions you don't want the answers to, Devon."

The soldier, Devon, sighs heavily. He closes the distance between them and pushes her cloak aside to reveal a wound he helps her clean and bandage, all in total silence, and the tension is so palpable that when she catches her breath, I do, too. The way he's looking at her is so intense, I feel almost like I'm intruding, even though it's just a TV show.

"This will be the final time," he says, his voice low.

"You do not order me about in my own home, sir. Do you forget that I am the future Lady di Silver? The fate of these lands, these people, rests on my shoulders. I do not answer to a common soldier who—"

"Who will saddle a horse, and leave with you at midnight." He straightens up, levels her with another weighted look. I think I gasp out loud at the turn in the story. *"This cannot continue, my lady; they will find you out, and your quest will take you far beyond the towns surrounding your father's keep. Honor compels me that I cannot let you go alone."*

"You'll . . . come with me?"

"I will," he responds, and as grim as he makes the promise sound, he hasn't taken his eyes off hers. *"Until the end."*

The screen goes to black, credits rolling with the title music, and this time I really almost do fall off the bed in my haste to spin around, looking at Jake with wide eyes.

"You didn't tell me this was a *romance*! Jake!" I cast about for something to throw at him, but his pillows are too far out of reach, so I settle for taking a playful swipe at his shin instead while he laughs, his eyes glittering at my reaction. "I would've watched this with you ages ago if you'd told me that! I thought it was all boring sword fights and casting spells and stuff."

"The sword fights are the *opposite* of boring," he tells me. "Have you even been paying attention to *any* of the scenes with Daxys? He's just . . . he's *amazing.*"

Max says, "And the spells are pretty cool, too." Then he laughs, and gestures at me as he says to Jake, "I told you she'd be a Silversmith shipper in no time. Called it."

"A what?"

"Lady Adanna di Silver, and Devon Smith, her . . . I guess you'd call him her bodyguard? A soldier sworn to protect her. They're a really popular ship in the fandom," Max explains. "People rooting for them to be together, you know, romantically."

I feel my cheeks warm. "I *know* what shipping is."

He doesn't acknowledge me, but carries on. "Especially because of the forbidden element—Devon tries to be really proper and not overstep when his duty is to watch her back, not, you know, fall for her. Although even half the Silversmith fans are convinced they're not endgame, and he'll die."

"He'll *what*? But—"

But that's not how it works! Don't they know? Haven't they ever seen a romance movie? The way they looked at each other . . .

"There's tons of theories about how he'll die protecting her,"

Jake tells me. "Especially with the foreshadowing in this episode. *'Until the end.'* People think he'll go down defending her."

"Oh!" I clasp a hand to my chest, already picturing it. "That's so tragic and romantic."

Is it weird if I ask Jake to rewind so we can watch that scene again? It was just *so good.* How can Jake have neglected to mention *this* any time he's waxed lyrical about his favorite series?

How is trekking through the forest and ragtag bands of rebels more worthwhile than an epic, maybe doomed romance?

"Okay, spoilers, *please*," I say, feeling the need to disclose after the constant jokes about it on Discord. I grab Jake's shin, leaning toward him with wide eyes. "Tell me they have *tons* more screen time together."

"*So* much screen time," he promises. "Four seasons' worth, so far."

"Amazing. Perfect. Yes."

He laughs, and I can't even be embarrassed about my unashamed fangirling. Even in the fantasy setting, the romance storyline works. Maybe it even makes it *better*?

"She'll be going home to find the fanfics now," Max tells Jake—and why, why does he keep talking about me like I'm not here? Am I invisible? Am I worth so little of his energy that he can barely even acknowledge me, and will only talk to Jake?

But my curiosity gets the better of me, and my face falls. "Fanfiction? What, like . . . like people writing stories about all of BTS falling in love with them on tour or something?"

"Kind of," Jake says, and then scoots down the bed to grasp my shoulders and stare into my eyes. It's not as intense as Devon and Lady di Silver, but I stare back, willing it to be. We're sitting on Jake's bed, my knees touching his thigh, his face only inches from mine . . . discussing *OWAR* fanfiction while his new bestie, *Max,* loiters nearby. This isn't how I pictured it.

But Jake's still talking, and I try hard to pay attention.

"Cerys, when I tell you this is a very dedicated fanbase, I mean it. Word has it there is a fic from a couple of years ago that's *eight hundred thousand words,* and two girls wrote it together in less than a year."

"That's . . . a lot," I say carefully. I know Jake will think I mean the word count, but in reality, I'm thinking that's a lot of time and effort to put into something that . . . doesn't really matter.

Didn't those girls have anything better to do? Didn't they want to do something more productive, or fun? How did they write almost a million words of a story that hardly anybody will read anyway, in less than a year? They can't have done anything else in that time. Isn't that sort of sad, a little weird? Isn't it . . . well, a *lot?*

I can't imagine pouring that sort of time and effort into an art project. I think of the abandoned pieces stacked under my bed, unfinished and cast aside whenever my inspiration waned or life got in the way.

Did they really decide to put their whole heart and soul into creating something just . . . *because?*

It's so bizarre I can't even wrap my head around it, but there's a burning sensation deep in my chest that feels like . . . jealousy.

I can feel Max looking at me, *judging me,* and wonder if he can hear the things I'm not saying out loud the way Jake sometimes does. Am I really so easy to read?

He says, in another cryptic "Is it a quote from the show or just Max being a dork?" phrase, "A daunting prospect indeed. The time to bow out is not yet past."

I ignore him, and say to Jake, "Let's watch the next one."

9

I'm on a high when the fourth episode finishes. Téiglin has made a reappearance, running into some council meeting of his fellow forest creatures, interrupting Minotaurs and fauns and a very large, badly animated owl, to report back what he found out about the evil royal family.

I'm still not sure why they're so evil, or what the whole drama is exactly, but Téiglin has solidified himself as an endearing, sort of bumbling character—and I'm here for it. Plus, it's given me some new inspiration for my art project, and I'm suddenly itching to get home to my sketchbook to draw, which is . . . new. I normally turn to art to while away time, rather than because I feel this burning need to put an idea onto canvas and see it come to life.

So maybe *Of Wrath and Rune* isn't all *so* awful and boring.

I'm not sure I'd call myself a "fan" at this stage, but when I tell Jake I'm excited to watch the next few episodes, I'm surprised to find just how much I mean it. The storyline hasn't captured me in the slightest, but the characters are making up for that.

"Are you around this week?" I ask Jake. "Maybe we can watch some more?"

Plus, I'll get to see him again, and maybe we won't have to put up with our third wheel this time.

But Jake hesitates, and in that split second, my stomach sinks.

"Oh, uh . . . I don't know, Cer." He rubs the back of his neck, and glances at Max for a beat too long. The usurper, the interloper. "We've got a *lot* of homework, and then it's soccer, plus the match on Sunday—we were gonna go out after that, and . . . I mean, you're working Saturday anyway, right?"

"Yeah, but . . ."

I trail off, swallowing the rest of that sentence. My shift at the H&M in town is only a few hours in the afternoon, but I'm getting the message loud and clear: Jake doesn't want to spend time with me.

I am being pushed out.

I am no longer the best friend he chooses to hang out with.

I hate hate hate Max with a passion. I don't even know his last name, but I *hate him.*

I can't bring myself to hate Jake; this wedge between us hurts too much, and I know that if I could just get rid of it, things might go back to the way they were before. If I take this betrayal and upset out on Jake, it could ruin us for good. But Max—Max is very safe to hate. *He's* the one who's taking this away from me, after all.

"Maybe next week?" Jake says, more hopefully. "We could make this a regular Wednesday thing! Max, you'd be up for that, right?"

Oh, goodie, weekly hangouts with Max.

But if the alternative is not knowing when I might have plans with Jake next . . .

I force a smile. "That'd be great! Yeah, Max, are you in?" *Please say no, please say no.*

He looks a little startled when I talk more directly to him, and he doesn't smile but does nod once, hesitant. "Sure, I guess."

Why? Why would he agree when he so clearly doesn't want to be here?

My smile strains. "Perfect."

Jake beams, looking genuinely thrilled, absolutely oblivious to the tension between me and Max. "Awesome! *OWAR* Wednesdays, it's on the calendar. You staying for dinner, by the way, Cer? Think Mom's doing a chili."

The "yes" is so ready on my tongue, but Max is slouched low in the gaming chair on his phone like he's already been invited and will be staying, so I hear myself telling Jake, "Thanks, but I should probably get home."

"You sure?"

"Yeah! Next time, though, maybe."

He brightens, and I reach for my bag, not realizing when I haul it upright that it's open.

"Got it!" Jake says, immediately diving to collect my schoolbooks that have fallen out. One catches his eye, though—a blue spiral-bound sketchbook. He was with me when I bought it. He lights up as he starts to thumb through it, and I freeze.

Like, my whole body. Turned to ice. Rooted to the spot. The world stops turning, except for Jake, who seems to be moving at a lightning speed I can't fully process.

"Ooh, what've you been drawing lately, Cer? Any nice profiles of yours truly? I am such a handsome muse, after all."

I'd laugh, but it's *not funny*, because the sketchbook contains worse things than a collection of portraits of the boy I have a crush on, like . . . *The Fangirl Project*.

I drop my bag—sending schoolbooks flying again—so I can snatch it off him.

Jake laughs, holding his hands up in surrender. "All right, Cer, calm down. Show me when they're finished, yeah?"

He says that last part more sincerely—genuinely wanting to see what I've been working on, knowing they're not actually pictures of him. I breathe easier for the out, and nod. "Course. I always do, don't I?"

After shoving everything back into my bag—the sketchbook secure so it can't make another accidental appearance—I tell Max, "See you," even though I really hope I *don't*. He waves goodbye, and Jake comes downstairs to walk me out.

It's the first time we've properly had a minute alone all evening—even though I can hear his mom on the phone in the living room to somebody and his dad puttering around in the kitchen, both home from work by now.

"Thanks for the watch party," I tell Jake. "I had a nice time."

"Good. Told you you'd like it, didn't I?"

He waggles his eyebrows and nudges me with his elbow until I laugh and say, "Yes, yes, all right, you're right, you always know best."

"And Max is pretty cool, too, isn't he? Don't you think?"

"He's . . . cool, yeah." *Frosty*, at any rate . . .

Jake bounces a little on the balls of his feet, his eyes warm and bright, and my heart swells in my aching chest; it's so important to him that Max and I get along, it'd hurt him so badly if he thought we didn't.

So, attempting a more sincere tone, I tell him, "Max seems great. I'll see you both next week."

While I'm pulling my shoes on and getting my coat, Jake asks me softly, "How's things going with your mom and dad?"

I can't repress a groan. Jake knows all the gory details—or enough of them, at least—that I don't bother pretending with him, even if things have felt off between us lately.

"*Weird*. Mom's got all these plans with friends suddenly, but that just feels like some guise so Dad has an excuse to see me, and we had this really *weird* family dinner over the weekend where they were all smiles and nicey-nice . . . It was like they'd had a full personality transplant. *And* they're seeing the couples' counselor again. It's just . . . I thought things were finally calming down, you know? Dust settling, and whatever. But it's almost like they're trying to go *back* to how things were—and they were never that good in the first place . . . Honestly?" I pause for breath; this is the first chance I've had to voice any of this out loud, and the weight off my shoulders is so abrupt, I feel like my knees might give way. "Honestly, it makes me feel sick. I hate it."

"Oh, Cer." Jake's eyes are shining with sympathy, and when he gives my arm a squeeze, it's suddenly all I can do not to burst into tears.

Jake pulls me into an embrace that's less of his usual rough-and-ready bear hug and more like a proper, comforting cwtch, squeezing me tight, his arms wrapping all the way around and his head tucking next to mine. I breathe him in, a familiar scent of bergamot, and instead of worrying about whether this is the kind of hug that's the start of a potential romance, I cling tight to him, glad for my best friend—even if it's only for these brief snatches of time lately.

"Well, remember," he says, when we finally part. I'm blinking my eyes dry before I really do start crying, and Jake has his usual broad smile in place, which makes me feel better already. "You can always move in here. Not sure what Mom and Dad would say about an extra lodger, or how Gin would feel if you stole her bedroom while she's at uni, but I've watched enough *OWAR* to know how to deal with them."

He leaps back a step to wield an imaginary sword, lunging right and swinging left, and a wobbly laugh spills out of me.

"I can be your Devon, defending the fair maiden—even if she's strong enough to fight her own battles most of the time."

Warmth blooms in my chest, and I say, only half a joke, "Until the end?"

He gives me another quick hug. *"Until the end."*

GIRLIE POPS! ✦

Daphne has added **Cerys** to the group chat

Daphne

Cerys omg we're all here like "why hasn't she texted us to let us know how it's gone?!?!?!" when I realized I FORGOT TO ADD YOU TO THE GROUP CHAT 😭

Nikita

It's because she secretly hates you.

Evie

NIK THAT'S SO MEAN

Chloe

SHE'S JOKING, CERYS

Daphne

@Nikita wow okay blocking u

Kidding

Me

Haha as if I hadn't had enough emotional whiplash already this evening!

Thanks for adding me

It was . . . not a successful date, I'm afraid to report

Chloe

Oh no!! What happened?

Nikita

Awh babe I'm so sorry! But, pls spill

Me

HE INVITED HIS FRIEND

Evie

NOOOOOOOO

Daphne

NOOOO

Okay, full debrief tomorrow morning! We need to hear EVERYTHING!

Me

Absolutely! I'm definitely going to need your help to figure out how to drop this third wheel . . .

Private chat with @runicrascal

@runicrascal
All right I've gotta know . . . what did you ACTUALLY think of ep3 and 4? You looked pretty into it?

@mythicwitch
Are you kidding??? SO into it!

@runicrascal
Was it the "who hurt you" trope that got you?

@mythicwitch
Kind of . . . But also, have you SEEN the makeup, the artistry? I can't believe it's all handcrafted for the characters. I mean the CGI is . . . something to be desired, but the design is there, you know? And the painted scenery, and when they do the sweeping shots with the miniature sets? It's beautiful

@runicrascal
Ah, no surprise you appreciate that aspect of things! How is the Téiglin fanart going?

@mythicwitch
It's going well! I'm thinking of using it for my coursework project actually. If my teacher's on board with the plan, I'm thinking I'll do some sculpture work for one of my pieces. Definitely better than the sad still-life rose I was originally working on!

@runicrascal
Nice! Can't wait to see it! ☺

@mythicwitch
I was gonna do some more tonight (maybe more actual fanart and less homework this time) but

@mythicwitch *is typing* . . .

@mythicwitch *is typing* . . .

@runicrascal
But?

@mythicwitch
Buuut the usual. My parents were acting suuuuper weird when I got home (Dad was here again? They had DINNER TOGETHER? Can't imagine how that went without me as a buffer lol. I honestly cannot WAIT for this divorce to be over with) so that kinda ruined the mood

Art's a really good escape until they suck all the inspiration out of the air and the whole house feels like I'm living in the middle of a storm cloud, you know?

@runicrascal
Damn. I'm sorry, Cerys

@mythicwitch
Thanks

@runicrascal
Here if you need a sounding board at all. Can't promise much in the way of artistic inspiration, but . . .

@mythicwitch
Haha, thanks. I appreciate it x

@runicrascal
The "storm cloud" line was some nice writing, though. Maybe you should give that a go, if drawing isn't working?

@mythicwitch

HA! Yeah, right! As if I've ever gotten more than a C for creative writing! That is in fact why I'm studying other people's work for A level English lit instead of making my own

Besides I wouldn't even know where to start

@runicrascal

I'm sure a romance lover like you could come up with a thing or two

---

OWAR Discord #324
#general

@runicrascal

All right **@everyone**—a call to arms! Newbie **@mythicwitch** is a few episodes into the show now and already seems to be a hardcore Silversmith shipper . . . Does anyone have any good fanfics to share with her?

@sirmoonypants

Noooo, Team Moonsilver all the way! You'll get there **@mythicwitch**, give it time ;) Glad to hear you're enjoying the show so far!

@silversmithhh

HELL YEAH THIS IS MY TIME TO SHINEEEEE

@fauningforhim

Haha, wondered how long it'd take you to show up!

@silversmithhh

What're we looking for, Cerys? In-universe canon-divergence? Gender swap? Spice? Or are we thinking more domestic fluff? One-shots? Omegaverse? Omg, I have some really good omegaverse ones I can send you

@wizeguy

Cool it **@silversmithhh**, you don't want to scare off the newcomers! Maybe start with a coffee shop AU?

@mythicwitch

I'm a little embarrassed to admit I don't know what any of those things are . . . Sorry, **@silversmithhh**! VERY much a newcomer haha

@silversmithhh

Oh no worries! Okay, so domestic fluff is just people being in love and happy and super cute. Canon is the stuff that actually happens in the books/show, so canon *divergence* is like . . . tweaking/changing certain aspects of that, but the story is still set in the show/books. AU is "alternate universe"—basically putting the characters into, like, Regency-era England, or a Star Wars setting, or a WWII drama! (I have a very good rec for one where Devon is a WWII soldier and Adanna is a spy . . .)

@runicrascal

How about something with Notting Hill vibes?

@mythicwitch

That would be perfect!

@silversmithhh

Don't worry, girl. I've got you

Of Love and Books by disilv8

Lady Adanna di Silver/Devon Smith, Lady Adanna di Silver, Devon Smith, Téiglin, Roach, Rogdan, Lady Helena di Silver, Guaranteed Happily Ever After, Fluff, Modern AU, bookshop AU, no beta we die like men, Devon is a grumpy bookworm who drinks too much coffee, Helena is an interfering witch when it comes to her daughter but what's new

Modern AU where Devon owns a bookstore and Adanna is an heiress who moves into town, trying to shake off her family legacy and the paparazzi, and gets a job in Devon's shop instead—much to his chagrin! (AN: updates weekly! Back on schedule after I broke my arm this summer trying to high-kick too ferociously in my audition for Shrek the Musical! Next chapter coming on Thursday!)

Words: 26,802   Chapters: 8/13   Hits: 18,004

THE FANGIRL PROJECT

Become an "OWAR" fangirl to convince Jake I am his dream girl and we are actually a match made in heaven:

1. buy the books ✓
2. watch the show ✓
3. remember to call it "OWAR" like a real fan ✓
4. go to a convention (cringe) ✓
5. . . . cosplay??!?? (something <u>CUTE!!!</u> that Jake can't resist)
6. <u>DO NOT</u> badmouth OWAR in front of Jake
7. who/what is "Roach"??? Find out! ✓
8. wear the new T-shirt Jake bought me next time I see him! ✓
9. join this fan-forum-chat thing on Discord (whatever that is?) and talk to Jake in it to prove that I really AM all in and therefore the love of his life ✓ ♡♡
10. GET. RID. OF. MAX!!!!
11. look up "Silversmith domestic fluff"

Daphne takes a long slurp of her pumpkin spice latte and gives me a critical look. "And you're *sure* it wasn't a date?"

Chloe leans closer across our table, pushing her designer glasses up her ski-slope nose. I'm honored to be not just included but *central* to this little before-school meetup in Costa. Plus, Daphne's added me to a group chat, which is a definite step in the right direction.

"Maybe he was nervous?" Chloe suggests. "And didn't know how to kick this Max guy out without being rude?"

"Maybe . . ."

"And he hugged you at the end, *and* saw you to the door," Nikita says. She pats her hair with marbled pink-and-gold nails, her natural chestnut curls smoothed and slicked into a pin-straight ponytail today.

"And he sat on the bed with you, too!" Daphne adds. Today, she wears various tones of beige and cream that complement her fair skin and deep brown eyes. Her jewelry is artfully mismatched silvers and golds that look like she just threw the look together; I'd have agonized over it for hours. "I reckon you're totally in. It's just . . . slow burn, that's all. I wouldn't worry about it yet, if I were you—it all adds up to him being nervous, like Chloe said. You said he's never been in a relationship before, plus you're really good friends, so he'll be extra worried about damaging your friendship by making the wrong move."

"So what do I do? It's turned into this regular group hang now, which was *so* not the plan, but I don't know how to get out of it . . ."

It feels so good to have some people to turn to for advice about this, people who are external to my friendship with Jake. Evie couldn't join us this morning, but I'm starting to think that if I just asked her to keep this a secret, she wouldn't gossip to any mutual friends. And chatting about this Jake romance drama, however one-sided it might be at the moment, feels like I'm really solidifying my place in this group. It's giving us something to bond over.

I haven't even had to mention all the *OWAR* stuff! A total bonus.

A split second later, I realize that even thinking about *OWAR* has jinxed it.

As the girls start workshopping ways that I might be able to see more of Jake *without* Max, or how I might be able to up the ante by flirting over text more obviously if he's not picking up any of the hints I've dropped so far, the door opens. I'm facing it, so my eyes are automatically drawn to who walks in.

It's Anissa, from my old school and my art class, who looked *too* long at my Téiglin-inspired sketch. She's wearing a long, checkered shirt under a boxy bomber jacket paired with purple leggings, and pieces of uneven brown hair fall around her face where the rest of it is pulled up in a messy bun.

Nikita notices me looking, and cuts herself off mid-sentence to whisper to us, "Oh my God, have you guys met her yet? She's *such* a weirdo. Dead quiet, and I don't think she's got any friends— although I'm not sure she *wants* any. It's not like I've seen her make any effort to chat with people. She's in my French class. She's got history with us too, hasn't she, Cerys?"

Daphne's eyes widen as she glances over and recognizes her. "Evie told me about her! Apparently she's like . . . a *witch*."

I've heard those rumors too; and right now, I notice the silver dagger-shaped earring dangling from one of Anissa's ears, visible with her choppy hairdo. It's arguably the least out-there of anything I've seen Anissa wear before.

Daphne is whispering now, and we all lean in to listen. "She has one of those evil-eye bracelets and has, like, a tarot deck and stuff, and Evie said she *cursed* someone. Some guy in the year above who was bullying her, and then Anissa cursed him—everyone saw her do it—and the next day he broke his nose in rugby."

"That's ridiculous," Nikita scoffs, but her voice has dropped, too, and there's a furrow in her brow like she doesn't quite believe her own scorn. I always assumed they were just rumors, people just being needlessly mean about Anissa, but . . .

Well, I wouldn't mess with her. Just in case.

"Never mind *that*. What on *earth* is going on with her hair?" Chloe asks us, aghast. She pats her own immaculate French braid. "Did she cut it herself, d'you think?"

"With blunt scissors, maybe," Daphne adds, because that's exactly how it looks, and we all giggle. "I had the *worst* luck with a hairdresser a couple of years ago, tried to get a long bob and ended up with . . . Hang on, let me find the pictures, you'll never believe . . ."

But just as she says it, Anissa looks over at us all.

Chloe gives her a little wave, though she's blushing and looking guilty. Nikita, sitting with her back to the door, has turned around to look and may or may not have been caught staring; she looks at us with puffed-out cheeks and wide eyes, not sure whether to laugh at her own embarrassment or not.

I duck out of sight best I can.

I can't shake the feeling that Anissa knew *exactly* where the inspiration for my sketch last week had come from. If she did, that means she's an *Of Wrath and Rune* fan like Jake and Max, but hearing Nikita talk about what an outcast she is only solidifies why I don't want them to know about my association with the series. I've only just shaken off my own loner status at school and found a friend group before it got too late, but Anissa has done the opposite.

I don't want to be like that.

Maybe Anissa is just shy, or maybe she's generally socially awkward, and those are totally separate facts from her liking *OWAR*. I know, rationally, the two don't go hand in hand. Look at Jake! And the Discord community seem pretty chatty and nice— @silversmithhh has been messaging me on and off over the past few days, dissecting our favorite romance tropes and recommending yet more fanfic and even some books she thinks I'll like. She's a first-year uni student at Cardiff studying law, and has a great appreciation for a longing look and grand romantic gestures.

But I think about Max with his off-putting attitude, and I also know that being an *OWAR* fan doesn't automatically make you a *likable* person, either.

What if Anissa outs me as a fantasy geek, when I'm not? I mean, yes, fine, I made some drawings of that one character, and I did stay up till two a.m. last night reading the entire *Of Love and Books* fanfiction so far, but that hardly counts!

Does it?

Crap, *am* I a fan? I thought I could just pretend, for Jake's sake . . .

No, I can't afford to be the weird girl obsessed with this niche, nerdy series. Not in real life. Not when Anissa might be like that, and look where it's gotten her—eating lunch on her own, completely out of touch with the world around her, and with no friends.

She places her order and comes over to our table.

"Hi."

Nikita looks ready to burst, and says in a strange, high-pitched voice, "All right, Anissa?"

"Did you have free periods this morning, too?"

"Yep," Daphne chirps, doing a much better job of making small talk. "We're just debriefing on a date that Cerys had last night. It didn't really go to plan."

"Oh?" Anissa says, her bright hazel eyes shifting over to me.

I don't know what to say. It's not like it'll get back to Jake through her like it might from Evie . . . and all my brain is doing is screaming a mantra of *You're going to blurt out that you watched OWAR with him and she'll know what that is and you'll start gushing about Lady di Silver and Devon and the others are going to think you've lost it, don't mention OWAR don't mention OWAR mention OWAR mention OWAR mentionOWARmentionOWARmention—*

I must be silent for a beat too long because Daphne saves me by explaining, "His friend was there, so it turned into a casual hangout instead of a date."

Chloe says, "We were just trying to figure out how Cerys can make the *next* one a proper date, and drop some more hints that she's interested in him *romantically*. Sort of ask him out *without* asking him out, you know?"

Anissa nods slowly, but doesn't offer up any suggestions or contributions to the conversation. Daphne shifts in her seat, and Chloe glances between us all, fidgeting nervously with her glasses. Nikita clears her throat, but seems at a loss for something to break the ice.

We're all rescued by the barista calling out, "Iced americano with vanilla syrup!" Anissa goes to collect her drink, leaving without so much as a wave goodbye.

"Do you think she heard us talking about her hair?" Chloe asks, worrying her lip between her teeth. "Should we have said something? Apologized? I could've shown her my hairdresser's Instagram?"

Nikita says, "D'you see what I mean, though? She's dead quiet and awkward."

"She went to my school," I offer up. "She's always been like that, as far as I know."

Daphne glances at the door, frowning, but it seems to be less irritation at Anissa and more like she's debating how that interaction could've gone differently. Then she sighs. "Oh well. Anyway, those pictures I was going to show you . . . Would you just *lock* at the state of me!"

She has us all in peals of laughter then, with her bowl-cut-esque style that looks totally atrocious, and Chloe shrieks, "No, I remember this! My mom said you looked like one of the Beatles!"

I join in, but my mind is still on Anissa, and my stomach squirms.

It was a lucky escape this time, I think. I'll have to make sure it doesn't happen again.

By Sunday evening, I'm listless and *bored*. I've done all my homework, I've done my chores, there's no work shift to distract me, and I've read all the *Of Love and Books* fanfiction that @silversmithhh sent me.

Mom is out with some friends for "book club," although I've yet to see her pick up a book for it and she usually comes back tipsy; Dad is here again, out in the garage mucking around with her car. Polishing it or checking the oil or something.

And I'm stuck in my room, bored out of my mind. I drop a message in the group chat that I'm now a part of, but the only responses are a photo from Evie looking melodramatically pained while she watches a BBC drama with her family, and Chloe saying she's bogged down with all the homework that's due in this week, which she neglected in favor of her dressage classes. The others must be busy, because they don't respond.

I have to tell myself that they aren't ignoring me, that there isn't a secret group chat I'm not in and this one is just to humor me. That's too paranoid, even for me.

It's just . . . *strange,* making new friends. I've never had to worry too much about this before. Friendships just happened—they were down to circumstance and proximity and shared experience and . . . well, and mainly, they were down to Jake.

Of course he didn't have any trouble making friends at his new school. He'd already joined a local soccer team, so he had built-in friends like Max by the time classes started. And anyway, it's different for boys, I'm convinced of it. *They* don't have to worry about being mocked for wearing the wrong lipstick or not knowing what sort of bag we're all using for school this year. Or being too quiet and having a bad haircut, like Anissa.

Thinking of Jake is threatening to send me into a spiral, and the rom-com I've put on in the background—*Red, White & Royal Blue*—feels mocking, somehow. The Fangirl Project has gone wildly off-track, and I need to find a way to bring it back. If he hadn't been busy with the soccer guys this afternoon . . .

I cast a glance toward my bedroom window. It's dusky outside, the sky a deep gray smudged like charcoal, rain pattering at the windowsills. I lament that I won't get my driver's license till I turn seventeen in April. Being so reliant on the bus is a pain, and trekking an hour across town this late in the evening isn't very appealing, even if Jake *was* free to hang out.

My doodling—an antique vanity with a mirror crowded with flowers and vines and antlers—falters, and I sigh as I toss my pencil aside, reaching for my phone instead as I slump back against the pillows.

It must say something about how phenomenally, colossally bored I am that watching a few more episodes of *OWAR* seems like the perfect solution right now. I'm almost *annoyed* that I have to wait until Wednesday to watch more. It's definitely boredom driving me, and not any sort of sincere excitement for the show. It can't be; I'm still not even sure what this elaborate plotline to search for the Eldritch King is all about—can you be *that* into a show when you can't really describe what's going on?

I open up the Discord, and my private chat with Jake is there. I didn't text him earlier—careful not to come off as too clingy or needy—but messaging first in the confines of this fan forum feels . . . different. Less pressure somehow, more casual. This is just bland nonsense about the show, it's not *real* that way.

> **@mythicwitch**
> So on a scale of 1–10, how fangirl is it of me to be super excited for Wednesday and want to watch the next episodes already?

He's online almost immediately, and my heart somersaults to see him typing a response.

> **@runicrascal**
> Like a 5
>
> **@mythicwitch**
> Only a 5!!! Have I earned no bonus points for finally giving in and getting into the show?

@runicrascal
Nah, a real fan would have smashed through them already, preplanned watching schedule with friends be damned 😏

@mythicwitch
Touché. I am tempted though . . . But it feels like it's more fun to share that experience in person?

@runicrascal
Based on how you reacted to the end of ep3, I'd agree

And there's some really fun stuff to look forward to in ep5 and 6 this week, characters beginning to interact with each other and such—that's more your thing than the sword fights, right?

@mythicwitch
Right. But at least between us we've got a well-rounded appreciation for the show!

@runicrascal
Haha true

How's your weekend been?

@mythicwitch
Not too bad. My shift was a drag but I'd rather that than any drama or stress with customers and stuff! I'd like to say I've had lots of super exciting super fun totally brilliant plans, but really I just got a lot of schoolwork done

How about yours? How did the match go today?!?!??

@runicrascal
We won!! 3–1

> **@runicrascal**
> Our goalie took off with his girlfriend in the second half so we had to bring in one of the subs lol. He's benched next week now, but that sucks for the rest of us more than it does him really

> **@mythicwitch**
> Is that Alfie? Ugh, I thought he'd split with his gf? I thought it turned into a whole mess that had them arguing at school?

> **@runicrascal**
> It did haha, but guess they patched things up. True love conquers all! Or something like that, right?

> **@mythicwitch**
> "Until the end"?

> **@runicrascal**
> Coming in hot with the big quotes! Congratulations, your fangirl score has just increased to a solid 6/10

> **@mythicwitch**
> What can I say? I'm a sucker for a good love story . . .

The hours slip away as we message back and forth over the Discord chat.

When I ask what else he was up to this weekend, he mentions how his dad drove his older sister up to uni yesterday; he asks me how things are with my parents, and I appreciate it. It feels different talking about it in the Discord. Secret, almost, like I can put it away and erase it if I ever wanted to, and it wouldn't ever be part of our real friendship, our real life. It makes it easier to talk about, so I say everything that's on my mind. Until . . .

Mom arrives home, calling to someone outside, "Thanks, Naomi!" and then staggering up the stairs to bed singing ABEA's "Waterloo" with a slur in her voice, and I hear Dad follow her upstairs, the two of them chatting—still with that annoyingly *reasonable* and *polite* new tone. Is he staying in the spare room *again*? That's a recent development only slightly less horrifying than if he was staying in their room. Mom even *giggles* at something, and I pull a face, slumping lower against my headboard.

Am I going to have to, like, reverse-*Parent Trap* them? I can't cope with the whiplash if they call off the divorce. Whatever's going on, it can't last.

Even though I meant it when I told @runicrascal I'm a sucker for a good love story, my parents' relationship brings out the cynic in me.

I turn back to my phone, reading through our Discord chat for comfort. His replies are more thoughtful than usual. Jake's always been valiantly sympathetic with me, but I know he gets awkward about deep stuff, using silly jokes to make me feel better when he can't really relate. His dad—his stepdad, technically—has been in his life since Jake was three, and Jake, Ginny, and their big brother love him. He and Jake's mom have been happily married—and sappily, disgustingly in love—since before Jake can even remember.

So while Jake has always been there for me, and is a great sounding board and always has a hug and a joke ready to cheer me up, he doesn't really know how to *help*. But behind the screen name, the weird sense of anonymity we have in Discord, he takes extra time to type out his replies, talks about how stressful and tricky it must be, and asks if I want to rush off to uni just to be away from it.

It feels really nice.

And maybe he feels the same way? That this is separate, a space that exists away from everything else, where we can be a little more honest.

And I like that when I tell him I don't really want to talk about my parents anymore, he changes the subject to tell me about some inane writers' room drama behind the scenes of *OWAR*. It sounds silly and dramatic, at least in Jake's version—he even embellishes the story with screenshots of old Twitter threads and digs made in the comments of Instagram posts—but it's enough to take my mind off things for a while longer.

It's pitch-dark outside by the time my eyes begin to droop, and I've moved from slumping against my headboard to being curled under the covers, still in my leggings and sweatshirt from this morning, and when I check the time I'm startled to find it's midnight. We've been talking nonstop for hours.

@mythicwitch
I should probably get some sleep, it is a school night

@runicrascal
Damn, I didn't notice it had gotten this late! I'm holding you personally responsible if I don't manage to finish my physics homework before class tomorrow, I was supposed to get to it tonight

@mythicwitch
You're a terrible procrastinator. It's very rascal-y of you

> **@runicrascal**
> Haha! I do suppose I've got a reputation to live up to
>
> See you Wednesday?

> **@mythicwitch**
> Can't wait 😊 x

> **@runicrascal**
> Me either 😊

> **@mythicwitch**
> Night!

> **@runicrascal**
> Good night, Cerys x

And even though I ended the conversation, it's impossible to sleep when, even after I plug my phone in to charge and leave it on my nightstand, I'm busy replaying the conversation over again in my mind, smiling to myself and with butterflies in my stomach.

I fall asleep daydreaming about kisses, and wake up the next morning from dreams of dark, intense eyes and a low voice saying my name like a prayer.

When Wednesday rolls around, I once again have a panic about my outfit—I can't bring myself to wear the fandom tee again and risk a full-on eye roll from Max this time. I forgo Daphne's assistance with my makeup this week, promising I'll try the look again soon but not sure I have the confidence for it right now, and instead make a dash for the bus with her calling after me, "Good luck! Go get your man, Cerys! Morning debrief at Costa with the girls tomorrow!"

I turn around long enough to grin and wave, already looking forward to it, glad that the free-period coffees sound like a staple in the calendar, one I'm firmly included in.

October has arrived with brisk winds, even if the sun is still bright and warm. The leaves haven't turned yet, and there's a summery feeling still clinging to things. Today, my outfit is the same blue floaty sundress I wore to the convention a couple of weeks ago, but layered with a woolly sweater and paired with sneakers instead of sandals.

Maybe it's not *quite* the weather for a sundress, but I've had to compensate for Max third-wheeling again by putting a little more effort into my look. My hair is piled into a bun, slicked back with some serum that Nikita lent me, and held in place by about a thousand hairpins. It's making my head ache after being so stiffly in place all day, but when I catch sight of myself in the reflection off the bus window, I don't dare mess with it. It *does* look really good. Sophisticated. Older.

Like someone who knows how to flirt with boys and signal to her best friend that she'd very much like for him to kiss her, thank you.

This time, when I get to Jake's house, I notice Max's car parked crookedly once more on the pavement. Ginny's car is there too, but only because she doesn't take it to uni with her; Jake's planning to use it to practice driving, much to her chagrin.

"Thomas never had to share *his* car" was her argument, according to Jake, to which their mom replied, "Yes, but Thomas had moved out and graduated uni by the time you were learning to drive. *Your* car is sitting here doing nothing, and since your father and I pay the insurance, you can share it with Jake while he's learning and you're at uni."

Mom and Dad have both said they'll take me out to learn in one of their cars since I got my learner's permit this summer, but that hasn't happened yet. It's another fight I've avoided causing between them, sure that *somehow* they'll use it to find another way to be at each other's throats and ruin the whole experience anyway.

I cast a glare at Max's car, annoyed—*jealous*—then steel myself and go knock at the front door. There are voices on the other side, laughter about something, and then it swings open to reveal Jake. He's in his school shirt and a pair of gray tracksuit bottoms, beaming at me but already moving back inside.

"All right, Cerys? Ready for another round of your favorite show?"

I laugh. "Don't you know it! Fangirl official, right?"

He doesn't send me upstairs like last week, so I follow him to the open-plan kitchen/dining room to help as he starts making snacks. Grilled cheese again, of course.

"Sometimes I think if we cut you in half, you'd bleed melted cheese."

Jake snorts. "That is weirdly morbid. And also, absolutely true."

"Sooo," I singsong. "How's school?"

"School's fiiiine," he sings back, a smile resting gently on his lips as he pulls slices of bread out of the packet to butter. I set the kettle on to boil and lean on my forearms on the island in the center of the kitchen, across from Jake.

I study the easy slope of his narrow shoulders, the lean definition in his arms that's appeared since the end of our last school year. He must've had a haircut since last week, because his sandy-blond locks are neater and shorter than when I saw him last, and as immaculately styled as if he'd only recently done it, rather than spent the day at school. There's a fingerprint on his metal-frame glasses, right in the middle of the lens, and I reach out to pull them from his face.

Jake jolts, but doesn't question me when I clean his glasses on the fabric of my dress, scrutinizing them to make sure they're properly clean before I hand them back. Then I course-correct, and place them gently back on his face, letting my fingertips softly graze against his cheeks. It could be passed off as just friendly, an accidental touch, but at the same time it feels almost recklessly bold, especially when I let my hands stay there just a second too long and smile as I say, "There. You're perfect."

His bright blue eyes blink rapidly—maybe just testing the clean lenses or, hopefully, reading into my gesture for what it *really* is—then he flashes a smile my way. "What *would* I do without you, Cer?"

"I really don't know."

"So, how's school with yoooou?" he asks then, drawing the word out brightly. It annoyingly interrupts the intensity of the moment we just had going on, but I suppose being hauled in for an impassioned kiss across the kitchen counter *is* too much to hope for.

I give him a more detailed answer than he offered me, although I suppose I am already fully up to date on his soccer drama, and Jake's always preferred chatting about his friends and his hobbies than his classes anyway. "It's pretty good. My lessons are all okay—history's a slog, but that's mainly because we get so much homework. *And* I think I'm officially part of the group now."

"With Evie from school and whatsherface, the *Bridgerton* girl?"

I giggle. "*Daphne.* Yes, that lot. We have Thursday morning debriefs now."

It's only after I blurt it out that I realize what I've said, and blush. Jake is too busy carefully layering slices of cheese to notice, at least, so he just asks, "Debriefs? That sounds very intense. What about?"

"Oh, um. Just. You know, how classes are going and stuff."

Mostly stuff.

Mostly *him.*

"This sounds like when my mom puts a 'weekly audit' meeting on her work calendar, but she's actually at spin class." He glances up at me with twinkling eyes. "Dad's been making fun of her since she let that slip. She asked him to take the garbage out the other night and he said, 'Sorry, I'm currently busy with my weekly audit'—you can imagine she was *not* impressed, so obviously we've all started doing it now."

Even though I laugh, the story leaves my chest feeling tight.

"I wish my parents would joke around like that instead of . . . whatever the hell it is they're doing these days," I confess. The kitchen is quiet but for the bubbling of the kettle, almost finished, and the scrape of the butter knife in Jake's hand.

He pauses, not quite meeting my eye before he says, "Maybe you should sign them up to clown school for their Christmas present. Nothing says 'shut up' like a mouth full of colored cloths that just won't stop coming!"

My laugh is hollow, but we both pretend not to notice. And I try not to miss the Jake who talked to me more openly, more deeply, in the Discord on Sunday night. But that's okay, I tell myself; I know he cares, and now that I know he *is* capable of that sort of heart-to-heart, however awkward he might find it in person, it only makes him more endearing.

The kettle finishes boiling and I find the mugs. I pull down the JUST DANDY mug and my mood shifts instantly, like it's a cursed object.

I could take it back. It's petty, maybe, but it'll be a victory. I'll be making a *point.*

But Max is Jake's new friend, close enough that Jake wants to include him in our weekly hangouts, so I suck it up to prove that I am a good person, a compassionate future girlfriend, and I switch it for Ginny's swearing pug mug.

Look at me, taking the moral high ground.

I am—and I'm sure Jake will see it any day now—*such* a catch.

This week, I sit farther up on the bed, closer to Jake but not quite *next* to him, and not near enough to the headboard that I might be tempted to relax into it; lying down on his bed with him feels a little *too* nerve-racking, even if we didn't have our third wheel to deal with. Instead, I sit with my skirt arranged prettily around me and my legs stretched out, crossed at the ankle, and prop myself back on my hand.

It's not very comfortable, admittedly, but that's beside the point.

Luckily, I don't have to exchange much small talk with Max beyond a hello because Jake immediately queues up the next episode for us all to start watching, and the show takes over. I can't believe how into it they both are—Jake is bright-eyed and smiling as he watches, even mouthing along to parts of the show, and Max leans forward intently, his eyes focused entirely on the screen. They both cry out at some apparent betrayal, both cheer at the appearance of a ragged, withered-looking man with stringy red hair turning gray and a broken pair of glasses, and they both wait for my reactions to certain moments with bated breath.

Mostly, it's whenever Lady di Silver and her guard are onscreen, though they aren't doing very much. For a good chunk of one episode, all they do is ride horseback down a road and discuss politics, which is nowhere near as entrancing as the scene in the bedroom—even if they *are* sharing a horse, and cozied up together.

Actually, most of the two episodes is politics and characters swapping ancient myths and legends about the long-lost Eldritch King who will bring the realm back to rights, and it's lots of dark, moody scenes in taverns and dramatic, foreboding one-liners that make the boys positively vibrate with excitement but go right over my head.

By the end of it, when Jake sits up to pause before episode seven—the season finale—plays, I flop back on the bed with a groan of despair, throwing my arm over my head.

"I thought you said there would be lots of characters to love this week," I grumble.

Max laughs, which makes me scowl. I drag my head up enough to shoot him a glower from beneath my arm, but he cracks a smirk to himself and shakes his head. I lie back down, but keep scowling.

Jake pats my arm. "Guess you'll just have to keep watching to get that sweet, sweet Silversmith content. Even if they're *not* endgame."

"Says you," Max argues, but it's playful, and sounds like a debate they've hashed out plenty of times before.

Jake laughs—loudly, a little brashly, and it's enough to make me pick my head up to peer at him, confused because it doesn't sound like his usual laugh, and a little hurt that there's obviously some *hysterical* in-joke between them I'm missing.

"You crack me up," he tells Max through loud guffaws, and pats me again to say, "Isn't he hilarious?"

"Uh . . ."

Wait, am *I* in on the joke? Did I miss something?

But Max also looks startled, catching my eye and obviously as out of the loop as I am, and I find myself giving him a shrug in this strange moment of solidarity between us when faced with Jake's sudden weirdness.

Jake sighs, recovering himself, seeming to catch the mood and realize we're not all rolling around in fits of laughter. He runs a hand back through his hair and leans forward to reply properly to Max.

"Oh come on, you're telling me you've got two insanely powerful characters with *huge* ties to destiny, a half-elf of noble birth with blood magick, and an elf warrior, a man of the people, with fated magick granted to him by the gods, and they're *not* going to end up together? Moonsilver all the way."

"Why's it called Moonsilver?" I ask.

"Spoilers," says Max.

"Next episode, actually. Do you guys want to stay to watch it? It's the last one of the first season . . ." Jake looks between us and I sit up properly now, under his gaze. I pull my dress back into place, laying it neatly around my knees. He smiles, hopeful, and turns to Max. "I don't think Mom and Dad will mind if you guys stay for tea—maybe I can convince them to let us order some pizza, or something?"

Max shrugs, looking so annoyingly *affable* that it sets my teeth on edge. Is he pretending to be friendly toward me, just like I am with him? "I don't mind. I don't want to intrude or anything."

YOU ARE, I want to scream. *YOU ARE INTRUDING! On this evening, on this potential romance, on all of it!*

But now they're both looking at me, and thankfully a more rational part of my brain takes over. I reach for my phone to check the time, and bite my lip. "I'm not sure . . . It's going to be really late getting the bus back home . . ." And I don't dare call Mom or Dad to ask them to come pick me up, but I can't mention *that* in front of Max. I don't need him knowing every horrible thing in my life.

The last time I stayed out too late, missed the bus home, and called for a ride home, Dad came to collect me and said it was no problem. Then I heard Mom snapping at him because it was encouraging me to be irresponsible and we should both know better. The time before that, Mom had picked me up and Dad told *her* that I had exams to study for and she clearly didn't care about the impact on my schoolwork as much as she cared about being "the cool mom."

Jake, of course, knows this, and he knows what I'm not saying, because his face creases in sympathy and he reaches over to give my hand a brief, wonderful little squeeze before he says, "Well, you could drop Cerys home, couldn't you, Max?"

I cringe just as Max glances my way, and my cheeks flame; I'm sure he caught that.

"She's only over by the garden center," Jake's telling him. "It's not that far out the way. You're that side of town anyway, aren't you?"

He cannot be serious. A car ride, alone, with *Max*? I would rather deal with my parents! It's a half-hour drive! *Thirty minutes,* when we barely filled three last week with small talk before Jake came upstairs with the grilled cheese. What would I even talk to Max about for that long?

"Really," I fumble to say, "you don't have to, it's okay. I can figure something out. We can just leave the finale until next week, or—"

"No way!" Jake crows, laughing. He scoots over on the bed to wrap his arm around me and give me a playful shake, and I can't even freak out at the fact that we're pressed together from shoulder to hip, that his leg is bumping against mine, or that he's pulled me against him. Oh, the irony, that this is the moment I decide to have what feels like an out-of-body experience, watching this nightmare unfold in real time. "There's no way I'm letting you go straight from the season finale into the next one. It ruins the whole dramatic effect!"

"It's all right," Max says quietly, in his low voice, the words even and measured, his gaze somewhere near my knees. "I don't mind, Cerys. And Jake's right—the finale is the kind of episode that needs breathing room before you dive into the next one."

I'm not so convinced—I haven't exactly been sucked whole-heartedly into the show so far, and I'm not sure how much that will change in the space of a single hour-long episode. But they're both waiting, both *expecting* me to agree, and I don't really know how to decline without making things weird.

"Come on, Cer! For me?" Jake wheedles, tugging me closer. "Please?"

And it's more time with Jake, isn't it? Wasn't that the goal here?

So I swallow, my mouth dry, and say, "Sure. Awesome. Thanks, Max. Sounds good."

Jake nips downstairs to ask his parents—home from work now—if we can stay and order some pizzas for dinner and, rather than waste any precious forced small talk on Max, I duck out under the pretense of calling my mom to let her know.

I *do* drop both her and Dad a text just to say I'll be home late (who even *knows* if Dad will be there—he shouldn't be, but I wouldn't want to put money on it these days), and I tell them I have a lift and won't need dinner.

But mostly, I hide out in the bathroom until I hear Jake running back upstairs.

I return to my spot in his bedroom, grimacing at a hairpin that's become lodged awkwardly and painfully in my hair after my dramatic flop onto the bed a few minutes ago. My whole scalp hurts, actually. I don't think this is a hairstyle that's meant to be worn for such long periods of time—or if it is, I'm just not used to it.

"What's up?" Jake asks, noticing.

"My hair," I say, then laugh because I don't think he'll under-stand. I roll my eyes and try to explain anyway, and Jake nods solemnly.

"Ah yes." He tosses his own head, as if shaking out a long mane of hair. "I, too, know the struggle. Beauty is pain, my dear Cerys, and how we both struggle. It is simply *not* easy, to look as lovely as we do."

My face warms and my stomach fizzes, but I'm all too aware of the interloper, dampening the opportunity for further flirting. Jake notices me glance over at Max and adds, "Alas, our tall, dark, not-at-*all*-handsome companion knows not of these pains, does he?"

"Cheeky bugger," Max mutters, flipping him off, and even I crack a smile at that.

Now that he points it out, though, I guess Max *does* have the whole tall, dark thing going for him . . . And while he's not conventionally handsome, not with that long hair, he's . . . well, he's not exactly *bad*-looking, I suppose. Really, I think, it's not fair that someone that annoying and judgmental shouldn't look as ugly as they are on the inside. Max's full lips and dark eyes framed with thick lashes are anything *but*.

He's a little shorter than Jake, but broader, more . . . filled out, sort of, and his white school shirt is undone a couple of buttons at the top, showing the rope chain of a necklace. Is it the same one he wore with his cosplay? Is it fandom-related, or something else, maybe more sentimental?

Aware that I'm staring, I tear my eyes away.

I feel too awkward to engage in the banter now—too awkward to flirt with Jake in front of Max, and I don't know Max well enough to poke fun at him without it coming off as mean—so instead I start taking my hair down, holding the hairpins between my teeth so I don't have to speak. The boys turn to talking about Alfie the goalkeeper and his frenetic relationship with his girlfriend; apparently, there's yet *more* drama there.

Jake and I would *never* be like that.

Whatever Max is saying, he cuts himself off mid-sentence—and mid-eyeroll, too—when he catches sight of me and turns his gaze more fully on me before letting out a loud, sputtering laugh he tries to hide behind a cough.

He fails miserably, blushing.

I sit up, indignant, and take the pins out of my mouth.

"What? What is it?" I scowl, but he's still laughing, and when I turn to Jake his eyes blow wide and he lets out a snort, too, before making a show of hiding me from view so he won't laugh. I scramble for my phone and swipe on to the camera to see, and—

Oh, crap.

My hair is a *mess*. A huge, puffy cloud of pale blond sticking out around my head in uneven bumps and not-quite curls, so voluminous it stands out several inches—except for the extremely stubborn flat section on the very top where I'd slicked it down with heaps of product this morning. I look totally ridiculous. I watch in the screen as my cheeks turn a bright, almost glowing shade of pink beneath all my freckles and the makeup I tried to cover them with.

Jake's seen me sweaty after an intense PE class, with some spots, or on a bad hair day, but *this* is . . .

This is straight-up hot mess—easy on the hot.

Taking a page out of Jake's book and opting for a joke so they can't tell how truly mortified I am, I whine, "You're both horrible, the pair of you. *Rascals.*"

Jake laughs even harder at that, giving my leg a nudge and saying, "See, you're getting into the *OWAR* spirit! I knew you would! Ah, Max, I take it back—*we* are the hot, handsome ones here, it seems, not poor Cerys."

Max, meanwhile, inclines his head low in an imitation of a bow, and drawls, "Here to service your rebellions and mischief alike, fair lady."

God, he is *such* a dork.

I settle for just rolling my eyes at him and pull my frizzy mass of hair back into a rough, looser ponytail.

I redirect the conversation with Jake to the almost-abandoned group chat with our old school friends, where there are halfhearted plans to organize a cinema trip. I assume everyone's just busy with school these days and that's why we don't talk as much. The longer the silences stretch, the more hesitant I am to reach out to any of them. It's not as if they've reached out to me, either. I *do* miss them, but I can't tell how much of that is because I actually just miss the extra opportunities to hang out with Jake . . .

But he shrugs and says, "I'm not sure if I'm going to bother with the cinema, to be honest."

"What? Why not?"

"I don't know. I just don't speak to anyone except you that much anymore."

I can only stare, horrified, because, while he's right, I can't wrap my head around his blasé attitude. He doesn't even sound like he *cares.*

"But . . . but they're our friends."

"Yeah, I'm not saying otherwise, it's just . . . you know . . ."

He shrugs, a resigned but mild expression on his face, and Mom's words about drifting apart ring in my mind again.

"No," I tell him, an edge to my voice. "I *don't* know."

Jake seems almost happy to distance himself from them, to let that distance just happen, and . . .

What if I'm next?

What if he decides to drift apart from me, too? It's already started happening, our lengthy Discord chats the only saving grace for how infrequently he texts me these days. And I know we've had these couple of Wednesday after-school hangouts, but with Max tagging along, what if that's not Jake wanting to include his new friend so much as trying to *exclude* me?

After the pizzas arrive, I resume my previous position on the bed as Jake queues up the final episode. But I can't stop my brain from worrying—if Jake fades out the gang from school, we'll have one less anchor in our friendship . . . unless *that's* intentional, too? On the flip side, I can suddenly hear Daphne and the girls telling me that Jake isn't trying to push me out completely, only out of the *friend zone,* and that this can only be good for proving to him how perfect we'd be together. If he sees me as less of a friend . . .

If he sees me as less of a friend, I think, determination pushing out the weird mix of grief and worry and sadness in my stomach, maybe he will start to see me as more of a girlfriend?

The alternative really doesn't bear thinking about.

***

The finale of season one is essentially a montage of main characters establishing that they are on various, semi-connected quests to defeat the evil rulers and seek out the long-lost Eldritch King, who's rumored to bring peace back to the land.

It ends with a scene that has both boys cheering: a hard-done-by yet conventionally attractive young man in the capitol, cursed (or blessed, depending on how you look at it) with fated magick and with a great destiny ahead of him, is forced to flee the palace guards and runs right into the path of the bedraggled redheaded man with broken glasses, Rogdan, leader of the rebellious Rascals, a ragtag bunch of people and creatures causing mischief and mayhem to disrupt the evil royal family.

Rogdan grasps the young man by the shoulder, after lecturing him on the wider plot of the series while a montage of the other characters on their quests plays out. And then, just before the credits roll, he asks in a gruff voice, *"So . . . be ye a Rascal, Roach?"*

I let out an audible *"Ohhh!"* at finally hearing the line from our T-shirts. It *does* pack a punch. And I do feel excited to see how things go next, and how Roach joining the Rascals will change the dynamics on the show.

"So? Worth the watch?" Jake asks, scooting a little closer to beam at me. His blue eyes twinkle, the light off the TV reflecting in them and his glasses. His hand is placed just behind my back and I can't help but think that if I leaned over just a *little,* it'd put our faces very, *very* near together.

I risk placing my hand over his on the bed as I enthuse, "*So* worth it! That was brilliant!"

I still don't know that I could explain the plot very well, or why this Eldritch King is so important, but I can see how people are so drawn to the characters. And the artwork and design is *mesmerizing*.

I'm genuinely looking forward to watching more.

I'm even a little disappointed that I missed out on that special-effects panel Jake mentioned at the convention, and say as much. In the Discord, it's easier to take a minute to think through anything I say about the show so I don't sound like an idiot or accidentally offend his love for *OWAR,* but I don't want Jake to mistake my quietness now for being fake.

Even if it did sort of, kind of, actually start out that way.

And even if I'll probably spend hours talking about it with him in the Discord later.

Jake grins. "See? Did you *really* think I'd lead you astray, all those times I said you should watch it?"

"Better late than never, though, right?"

"Oh, always." He winks, and butterflies flutter in my stomach even as he pulls his hand from underneath mine, turning to look as Max stands up, stretching his arms above his head. His shirt rises, revealing a sliver of lean stomach beneath. He drops his arms with a groan, then grabs his blazer where it's slung over the back of the gaming chair.

"Are you leaving?" Jake says, looking as dismayed as I feel; I file that look away to tell the girls about tomorrow, sure it must mean something. "Already? But . . . You can't go now! I mean, we haven't even grilled Cerys yet about her favorite parts of the season."

Max scoffs, glancing my way only briefly before replying, "Please, I think we both know the answer to that. That tower scene was a pivotal moment for the newbie over here. But yeah, I've gotta get going—it's already nine o'clock, mate, and I've got that math homework due for second period tomorrow that I never got around to finishing."

"*Still?* We've had that since Monday!" Jake *tsks*. "D'you want to just borrow mine? You can give it back to me in class."

"Nah, I need to get my head around these differentials. I've only got a couple of problems left to work through."

"And they're due tomorrow?" I say, and return Max the favor of not looking at him when I talk about him, instead laughing as I push Jake gently in the shoulder. "This one's a serial procrastinator, too; you're as bad as each other! Either that or he's just a *terrible* influence."

"The *worst*," Jake croons, his eyes and smile full of mischief and shared memories of the two of us cutting class, or scrabbling to swap homework answers at the last minute. My cheeks turn warm under the intensity of his gaze.

I want to whisper, "Rascal," like it's a private joke—which it is, in a way—and then lean in, imagining how he'd lift a hand to cradle my cheek and we'd stare into each other's eyes for another long moment before he finally kissed me . . .

But there's Max, making a racket as he takes his car keys out of his pocket and asks for my address so he can plug it into the maps app on his phone, robbing us of the moment.

Regretful, I peel away from Jake, but after he walks us to the door I throw my arms around him for a quick hug.

"See you soon?" I ask, hopeful, terrified, remembering how he didn't care if he didn't see the group from school.

"Couldn't get rid of me if you tried, Cer."

Oh, I hope not. I really, really hope not.

I linger just a beat longer, before I have to turn and go after Max.

Max's car is so clean, I'm almost terrified to put my feet on the floor mat in case some dirt comes off my shoes. I hug my bag on my lap, sitting bolt upright and tense, not sure whether that has more to do with the pristine car or him.

Who am I kidding?

It's at least ninety-five percent to do with him.

I'm fully prepared to eke out the silence for as long as we can get away with, if only to stretch out the snatches of stilted small talk I fully anticipate. I'm even already considering which directions I can mention as he drives, just for something else to talk about.

But as soon as Max turns on the engine his phone connects automatically and a voice begins droning out of the speakers: *". . . phantom pain lanced through his damaged wings, once more magnificent than any of his Greater Fae brethren's. Daxys thought again of the friends he had left behind in the palace, the brothers-in-arms who had turned their backs on him . . ."*

An incredulous bark of laughter bursts out of me, even as Max is already reaching to turn down the volume and fumbling with his phone to find something else to play.

"Is that the *OWAR* audiobook?" I say, even though I already know. Daxys is Jake's favorite character—a huge, buff, winged warrior, played by an actor that Jake's described as "a real teddy bear with golden retriever energy." I raise an eyebrow at Max. "How many times have you read these books?"

"This is only the second time," he says, looking awkward. "It took me a year to work through them, but they've just released the complete audiobook series, and I'm finding those way easier to get through. It's nice to experience them again and find all the details I missed the first time around, now that I'm more comfortable with the whole worldbuilding side of things and know the ins and outs of most of the series."

"Er . . . right."

There's a beat of silence—awkward and stilted and oppressive—before Max asks, with an almost deliberate politeness, "How's your foray into the books going?"

I readjust my bag on my lap. My copy hasn't left the bottom of it in about a week and, despite being pretty battered at this point, is largely unread.

"It's not," I admit, and Max lets out a short, sharp laugh. I scowl. "Hey, you can't judge me when *you're* so much of a die-hard fan you go out in cosplay and—"

"I'm not judging you," he says, and I scoff because *yeah, right.* "I'm just not surprised."

"That kinda sounds like you're judging me."

"Hmm." He clears his throat then, and when he starts another playlist I see on his phone screen it's the soundtrack from *The Witcher*. He skips it, and something that I can only describe as a jaunty folk tune on a lyre starts up. I raise my eyebrows; I didn't ever imagine anyone listened to this sort of stuff. Max skips through a few more weird-sounding songs and finally settles on an album from a moody indie punk rock band. That must be about as mainstream as he can think of, and I don't feel like I can really question or insult his music tastes further when he's doing me a favor and driving me home.

But I can't help asking, "Is this the sort of stuff you normally listen to?"

"What do *you* normally listen to?"

It sounds so accusatory, I question if my own tone was that sharp, but I'm sure it wasn't. It's just Max being his usual difficult, prickly self.

I flounder for an answer to him, confused because I thought my music taste was fairly normal—Sabrina Carpenter and Olivia Rodrigo and a lot of Taylor Swift. Finally I say, "Not *that*."

"See, now it sounds like *you're* the one judging *me*, Cerys."

Max gives me an arch look, then puts the car in gear and pulls off, with me sufficiently chastised. I bite the inside of my cheek, the lack of conversation between us stewing, thickening, like some physical thing in the car with us. I'm glad for the music, even if it doesn't provide much of a buffer.

Feeling like I may have gone a bit *too* far, I offer a truce. "This stuff isn't too bad, though. They sound good."

"Argonauta. It's these three sisters from Leeds. All their songs have some kind of reference to Greek myths—mostly the tragedies, I think."

I repress a sigh; just when I thought we might have found some common ground that *isn't* Max having a nerdy, niche interest . . . But this time when we lapse into quiet it's to listen to the music, and nothing jumps out at me as being the story of the Trojan horse or Medusa or anything like that. It's just a catchy song about revenge after a breakup, with gorgeously layered vocals and a violin blended with otherwise modern sounds in a way that's kind of entrancing.

"What's this one about?"

"Clytemnestra." He says the name carefully, like he's trying to remember each syllable correctly. "I forget the details, but I think her husband was awful, so she ended up cheating on him, stealing his throne, and killing him?"

I'm momentarily speechless, but recover enough to say, "Well, if this song is any reflection of the story, I think I want to say good for her."

Max laughs, and at once the mood shifts, eases, lightens. He relaxes, shoulders shuffling against the back of his seat, his fingers drumming absently on the steering wheel in time to the song. "Why does that sound rich, coming from someone who obviously loves a romance?"

I shrug, not knowing how to reply to that. It's jarring that he knows that about me, even if I guess I have made it obvious; and I think it only feels so weird because I know so little about him, outside of the context of him as Jake's new fandom/soccer/school buddy.

Maybe he wouldn't be *so* bad if I tried to get to know him?

But then he says, "They're coming to Cardiff next month. Me and Jake have got tickets. I don't know if there'll be any left . . ."

It's half an invitation, but not really, and sounds almost reluctant. And it twists a knife in my gut, reminding me exactly why I don't like Max, just on principle. Jake never mentioned he liked this band to me, has never said anything about listening to this sort of music, but suddenly he's enough of a fan to go to their concert with Max?

I swallow the lump in my throat. "I'm sure that'll be great fun for you guys."

We're quiet another few minutes while Max concentrates on driving. The next Argonauta song starts, but I decide not to ask him what this one's about. The vibe and lyrics are packed full of sorrow and longing, something about unrequited love, and that hits a little too close to home for me right now.

Instead, I think of a hundred questions I suddenly want to ask Max, but they're all so invasive—borderline judgmental—that I don't dare open my mouth. I don't need to stoop to his level.

But doesn't he *care* how he comes across? Doesn't it bother him that he's gone so far into this fandom and other non-mainstream things that he's alienating himself from those of us in the real world?

Does he think I should give the audiobooks a go, instead of trying to tackle the paperback?

Finally, we turn on to the main road that leads to my neighborhood. It's pitch-dark, the lengthy, dusky summer nights that lingered having vanished all at once, and I'm glad I didn't have to get the bus this late.

"Thanks," I say. "For the lift home. I know Jake put you up to it and that must've made it awkward to say no, but . . ."

"It's all right. You're not very far out of my way."

"Well, thanks," I say again, and even though I mean it, it comes out sounding so stilted that I wince. Max, noticing, smirks, and it makes irritation prickle beneath my skin just enough that it feels more normal between us.

"By the way, I don't know if Jake got around to mentioning it yet, but Cardiff Comic Con's in two weeks. We booked it back at the start of the summer—they'd announced the guest list and a couple of *OWAR* actors are going to be there. There's definitely still tickets available for that one. We were planning to go on Saturday. You work then, right?"

Is this another non-invite? I can't work it out.

Hedging my bets, I say, "I could probably try to swap my shift."

"Cool."

My nose wrinkles before I can stop myself. "Are you going in cosplay again? Is *Jake*?" Is that why he didn't tell me—was he embarrassed? Or is it because he booked it so long ago he forgot and didn't know if I'd be engaged enough with the fandom to want to go? That sounds more likely.

Max's mouth cracks into a crooked grin. "Obviously I am. Don't know about Jake. He was toying with it, but I don't know how committed he was to actually making the costume. You know what he's like," he adds with an affectionate chuckle that rubs me the wrong way. "Lady di Silver would be pretty easy to cosplay. I've got some spare elf ears you could borrow."

Oh my God.

Is this truly what my life's come to? Secondhand elf ears from a boy who's practically my archnemesis in my quest to prove myself to Jake?

Using words like "archnemesis" and "quest" like they're part of any halfway reasonable person's daily vocabulary?

"I'll think about it," I mumble, which feels like the most polite reply I can muster. I'm not even sure I'll wear the T-shirt Jake bought me at the last con; I don't know how Max can expect me to get on public transport in full cosplay. Just because *he* doesn't care what he looks like . . .

"Sure, just let me know." We're at my house now; I point it out by the cars outside, and Max jolts up onto the curb, engine idling as I unbuckle my seat belt. Just as I'm about to thank him one last time for the lift, he says, "I can't make next Wednesday, by the way. I've got some stuff on."

"Oh! You do?"

Yes! *YES!!!* This is the best thing he's said all night! I'll have a full evening alone with Jake at *last*. Maybe we can even forget about watching any new episodes and actually talk, actually spend time together like we haven't been able to do for the past couple of months. That'll be so nice. Even though I've only just seen him, even though we talk most days, I *miss* him.

And maybe next week we can finally get that kiss it felt like we were leading up to tonight.

Max nods, then hesitates, and I'm not sure if he's being purposely elusive or simply doesn't like me enough to bother telling me. I guess he must decide he looks rude by ignoring my prompt, though, because he finally mutters, "Just some family stuff. But I look forward to hearing your play-by-play breakdown of the next couple of episodes."

That's *definitely* a dig, because I'm so *not* forthcoming about any debrief and dissection of the episodes we've all watched together so far.

"Believe me, my thoughts will be every bit as riveting as the books themselves," I quip, and throw open the car door. "Thanks for the lift," I say one last time, and then mutter, not quite under my breath, "Rascal."

It's really the only word for him. He's *such* a pain. Causing trouble and stirring up best-laid plans and just—just—*UGH.*

He's laughing when I slam the door shut.

Shut up in my bedroom a little while later, I decide to bite the bullet, book the Comic Con ticket—which thankfully is not much more expensive than a trip to the cinema with some popcorn—and send a screenshot to Jake via text.

He replies almost instantly, first with a string of party emojis and then:

Jake

> WHOOP! A full convert! You're officially one of us now! You going to cosplay? Max has tried to persuade me, and I am kind of tempted. I've totally got the good looks to pull off a Daxys costume, right? Or maybe Roach . . . ?

Me

> Maybe Rogdan . . . ? Grizzled and a little like Fagin from Oliver Twist, very you

> And you DID smash your glasses that one time . . .

Jake

You wound me, Cer. 🗡️ 💔

He makes his point with a broken heart and knife emoji, and I laugh.

Me

Or Devon would be an easy costume?

Which, fine, maybe it's the only idea I put out there because if I'm going to be strong-armed into cosplaying too, then I can be Lady di Silver and we can go as Silversmith, a couple's costume, and that might just be cute enough to mitigate the general weirdness of wearing a set of rubber elf ears out in public. And it'd definitely fit in with The Fangirl Project. It might even be romantic?

Jake

DEVON! Yes, that's a shout! I'll keep you posted!

Although thinking about it, Max has said he'd help me make some wings for a Daxys cosplay . . . I'll see!

Also, really sorry but got to bail on next week ☹️, and the week after, Thomas is visiting (he's looking at some houses and thinking about moving back here!! How awesome would that be?!) so can't do then either

Maybe you can go ahead and watch the next few eps without us? You could probably finish season two easy before Comic Con, and even s3 if you're not waiting around to watch with us!

Me

Exciting about Thomas maybe moving back this way! I know you've been missing your Dungeons & Dragons stuff with him

How come you can't do this week btw? But no worries, will go ahead and watch! I'll keep you posted on all my reactions 😊 can live-text them to you to make up for it haha

Jake

Definitely do! I love how invested you are! Wish we'd done this ages ago lol x

Me

Me too x

Why has he canceled? Is this because of Max not being able to make it—does he not want to spend time with me, like he doesn't want to with the gang from school? Is it a total coincidence? Why did he ignore that part of my message?

I take a breath to calm my racing thoughts. Knowing Jake, it's because he responded faster than he thought and just didn't even notice that he hadn't answered my question. And he seems *genuinely* excited about me joining them for Comic Con; I believe that.

My stomach sinks as I stare at our text conversation, my message left on read even though I don't really know what he would've replied anyway.

And then a notification slides down the top of my screen, a Discord message from Jake—a link to Instagram posts of Lady di Silver cosplays—and I open it with a little more enthusiasm than I'd shown Max in the car.

If wearing some elf ears is the way to Jake's heart . . . Well, if I've learned one thing from all those rom-coms, it's that a little dent in my pride and dignity is a small price to pay for true love.

For the next two weeks, Jake goes quiet. Over text, he tells me that he's too busy with school stuff; on Discord, I learn that he canceled our Wednesday watch party because his dad wanted to take him out for dinner and talk about universities. It sends me into a spiral of my own, and in a panic I order about twenty prospectuses despite having no idea what I'm even *looking* for in a uni, if I want to go, or what I'd study.

There's a little flutter in my chest that screams *ART!!!*, that dreams of being able to work on sets and designs like the ones on *OWAR*, but I shove that ridiculous notion away as soon as it rises to the surface.

Dad sits with me after my shift on Saturday, helping me look through all the brochures. Then Mom takes me for coffee and cake on Sunday morning before I go to work and we make a spreadsheet of different unis and their courses and their merits. I don't know if they're trying to one-up each other, if they're genuinely working in tandem, or if they simply never communicated to each other how they're both trying to help, but I don't worry about it too much. It *does* help put me at ease about university, and it's nice to spend some time with them both.

I get invited to Daphne's house to hang out with some of the girls after school one day, and I feel firmly, solidly One Of The Group. Now that I don't feel I have to work so hard to keep up or make sure they really *do* like me, I enjoy their company even more. I don't even mind mentioning Jake more openly around Evie, who promises not to tell anybody from our old school but tells me, "I always thought you two had kind of a thing going on. I'm *so* here for it, you'd be such an adorable couple."

They're fun and cool and so easy to be around, and I'm so busy basking in it that the cinema trip with the group from my old school comes and goes without me even noticing. It does make me realize maybe I don't *really* miss them very much, though; and that, in comparison to the girls at school, my old school friendships were very surface-level, especially because they were mostly facilitated by Jake. I was never as excited to see them as I am Daphne and the girls, have never connected with them in the same way. My feelings have a lot more to do with losing Jake than it does *them*, and I'm surprised by the sense of absolute relief in accepting that we've grown apart . . . and that's okay.

It's okay because, like Mom said, sometimes it happens. It's okay because I still have Jake. But mostly, it's okay because I have the girls.

And it feels *nice* to have proper friends of my own.

Still, I don't mention Comic Con and the couple's costume to Daphne or Nikita or anybody, not sure how to bring it up and aware how pathetic it sounds. Finding a costume isn't half as difficult as I thought it might be—this time of year there are plenty of cheap black cloaks and sword belts and wigs available online, and when Mom or Dad asks about the parcels I've been ordering, I can pass them off as a Halloween costume without too much further inquiry.

Plus, thanks to some assistance from @runicrascal, a little further research of my own, and a few pointers from fellow Discord fangirl @silversmithhh, I learn that one of Lady di Silver's more notable outfits in the show is a green embroidered dress that she apparently wears to a ball. There's some truly gorgeous fanart, and incredible videos from women who have re-created the look for themselves on a sewing machine, which I can't help but be impressed by. The style is very medieval, but I think a plain green dress would do the job just as well, and that won't feel as weird to wear out in public as a *full* costume.

Plus, it's a lot cheaper to find a dupe online than something more show-accurate, and I'm not made of money. The *literal* price of doing this in the name of romance would be steep otherwise.

The Friday night before Comic Con, I lay my outfit on my bed. A brown wig styled into a braided updo that I spent hours wrestling into place with hairpins trying to make perfect, the green dress (which really looks like more of a tiered midi than something medieval but is at least the right shade of emerald), along with the sword belt (with a cardboard hilt I crafted and covered in bronze and silver paint) and my Amazon-purchased cloak.

It's a solid costume. *Cosplay.* Especially for a first attempt, done on a budget and on a time crunch. It'll look brilliant next to Jake's costume, I'm sure of it, and the green dress won't even be too weird to wear on the train into town.

But when Saturday morning arrives, I stand shaking in my room with the cloak bunched in my hands, not sure why I feel so sick with nerves. I imagine walking into a hall full of people *not* in costume; this isn't an *OWAR*-specific event like the last one, after all, so what if I look completely out of place and nobody recognizes who I'm supposed to be? Or the *OWAR* fans (cough, *Max*, cough) ridicule me for grossly misunderstanding, for being such a fake fan?

And what if Jake doesn't even go through with *his* cosplay? If it's just me and Max, two weirdos together, everybody pointing and laughing and whispering behind their hands? What if I see someone I know? Anissa might be there and tell someone at school about it, or maybe a photo of me dressed up could end up online . . .

I can't do it. I can get into this convoluted show with its tangled plotline, I can read the fanfiction for the romantic storyline, I can even put up with a third wheel every time I hang out with Jake, but I *can't do this.*

I shove the cloak, sword belt, dress, and wig into the bottom of my wardrobe next to a half-done watercolor painting of Lady di Silver's tower and a shoebox of painting supplies, and throw on a pair of jeans instead. I leave the BE YE A RASCAL, ROACH? T-shirt Jake got me in the drawer, ignoring it in favor of a woolly sweater.

It's too cold for a T-shirt anyway. He'll understand. I'll just say that the dress didn't fit, or the cloak didn't arrive in time, or something.

He'll understand.

I just can't do it. I can't be that person.

Look at Anissa. Look at Max—I don't know if he even has friends outside of Jake and *maybe* the soccer guys. Look at *Jake*, withdrawing from all his old friends from school, and even from me.

When I get to the concert hall in the middle of town, I'm relieved to see that most people walking in are dressed more casually—jeans and hoodies, similar to my own outfit. At least I won't be as out of place as I was the last time.

I arrive first, but soon spot Jake and Max. They're deep in conversation, smiling as they talk, and Jake bumps him playfully on the shoulder about something. Neither of them has noticed me yet.

Max strides along in the same cosplay as last time, cloak billowing behind him, his loose old-fashioned shirt buffeting against his chest in the brisk October breeze; the long blond wig is drawn back in a low ponytail, pointed elf ears sticking out. He's covered in the same leather armor pieces that I've since learned are called a bandolier, bracers, and pauldrons.

Jake, beside him, is in jeans, and I can see the glint of the circular runic pattern of his *OWAR* T-shirt underneath his jacket. Anger flares, hot and red, in my chest.

I can't believe he didn't tell me he was going to flake on the costume!

Was he really going to let me show up in a medieval ball gown (or, you know, close enough) and not even at least look like an idiot with me? Ugh! I'm so glad I changed my mind.

I can't *believe* he would do that to me.

But, then again . . . maybe this is a sign that we're so in sync and therefore totally meant to be together?

Max notices me first, just as they're waiting to cross the road. An expression I can't identify tugs at his eyebrows, pulls his mouth downward, and he says something to Jake that makes my stomach knot—I get the impression it's not very favorable.

Did Max really expect me to show up in cosplay? In the span of me saying I'd "think about" borrowing his spare elf ears, did I really give him the impression that I'd do it? Is he still *that* much of a superior jerk that he thinks I'm a fake fan for not doing it?

Then Jake looks up, smiling, and gives me a big wave that cools the anger in my chest a little.

By the time they reach me, Jake comes forward to wrap me in a big hug, talking a mile a minute about how—"the wings broke! I'm so gutted. We spent *ages* trying to get them to look right, taping them together and painting them, and they totally disintegrated as soon as I stepped outside. Max told me I should've used something better than craft paper and chicken wire . . . and we put *so* many hours into it, too! Getting them to fit, measuring, trying different types of glue or tape . . . Lesson learned: Max is always right. Especially when it comes to this stuff!"

I hide a wince. So this is why he's been so quiet lately: he's been holed up with Max every spare moment, the two of them building a set of costume wings. Something fandom-related that he *could* have involved me in, but chose not to.

It stings more than it has any right to.

I never thought I'd be so jealous of Max, or so desperate to be a cosplay guru.

I glance his way, find his eyes searing into me, and tear my gaze away instantly.

Jake doesn't even notice when I fight to craft a more neutral expression to hide my hurt, and he's too busy still chattering away to notice my breath tremble on the exhale.

He says, "The costume just didn't look any good without them. You were right, Cer. I should've gone as Roach instead, or Devon. Oh well. Next time, right? What happened to yours? I thought you had a dress sorted? Didn't you style a wig?"

I grimace, feeling Max's dark eyes boring into me, and tell Jake, "Mine didn't really work out, either."

Jake's face falls; I'd gushed in the Discord about how pleased I was to find pieces to pull the look together and how happy I was with how the wig turned out, but before he can be too sympathetic I put on a smile.

"Next time, right?" I repeat, and he nods, grinning once more.

"I'll hold you to it. Never mind. We've still got Sir Grayson here, huh? One of us managed it! And *killed it,* of course." He slings an arm around Max's shoulders, admiring his outfit, and I fall back half a step, blinking rapidly as I take it in myself. The white-blond hair, the ears of a half-elf character, the dark armor and sturdy boots and . . .

Oh, God.

I don't know how I didn't realize this before, but Max's cosplay character is Sir Grayson—the Moonwalker—one half of the other popular ship in the fandom, Moonsilver. As in, the Moonwalker and *Lady di Silver,* who I almost came dressed as.

I cannot *believe* I almost showed up in a couple's costume with Max!

Thank God I freaked myself out of wearing the dress. My intuition must have been tuned all the way in this morning. I would never have lived it down anyway, but a couple's costume with my crush's best friend . . . That'd be a surefire way to kill The Fangirl Project.

Unless it would've made Jake just a little jealous . . . ?

It's too late now anyway.

Who knew fandom could be such a vessel for romance and flirting and missteps in love?

Jake's been saying something I'm totally oblivious to while I've been staring blankly at Max's outfit, and I jolt back to reality when I hear my name. Not sure I want to have been caught staring (even accidentally) at Max, I just smile and hope Jake didn't ask me anything that needs a response.

They're both pulling their phones out of their pockets, though, and I catch on—we're finding our tickets to go inside.

Jake bounds up the stairs ahead of us, so fast that Max and I get separated from him in the ticket line by a group of uni-aged guys.

"Guess I didn't need to bring those spare ears after all," he says rigidly, and he sounds disappointed in me. Like I've offended him somehow. Like he has taken my own normal, everyday attire as a deep personal insult.

The tone alone makes me feel guilty, which is stupid when I owe him *nothing,* and I find myself spinning around to snap back at him, "Probably just as well—I wouldn't want to have given every-body the wrong impression."

He frowns, gaze darkening as his chin ticks up. He's standing on the step below me; like this, we're eye level. My chest rises and falls shallowly, angrily, blood thrumming in my ears.

It's not Jake I'm still angry at, of course; I could never be, not really. This is all about Max. Max, who's responsible for taking Jake away from me, for driving that wedge between us. For being so downright insufferable to be around, *all the time*.

"And what impression would that be?" Max asks, his voice low, almost intimate, his words prickly and curt. His jaw clenches, though he doesn't take his eyes away from mine, and I don't look away, either. I refuse to let him win, even though I have no idea how we even got into this battle in the first place.

That I'm a freak like you, I want to spit, but even with the words on the tip of my tongue, even with Max being his usual awful self, I can't bring myself to say them, however true they feel.

Instead, I tilt my head and smile dryly, lips pressed into a thin line, and I give him the haughtiest look I can muster before I, the "newbie" he's so derisive of, use his own beloved fandom against him.

And I tell him simply, "That I think there's any universe in which Lady di Silver belongs with Sir Grayson."

As soon as my ticket is scanned I stride forward to where Jake is waiting and loop my arm through his to enter the fray, under the guise of not wanting to get lost in the crowd.

Max falls behind, and I don't look back.

Comic Con is . . . a strange experience. But despite it being busier and bigger than the convention I went to with Jake in September, it's a lot less intense and overwhelming—probably due to the presence of more mainstream fandoms like Star Wars or Marvel. Max ends up not bothering with a panel Jake wants to see and we lose him for a while afterward, so I actually get to spend some time alone with Jake, which is a relief.

Or it would be, if I didn't feel like Max was suddenly avoiding me. I don't even know what I did to upset him so much that he suddenly can't bear to put up with me, and while I think that's more of a him problem, I still feel guilty that I might have spoiled his enjoyment of the day.

Still, Jake and I get to hang out just the two of us, and it's like old times.

It's *better* than old times.

Maybe that's just the recent distance talking, but I think it's got more to do with how he'll take my hand every so often so we don't get separated. Without Max third-wheeling, we both get swept up in the atmosphere of the convention—or, rather, Jake does, and his excitement is so infectious that I'm just happy to share it with him. He darts between stalls selling merchandise and autographs and samples of mead we're not old enough to taste even though he tries valiantly to persuade the stall owner; he gushes about celebrities and snaps photos from afar of them at their signing tables, and I get a little thrill at seeing some of the *OWAR* cast in real life, although my favorite characters aren't here. Then, when Jake spots someone dressed in a really high-quality *Mandalorian* costume, I offer to take a photo of him, but he insists on asking a stranger so we can be in the picture together.

He grins at the photo afterward, both of us striking silly poses while the person in cosplay looks more like a professional from the Disneyland parks, and uploads it to Instagram—making me *so* glad I'm not in cosplay, and dressed cute instead.

"An official memento of our first Comic Con together," he tells me, beaming so wide that his mouth splits from ear to ear, and my heart flutters—it sounds like he's saying it'll be the first of many things the two of us do together, and I like that thought a lot.

Taking full advantage of our alone time, I do my best to flirt with Jake. When we look at the lightsabers on sale, I make him teach me how to hold one, relishing when he stands behind me with his arms all the way around my body, encasing me against him while his hands settle over mine, guiding my arms . . .

Although he does make all the "whoosh" noises in my ear, which puts a real dampener on the romance of the situation.

I no longer hesitate to reach for his hand, even when the crowds aren't too thick, and he tugs me along eagerly to each new corner of the convention, his fingers interlocked firmly with mine, his palm warm and smooth. When we wait in line to get some bottles of water, I play with my hair and tell him how good he looks today, how nice *his* hair looks, how brilliant it is to see him in his element like this and how glad I am that we get to share it. Then I purposely don't buy my own drink—and Jake, of course, offers me a sip of his, which is hardly the first time but feels *different* now, like this, when there's just the two of us, and it's not some big group outing to Barry Island in the heat of summer, passing around a Diet Coke.

I really try my best. I go all in, as bold as I dare to be.

The place is so packed, it almost grants us privacy: everyone is too preoccupied to pay any attention to us.

Unfortunately, though, every time I think Jake and I are truly having A Moment and something is going to happen . . . *he* gets too preoccupied by something else going on around us and it never gets a chance to fully manifest.

Now, though, we're squashed into a standing-room-only panel that includes the guy who plays Daxys in *Of Wrath and Rune,* and Jake is forced to stand flush against my back. I'm acutely aware of everywhere the lines of his body are pressed into me, far closer than when we looked at the lightsabers, and the unexpected proximity makes me positively vibrate with excitement. *He* initiated this one, I'm sure of it. He could've kept a bit of space between us if he *really* wanted to, right? I have to fight to stand totally still.

Jake leans his chin on to my shoulder, the side of his forehead resting against mine. "You all right? You're stood all funny."

"Fine!" It comes out thin, and he tries to shuffle back to steal another inch of space so I can be more comfortable, putting an arm lightly over my shoulder as if to buffer me from the person on my left. I can't very well explain that it isn't the crowds that're making me so awkward, but I appreciate the chivalry and throw him a grateful smile. When he stands holding me so casually like this, it's as if we really are boyfriend and girlfriend. I let the daydream take over and relax. Jake rests his head against mine again to see the panel better, and it's so lovely that I never want it to end. My skin tingles where he touches me, even through all the layers of clothes between us.

If this was real, I think, if he'd just *ask* me to be his girlfriend, we'd never have to think twice about this sort of affection . . .

Jake is just perfect boyfriend material. He's truly the sort of guy that rom-coms are made of: kind and sweet and funny and attractive, so inherently likable and lovable, and we go together so well. It'd be impossible *not* to have a crush on him.

I just wish he'd *realize.*

Short of outright declaring my feelings for him by singing "Can't Take My Eyes Off You" as I dance down some bleachers, *10 Things I Hate About You*—style, I just don't know what else to do to make him see it.

By midafternoon, we still haven't found Max, and Jake insists on getting out of the crowds to text him and try to track him down.

But we were having such a good time without our third wheel . . .

"I thought you wanted to try and beat the line to see that guy from the *Lord of the Rings* show?" I say.

Jake winces. "Isildur will have to wait."

"But you said you wouldn't have time to see him *and* get a picture with Daxys." It's not that I don't want to find Max, but . . . I mean, he's seventeen, he's a big boy, he can look after himself, and it's only some hall full of nerds.

Jake, though, shakes his head. "It's okay. I already got him to sign my poster at the last one. I just didn't get a photo with him . . . But we should really find Max, it's been ages. And this sort of thing is way more fun with others than by yourself."

I barely hide my flinch, realizing that the tables have turned: here, *I* am the third wheel, I am the one who's gotten in between them and spoiled their day together, sharing in something they love and have been looking forward to for months.

I am the one who was pointedly not invited to evenings spent building cosplay wings together.

So I wait patiently as Jake tries phoning (it goes to voicemail) and then sends a couple of texts. It is good of him to check in on his friend, I suppose, and it does feel like maybe it's my fault that Max has gone AWOL . . .

I'm sure he has no such conscience when *he's* the one interfering.

Jake looks agitated, gripping his phone in both hands and staring at the screen as if he can will Max to reply. I put my hand on his arm, my fingers curling around lightly, ready to pull him along.

"Shall we do a loop of the hall?" I suggest. "He'll be here somewhere. And he should be easy to spot, especially with his wig."

"Between the Legolas, Daemon Targaryen, and Witcher cosplays that are here, I wouldn't be so sure . . ."

Of course he's right; I quickly realize there are an unprecedented amount of guys in long white-blond wigs. But we do a circuit of the hall anyway, eyes raking over queues for autographs and the crowds around lightsaber displays, until there's a cry not far off, several voices in unison yelling, BE YE A RASCAL, ROACH? and descending into cheers and laughter.

I cut Jake a look, finding he's brightened considerably. "Do you think that'll be him?"

He laughs, and starts off at a jog toward the group of *OWAR* fans behind a row of merch stalls. There are two girls in Lady di Silver cosplay, though both wear her usual armor rather than the green dress; a guy with a very impressive set of huge, leather-look mechanical wings as Daxys; two more less-impressive Moonwalkers; and a few other miscellaneous character cosplays—including a guy with a Minotaur head tucked under his arm.

In the midst of them all, in his wig and pauldrons, is Max, and—

"Holy shit," Jake breathes, now that I've caught him up. He grasps my arm tight, though his eyes are wide and fixed ahead. "*Holy shit.* Cerys, is that . . . is that . . . ? That's . . ."

It's Daxys. Well, the actor who plays him.

And he's got his arm slung around Max like they're good buddies. He's such a huge man—easily six and a half feet, barrel-chested, and bald, with a smile that crinkles his eyes—that he practically dwarfs Max by comparison.

The group of fans gathered around them are reacting to his presence much the same way as Jake: eyes bugging wide and hardly blinking, mouths fallen open in glee, their entire bodies positively vibrating with excitement at this unfiltered, unguarded interaction with a favorite character and beloved actor.

Max, for his part, has on his usual cool, borderline-bored expression, as if he could not care less that he is currently being embraced by Jake's idol. Daxys (what *is* the actor's name? For all Jake's talked about him, my brain blanks now. Bryan? Bernard?) is chatting affably with Max and the group.

"Go over there!" I whisper to Jake. "Go say hi."

"Are you crazy? I can't!"

"You already met him. You were literally going to pay thirty quid to get a selfie with him."

"Yeah, but—but—"

He's totally starstruck, and I can't blame him. This guy is his Anne Hathaway, his Joey King, his Zoey Deutch.

Lucky for Jake, I'm not felled by quite the same affliction, and hook my arm firmly through his before raising my other hand in a wave to call, "Max! We've been looking everywhere for you!" I pull us through the crowd toward Max. And then, to the actor, I add, "Hi, hello."

When he turns to look at me, my body threatens to turn to jelly simply from the full force of his blatant charisma and the sudden realization smacking me in the face that *a TV star is two feet away from me, looking at me, saying hello.*

He grins at us, then says to Max, "Friends of yours, Moorwalker?"

"Oh my God, I'm dead, I've died," Jake whispers to me.

Max nods, but his eyes linger a moment on me. I expect some

snarky remark from him about how I, too, was meant to be in full cosplay, but he just says, "This is Cerys, she's very new to the fandom—"

"Oh, nice! How're you finding it? I'd ask your favorite character, but obviously I know the answer's going to be me!" Daxys winks, laughing, and it's a jolly sort of laugh that makes him sound more like Father Christmas than a professional warrior faerie. "You're enjoying the show, though?"

"Absolutely! Yes! I love it!"

As if I'd dare say anything but when face to face with one of the leads like this, but I *did* genuinely enjoy it. I must overdo it, though, because Max raises an eyebrow at me.

He interjects, "And this is my friend Jake. He was meant to come dressed as you, actually, but had a wing malfunction."

"Hey," jokes the actor, "been there! Very on-brand-for-Daxys of you."

Jake goes to say something, but instead it comes out as a high-pitched warble. I say for him, "He's a huge fan. We were at the Worlds Beyond con last month, too." Look at me, using the lingo, calling it a "con"!

He snaps his fingers, shaking his hand at Jake as he nods. "Yes! Dude, I remember you. You had that sick original poster that I signed. I was just saying to your friend here that I remembered him. One of the best Moonwalker looks I've seen on the circuit. The bandolier looked fresh off the set—even got the stitch marks from where Grayson repairs it after he gets stabbed."

He claps Max on the shoulder with another broad grin, and Max mumbles, shrugging as if it's no big deal.

Judging by the reaction from the little crowd around us, it's a *very* big deal.

A woman in a lanyard and a black T-shirt slips forward as if from nowhere, and despite being all of five foot nothing, murmurs quietly in the actor's ear and he nods, expression serious, before turning to all of us.

"Sorry, everyone, that's my cue to get going. I'm over on the signing tables now if you want to come by and get a photo or an autograph, and we can chat a little more. But . . ." He grits his teeth, bounces from one foot to the other, and sighs before saying, "Ah, I'm not *strictly* allowed to do this, but let's grab a group selfie, yeah? I'll put it on my socials later for you guys to find. Okay, everyone get in. Moonwalker Max, get in here! Come on, guys, we all ready?"

He crouches at an odd angle to get all of us in the shot, his arm slung around Max's shoulder still, and twenty or so of the rest of us grinning behind them. Jake's face presses close to mine as he squashes in, and I feel a fizz of warmth to experience his joy secondhand.

I'm not worried about anyone I know seeing *this* photo; they'd have to be an *OWAR* fan themselves for it to show up on their feeds at all.

The actor tells us all goodbye, and most of the group disperses to follow him to his signing table, chattering loudly. Jake clings to me with sweating palms and shallow breaths as a few stragglers chat with Max.

"This is the best day ever," he whispers, almost to himself, then gives me a quick, fierce hug and a kiss on the cheek. "You're the *best*. Thanks, Cerys. I owe you one!"

My whole face turns hot, the place where his lips pressed into my cheekbone for that too-brief moment sparking like he's ignited a whole host of fireworks beneath my skin, and I'm breathless, so taken aback I can't react—can't even turn toward him and take his hand, keep him close, hope for a *real* kiss.

He's never done that before! He's a hugger, but that kind of affection, a kiss on the cheek . . . that's wildly out of character for Jake.

It has to mean something, doesn't it? All my attempts at flirting earlier must have paid off, hints he's finally, *finally* picked up on, to make a little move of his own!

Jake, luckily, is too caught up in the adrenaline of everything that just happened to notice my internal screaming.

The others finally split off, leaving just me, Jake, and Max.

"Holy shit," Jake says again. He's shaking, and holds his hands out to demonstrate before raking them through his hair. Then, all at once, he blinks and surges forward to grab Max tightly by the pauldrons on his shoulders, standing close as he says, "Brayden Brown knows who I am. He knows who *you* are. He knows your *name.* Holy shit! Did that really just happen? How did you even get talking to him?"

"I—I didn't, I just—it sort of . . ."

Now, suddenly, Max is flustered. The aloof demeanor has vanished and his face is almost ashen, mouth slack and eyes tracking back and forth without really seeing anything. I'm so stunned that all I can do is gawp at him.

I'd never have guessed he was just *playing it cool* in front of Daxys. I thought he was just being . . . Max.

This show of such raw emotion is so unlike him, my jaw actually drops to see it.

"What happened?" I ask. Somehow, I don't think Max—a diehard fan and beyond starstruck beneath the surface—just approached the actor out of nowhere.

He rubs his jaw, not looking at me as he answers—although this time he's not really looking at Jake, either, so I don't take it personally for once. "I really don't know. I just got talking to a couple of people, some *OWAR* fans who wanted to grab a photo because of my cosplay, and then he just walks up out of nowhere . . . I guess there's a greenroom or something nearby. He *came up to us*—to me. He said he remembered me from the Worlds Beyond con and had meant to say hi because he liked my costume, thought it was impressive. And then all these other people started gathering around and . . . I think I blacked out."

Then he looks at Jake, a disbelieving laugh on his lips, and he grabs Jake by the shoulders, too, both of them tangled up and foreheads close.

"Brayden effing Brown *knows who we are!*"

I watch them both freak out, and I can't pinpoint what exactly causes the shift, but this time Jake's excitement isn't infectious. It's like someone dropped a curtain between us, and I'm on the sidelines watching it happen, not part of it anymore. It leaves me deflated, robbed of my own joy at Jake finally making a move to kiss me on the cheek, and how *good* our day together was.

My eyes shift from Jake, chattering breathlessly and a mile a minute, to Max as Jake recounts every moment of his interaction with Brayden Brown and his shock at us finding Max in the middle of it all.

The culprit. The interloper.

The reason Jake and I have had so many almost-moments and near kisses lately that have led to nothing at all. Because *he's* always there.

I *have* to find a way to get rid of him, before I lose my chance with Jake for good.

Private chat with @silversmithhh

@silversmithhh
CERYS!!!!

@mythicwitch
!!!???

@silversmithhh
Cannot believe I missed you at Comic Con Saturday 😭 I was on the lookout for your fab cosplay but didn't see you anywhere!

@mythicwitch
Oh I didn't end up wearing it! To be honest I chickened out . . . Cosplay is NOT my usual sort of thing lol, it felt too weird. But at least I have it ready if I ever change my mind for the next one! I'm sorry. Thanks for the help with ideas to pull the look together though x

@silversmithhh
That's totally fair enough, everyone approaches fandom differently and shows their love for it in different ways too! You don't need to apologize to me haha, I had fun helping you search for ideas! My own Adanna di Silver cosplay is very much armor-focused

@silversmithhh sent 1 photo

@mythicwitch
You look BADASS!

Wait

This might sound really weird but did you see that selfie Brayden Brown took? And the guy dressed up as the Moonwalker?

@silversmithhh
DID I SEE IT

Honey I was IN IT

Hang on, isn't Runic Rascal your friend who introduced you to the fandom/Discord/etc? I didn't get the chance to chat with him properly!

@mythicwitch
Yes! And I was in the photo too! I thought I recognized you in your pic—I'm literally two people left of you in the Brayden Brown selfie!

@silversmithhh
AS IF

I CANNOT BELIEVE WE WERE RIGHT THERE AND HAD NO IDEA! Internet friendships be wild, man

@mythicwitch
Haha tell me about it! At least we know who we're looking for at the next one!

@silversmithhh
Yes! BTW, this fic *just* completed . . . It's an arranged marriage AU where Devon accompanies Adanna to the capitol for her to marry into the royal family, which OF COURSE doesn't go according to plan

It's honestly just tooth-rottingly sweet fluff with a top-tier kiss scene, and zero plot spoilers for the show

@mythicwitch
Count me in!

GIRLIE POPS! ✦⁺

Evie

Umm Cerys why has Jake tagged you in a photo at COMIC CON?! I thought you said you guys were just hanging out this weekend! You didn't say anything about this!

Daphne

HE TAGGED YOU IN A PHOTO?!?! Omgomgomg

Nikita

HUGE NEWS

But also . . . Comic Con? Really????? Haha

Chloe

Sounds like a cute date idea! Putting the "convention" in "unconventional" at least

Evie

That was TERRIBLE Chlo lol

Daphne

It's a cute pic though! You guys look ADORABLE together! But yeah why didn't you say he was taking you to Comic Con?! That's . . . kind of a choice from Jake!

Me

Haha it was kind of a last-minute thing, he thought it'd be a laugh

Nikita

Oh like an ironic thing? Lol love it

I can't believe people actually PAY to go to these geekfests?! It's so weird

Evie

I so do not get it. Like don't you have better things to do than watch people talk about Star Wars all weekend?

Chloe

I could NEVER!!!

Daphne

Pls say the annoying third-wheel guy didn't tag along again?!?

Me

Sadly HE DID

Evie

Jake needs to learn what
boundaries are, wtf?!

Me

I know . . . But!!! He was off at some of
the panels and stuff so me and Jake got
to hang out a lot just the two of us

AND

GET THIS

He kissed me!!!

Well

He kissed me on the cheek, but still! It's a
move in the right direction, isn't it?

Daphne

SCREAMING

Nikita

Yasss girl get your man

Evie

That is SO cute

Chloe

I need a FULL debrief on this asap!!

THE FANGIRL PROJECT

Become an "OWAR" fangirl to convince Jake I am his dream girl and we are actually a match made in heaven:

1. buy the books ✓
2. watch the show ✓
3. remember to call it "OWAR" like a real fan ✓
4. go to a convention (cringe) ✓
5. ... ~~something~~ 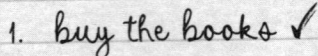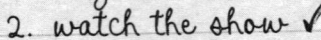thing CUTE!!! that Jake can't resist)
6. DO NOT badmouth OWAR in front of Jake
7. who/what is "Roach"??? Find out! ✓
8. wear the new T-shirt Jake bought me next time I see him! ✓
9. join this fan-forum-chat thing on Discord (whatever that is?) and talk to Jake in it to prove that I really A-M all in and therefore the love of his life ✓ ♡♡
10. GET. RID. OF. MAX!!!!
11. look up "Silversmith domestic fluff"
12. write some Silversmith fanfic . . . ?

Jake isn't very talkative in the days following Comic Con, and the Discord chat goes quiet too, only solidifying the need for my recent adjustment to The Fangirl Project—an additional, slightly sideways step that involves pushing Max totally out of the picture.

I try stalking his social media to find some bad takes—something that would prove Max isn't such a great person after all—but there's *nothing*. His Instagram looks inactive, and I can't find a trace of him anywhere else—no Facebook or Snapchat or TikTok, and he's not even in the Discord channel that *he* first mentioned to me. He must have some cryptic username keeping him anonymous—but there are so many Moonwalker/Sir Grayson–related names in the forum I don't know where to start looking for him.

After school on Wednesday, I'm hanging out with the girls in a field near campus. It's cold, and the weather switches between light drizzle and a loitering mist every few minutes, but there are some guys playing rugby there, including one Daphne is sort of talking to, so we sit huddled on a picnic bench pretending not to look like we're watching—or shivering.

I've spilled all (well, *most*) of what happened on the weekend to them in person now as well as in the group chat, avoiding any mention of *OWAR*. Their reaction to Comic Con was exactly what I'd been afraid of, so I *can't* let them find out about the fandom thing. I'd be totally ostracized. It's not worth it.

Besides, I'm only doing it for Jake.

Mostly. Sort of. Anyway.

Nikita suggests confronting Max. "He sounds rude as hell, too. I'd call him out."

"Maybe you can tell Jake?" is Evie's advice. "He's super sweet, I bet he'd understand if you told him this other guy is being a pain in the butt. You can always call it a 'personality clash' or something."

"But what if he chooses *him* over me?" I say, and she grimaces, not having an answer to that.

"Doesn't this Max guy have other friends?" Daphne says, and I admit that I don't know. Even if he does, it's clear that he and Jake have become best friends and near inseparable these days. Like we used to be.

It's Chloe in the end who says offhandedly, "Maybe *he* needs a girlfriend. Or a boyfriend! Maybe it's not about spending *less* time with this guy so much as inviting him to more things and trying to set him up with someone, or finding out if there's anyone he's got a crush on that you can help him with?"

I snort. "I don't think I'm very well equipped to help anyone else with romance when I'm failing so spectacularly with Jake."

"You're not failing!" Daphne cries, reaching to give my hand a squeeze. Her brown eyes are wide and earnest; the damp weather has made her usually pristine dark hair frizz in a halo around her head. "He's definitely into you. The *kiss on the cheek*? Hello? Are we forgetting that? And he made that really cute Instagram post of the two of you! *Plus,* you spent the whole day at Comic Con with him, and I don't know many people who'd put up with a hall full of obsessive nerds just for someone else's sake."

The others laugh, but I find myself biting down a comment about how, actually, I'd . . . kind of enjoyed it, up until we reunited with Max and I felt so pushed aside.

But Daphne's got a point. Saturday wasn't a complete failure; and maybe Chloe's right, too, although where I'd even *begin* to set Max up with someone is beyond me . . .

Friday, our art lesson runs into lunchtime. The classrooms are always open during breaks for anybody wanting to come and work on their projects and portfolios and, today, I decide to stick around.

Evie packs her things up and comes over to the easel I'm working at, in the corner. And while I can hardly hide my coursework piece, a surge of panic rises up from the pit of my stomach, remembering how the girls reacted to Comic Con.

But when she gets close she gasps, and says in a tone of quiet awe, "Omigosh, Cerys! The way you've captured the light . . . it's like it's *actually* sparkling. How'd you do that?"

The comment makes *me* feel like I'm sparkling, too, positively glowing with pride. Having moved on from my sketch, I'm focusing on the acrylic backdrop to my next Téiglin-inspired piece, and have spent most of the last week adjusting the sunlight streaking through the glade in my painting, trying to capture the magic of *OWAR*.

Or I guess, since it's OWAR, the *magick*.

Suddenly, I don't even mind that I've become the kind of person who actively thinks things like that.

"A *lot* of patience" is my only real explanation, and Evie laughs.

"You're going to have to help me when I get around to mine. I *hate* working with acrylics, but apparently I have to 'expand my artistic horizons' if I'm serious about getting into a good university course . . ." She casts a glare over her shoulder at our teacher, but grins, relaxing, when I promise I'll help her if she can give me some tips on working with pastels, which is her strength.

Evie looks at the paints still spread around me. "Aren't you coming for lunch? Nikita's driving us to the retail park, remember?"

"Oh, um . . . I actually want to try and finish some stuff on this. It's nearly there, you know? You guys have fun, though!"

A tiny panic siren sets off in my mind, one that screams FOMO. Like if I say no to things they'll stop inviting me altogether, and I'll lose the group just when I feel like I've found my place with them.

But it's only this once, and my agitation to get back to my painting wins out. I haven't felt this inspired in a long time, and for once I don't feel like I'm finishing pieces for the sake of a good grade in class, or losing steam and abandoning them before they're complete. I keep finding my mind drifting to them, my fingers itching to reach for a pencil or paintbrush. It's like a fire in my veins, energizing me.

I'm worried if I don't take advantage of it, it might disappear entirely.

Evie only shrugs, though, and says, "That's cool. See you later, yeah?"

Once she leaves, I slip my earphones in and get back to work. I'm trying out the first *Of Wrath and Rune* audiobook, and even though I'm not giving it my full attention I'm sure something will sink in. Plus, the narrator's voice is really soothing, so it's at least nice background noise.

Right now, conveniently, he is narrating a very long-winded passage about the Gilded Glade, where Téiglin and so many other creatures have taken refuge since the Eldritch King went missing decades ago, and one of the few places where magick is kept sacred. The book describes it just like it was in the show: shafts of golden light filtering through great oak trees and majestic pines, casting dappled shades of emerald and amber on the forest floor; a place where the world seems to almost stand still but for the rustle of leaves and lilting birdsong. Fresh brown earth and vibrant purple mushrooms and crawling vines of ivy, clusters of pure white daisies and swaying dandelions with their puff caught in the breeze—*"as if the glade itself were making a wish."*

The sudden mention of a dandelion has me gritting my teeth. I'd daubed a couple in, but now it only makes me think of that JUST DANDY mug, and Max.

I swap out my paintbrush for a finer one, meticulously dabbing in the tiny grayish-white seeds floating in the air, and make wishes of my own. *I wish he wasn't always lurking around spoiling things. I wish Jake would see me, really see. I wish he'd kissed me on Saturday, I wish this didn't feel like the be-all and end-all, I wish he'd just message me back already . . .*

Jake's been annoyingly quiet all week. He's replied to most of my texts, but none of it has been with his usual enthusiasm. It's always curt, cursory, polite. When he didn't reply to me asking if we'd be resuming our Wednesday watch parties, I went ahead and watched a few more episodes myself . . . and then a few more. Even if Jake wasn't inviting me over, I could still prove myself to him—and if I'm being totally honest with myself, I *did* get a little sucked into the show. I'm up to season three now, the action really starting to kick off, but the message I sent Jake in the Discord to chat about it, thinking *OWAR* was some safe, neutral ground, got a similarly short response, so I didn't bother after that.

Jake must have some stuff going on. Maybe with his family? Or school? Perhaps he's just really busy, or not feeling too well, and he'll be back to normal in a few days, and it's nothing personal.

Or maybe I did something wrong?

There has to be a *reason.* Jake wouldn't just . . . vanish. We've been best friends for too long for him to ghost me like this.

I'm so lost in my painting and mulling over every minuscule interaction with Jake and trying to pick apart where I've messed up or haven't noticed something going on with him, that when the bell rings to signal the end of lunch I yelp and practically topple off my stool, knocking my bag over and dropping my paintbrush.

A couple of girls in the year above, who've come in to do their own work, giggle at me.

Face flaming, I pull out my earphones and set them aside, along with my palette. I pick my paintbrush up and see that practically *everything* has spilled out of my bag. A loose tampon, the lip gloss Daphne used on me a few weeks ago that I bought in a different color in the hopes it would suit me better, all my notebooks and some pens . . .

I'm shoveling it all back in, knowing I still need to tidy up and get to my next class, when someone steps over in a pair of lilac Converse and tights with a run in them, bending down to help me gather up my things.

It's Anissa. She's cut her hair again—shorter, matching the length of the choppy pieces that used to hang at the front of her face. It's tousled, not quite straight and not quite wavy, but looks much better now. Her bangs are in her eyes, and her eyeliner is either smudged kohl or yesterday's mascara. Her fingers glint with three different gemstone rings, and I notice a rope bracelet around her wrist with the evil eye stone braided into it, reminding me of all the silly "witchy" rumors about her.

"Thanks," I say, taking the pens she's holding out. The last real interaction I had with Anissa was that Thursday morning debrief in Costa, when we thought she'd overheard us commenting about her hair. I wonder if she remembers it, too; it'd be burned into my mind, I think, if things were the other way around. As an olive branch, I tell her, "Your hair looks nice. That length really suits you."

She rolls her eyes. "My mom didn't give me much choice. I made a real botch job bleaching some of it a few weeks ago."

"Is that why you . . . ?" It's too awkward to say *had those awful, uneven chunks at the front*, so I mime a pair of scissors near my face instead.

"Yeah." She laughs, a brash and short sound, but not unfriendly. "I was trying to dye it purple and after I started thought maybe I should just do a test patch, which is just as well because I basically fried it."

"Oh shit! Well . . . it . . . looks . . ."

Better, I don't quite say, but she obviously knows that's what I meant, because she holds my gaze, and there's a little more spark to it compared to any other time I've seen her. This is also the longest conversation we've ever had, and the most I've heard her say in one go.

I stand up, bag haphazardly packed, and Anissa stands, too, holding something else out to me.

Of Wrath and Rune: Book 1—The Wakening.

Crap. Crap, crap, crap!

It's mine, it's definitely mine, with the pages crinkled, the front cover creased where it bent in half in my bag, and a makeup stain on the side where I spilled some foundation. My heart thunders in my chest. She might as well be handing me a hive of angry wasps.

I stare at the book in horror, too alarmed to even try to play it cool—*oh, I'm just hanging on to it for a friend*—and Anissa gives me a soft, barely there smile.

"I thought it looked like Téiglin that you were sketching before," she says. "And I saw that photo of you and Jake from school at Comic Con over the weekend, with the guy who plays Daxys. That was really cool."

"It . . ." I swallow the lump in my throat. The classroom is empty now, but it won't be for long. "It *was* pretty cool actually, yeah. He was really nice. He liked my—" *No, not "my" friend, Max is not "my" friend by any stretch.* "He liked Jake's friend's cosplay."

"Was that the guy dressed as Sir Grayson?"

"Yeah. Max."

"Omigod," she gushes, suddenly animated, her hazel eyes bright. She smiles wide enough to show a gap between her front teeth I've never noticed before. "He looked *so* cool! That's so amazing. I can't believe you guys all got to meet Daxys like that." Her eyes skirt past me then, lingering on my painting. Her mouth falls open as she drinks it in. "Is that the Gilded Glade?"

"Yeah." I point to an area of the trees. My heart is pounding, but it feels more like excitement to actually *talk* about my piece than worry at being found out. "I've gone for a kind of more abstract look, but if you squint you can sort of make out—"

"Téiglin!" she cries, and laughs, the sound lighter this time as she tilts her head to see the vague shape of an antlered man blended into the trees, her eyes tracking across the canvas and picking out the subtle, half-hidden shapes of fauns, a Minotaur, gnomes . . . You wouldn't know unless you were looking for them, and it's unrecognizable as *OWAR* fanart except to those who know.

And Anissa, unquestionably, knows.

"I didn't realize you were a fan too," she tells me as I wash my paintbrush at the sink. Splotches of dried paint are caked onto my fingers, but I'll have to deal with that later—I need to get to class. "How long have you been into it?"

"Er, not long. How about you?"

"Since always. I think I found the first book in the library when I was about ten, and I never looked back."

"Ten?" I echo, jaw dropping, and I blurt, "I can't even make it through more than a few pages of the book now; I can't imagine reading them as a ten-year-old."

She shrugs, looking embarrassed, though I didn't mean it badly at all.

"So are you into all the other stuff, too?" I ask. I wonder if I've exchanged messages with her in the Discord without even realizing it, or if she was wandering around Comic Con or the Worlds Beyond convention last month and we missed each other.

Anissa cocks her head, frowning at me. "Other stuff? What, like . . . *Game of Thrones* and *Lord of the Rings,* you mean?"

"No, like the fandom stuff. Like Comic Con. You know, OWFR cosplays and fanfiction and Discords and that kind of thing."

"I . . ." Her frown deepens, and she searches my face, almost like she's looking for the lie in my words, some kind of trick. "I've read a couple of fanfictions, but . . ."

I have the sudden urge to ask if she's a Silversmith shipper, too, what she thinks about the theory that Devon will die protecting Lady di Silver, to say how excited I am for Lady di Silver and Roach to cross paths (which I'm sure they inevitably will in later episodes) because I've become convinced they'll end up having a really strong platonic bond, like siblings.

The thoughts pour in so thick and fast I can't pick which one to ask first, and they're followed swiftly by the realization that I *care* about her answers. About this fandom.

And not even for Jake's sake, but . . . just *because.*

I end up swallowing all my questions, and Anissa is still staring at me funny. She looks almost distrustful, as if whatever tentative bridge we just formed is going to shatter if she tries to step across it.

People are starting to stream into the classroom now, and I'm going to be late for my next class. I *am* late, probably. Anissa will be too, because she stayed to help me.

"We should get going," I say.

She nods, and I wait for her to grab her own things, though we leave in silence. I can't quite pinpoint what I said that shifted the conversation for the worse, and understand much less why it bothers me so much.

Do I even want to be friends with Anissa? The quiet loner girl I was so keen to avoid, worried I'd be tarnished by association? Or *cursed,* like Evie suggested she was capable of?

At the end of the corridor, we part ways, and I mutter a good-bye. Anissa hums, not quite saying anything, and we move in opposite directions to our next classes, other stragglers cluttering up the hallways.

I only get a few steps before I spin on my heel and run after her. "Wait! Anissa!"

I catch up to her and she looks at me with that frown still in place.

"There's a Discord—a chat room forum thing—for some local *OWAR* fans; they're all really nice. There's, like, channels within it for discussing theories or sharing links to fanart, and they organize meetups sometimes, although I haven't gone to any of those. Mostly they just talk about the show. The books, whatever. I could send you a link, if . . . if you wanted?"

The crease in her forehead and the pinch between her eyebrows eases away, and she blinks at me, owlish, before nodding.

"Cool, okay. Yeah. I'll, um . . ." I don't know why I'm so flustered. It's just—it's weird, sharing the fandom with someone in real life, someone who's not Jake. It's also weird to think that a long-established fan like Anissa, who's been into the books for six or seven years, isn't already invested in every facet of this bonkers little community. "I'll send you the link."

"That'd be really nice. I never get to chat about *Of Wrath and Rune* with anybody."

"Well, now you can."

She smiles, showing that gap in her teeth again, and there's something almost Jake-like in her grin that makes me smile back.

OWAR Discord #324
#general

@mythicwitch
Happy Friday, folks! How're your weekends looking? I just wanted to welcome **@ladyanissadishipper** to the group, she's a longtime reader but new to the Discord 😊

@sirmoonypants
Hey!

@fauningforhim
Hi @ladyanissadishipper!

@silversmithhh
Greetings, fellow fangirl!

@runicrascal
Welcome to the chat

@wizeguy
sup **@ladyanissadishipper**, great to have you here

@thesebootsweremadeformoonwalking
BE YE A RASCAL, **@ladyanissadishipper**?!

Private chat with @ladyanissadishipper

@ladyanissadishipper
Thanks for the invite Cerys 😊 can't believe I didn't know things like this existed for the OWAR fandom! And everyone seems so nice!

@mythicwitch
They've been very helpful to a newbie like me haha. And silversmithhh has some great fanfic recommendations (three guesses for which romantic pairing)

@ladyanissadishipper
I think this will be where I leave you, sorry

@mythicwitch
?

@ladyanissadishipper
The books made me Team Sir Grayson the Moonwalker before I even knew what shipping was lol. I get what the show is going for but . . . you won't convince me she isn't destined to end up with Sir Grayson

@mythicwitch
You're right, this is where we leave each other

. . . but say more. I started the first audiobook a
few days ago, maybe there's some Moonsilver
foreshadowing I need to be looking out for

@ladyanissadishipper
DEFINITELY. I mean, they've both got these HUGE
ties to fate and so many parallels with their journeys of
links to noble blood/duty that they twist out of to serve
a greater good, and in this essay I will . . .

I'm not *avoiding* Anissa at school, but our paths naturally don't cross very much. There's no strict assigned seating in classes, and this far into term everyone's picked their spot for the year, so in the classes we share—art and history—we both gravitate to our usual seats; but I smile her way and she says hi when we see each other around.

It's a small shift, and while it feels nice, I'm also horribly, self-ishly aware that the others might think it's weird I'm suddenly friendly with an outcast like Anissa, and I know they'll *definitely* judge me for building a bond with her over *Of Wrath and Rune,* of all things.

My emotions about *OWAR* have become a tangled mess with-out me even realizing it. I thought I was just in this for Jake—it was a means to an end, a necessary evil, hours inevitably wasted learning the ins and outs of this series all in the name of romance.

But now I've genuinely started to enjoy it, beyond thinking of Jake or even proving to horrible Max that I *am* committed to this fandom. I look forward to getting home and finishing up home-work so I can watch another episode, staying up late for some more if one ends on a cliffhanger, even rewinding scenes to watch again and trawling through the fanfiction for more heartwarming, squeal-worthy Silversmith content . . .

It's *fun*. I *like it*.

And I even feel like I know some of the others in the Discord more now. @wizeguy is twenty-six and Greek; he's gotten his grandma into the books and helps her learn English with them. @fauningforhim is a stay-at-home mom of three who likes to tell us about ridiculous things her young kids have said, and claims that fanfic and this community were a lifeline when she first moved to South Wales for her husband's work. There's @sirmoonypants, aka Sam, who has a wicked-sharp sense of humor and has just started studying for a PhD in economics. And, of course, @silversmithhh, the first-year law student and fellow romance aficionado whose name I've learned is Heather.

I realize it's all online and I don't *actually* know any of them, but . . . in the Discord, it feels like they're my friends just as much as Daphne and Nikita and everyone are at school.

Anissa and I chat in the Discord, too, sometimes about day-to-day stuff or school, and sometimes about the show. I notice she's quite active in the main chat and gets into heated debates in one of the theory threads, posting even while we're in class.

People leave casual messages in the main chat about things going on at work or school, or send photos of a book haul they just bought, or post memes and links to TikTok videos they want to share. It's not all obsessing over characters and theorizing—although I *have* started to delve into those channels a little, too, interested in ways the show has deviated from the books and what storylines I might be missing out on.

It's a different kind of friendship—low stakes and no pressure, nobody minding how little I know about the fandom or if I have silly questions about the lore of the show I don't quite understand. I don't feel like I have to work so hard to cultivate it, or to keep my place there. They're always *there*, whenever I want to be part of it.

It's nice.

It even goes a little way to filling the gap left by Jake's unexplained absence, although it can't distract me completely from it.

My best friend hasn't exactly dropped off the face of the earth— every few days, he sends me a funny post he's seen on Instagram, and he does reply to *some* of my texts, but I still get the sense he's holding me at arm's length, avoiding me somehow. The Discord private chat has been dead since his last too-brief reply in it.

I don't know whether I'm more upset or worried; if something was *really* wrong, wouldn't he tell me? His sister Ginny's Instagram posts are all very normal—her out with friends, sharing memes, cute outfit pics—so I don't think anything's up with his family . . . Whatever it is, it must be personal.

Would it be too pushy to just message Jake and ask him what's going on, if something's wrong? But I don't want him to just brush me off . . . Should I try phoning him? That seems better than showing up uninvited on his doorstep, but what if he doesn't answer? Could that missed call become the nail in the coffin for us?

I hate that navigating my crush is making our friendship suffer, but it's so hard to let go of it.

He'll tell me when he's ready.

He won't just disappear on me. He *wouldn't*.

Would he?

It doesn't help that things at home have also been weird, and I'm dying to talk to Jake about it. I don't want to bring it up with the girls—their families seem so uncomplicated, and it's kind of nice pretending mine is, too. It's nice having that escape where I can almost convince myself there's nothing going on worth talking about.

But Dad's been over more and more, including for more of these weird, too-civil "family dinners" where he and Mom seem to be *getting on,* and Mom's out with friends a lot more, so Dad keeps staying over in the spare room, and his toothbrush has appeared back by the bathroom sink, so I can't shake the horrible feeling that he's moving back in and they're trying again.

I know I should be happy about that, but it feels like it'll only blow up in their faces—and mine—before long. It has every other time. And I'm so exhausted by it. I'm so *tired* of being caught in the middle.

Jake would understand. Or rather, he'd be a good sympathetic ear to vent to about it all, which is really all I need. But as he's not really talking to me, it feels selfish to dump all my shit on him when we're like this, so I keep it to myself and distract myself with more *OWAR* episodes and the Discord and my new fanart projects.

When another Wednesday comes and goes without our weekly watch party, I ache with how much I miss Jake. His easy laughter and quick smile, his warm hugs, all of him. I even miss *Max*—if only because seeing him meant spending time with Jake, too.

Maybe I need an icebreaker in the Discord to get us talking again. Maybe if we can talk about *OWAR,* it'll lead to deeper conversations about *us*? That's worked before, with both of us opening up in there, all those late-night honest conversations where we moved on from talking about the show and messaged for hours.

I *miss* those conversations; I think I miss them more than I do hanging out with him in real life.

I'm up to the season three finale, and I go ahead and watch it on my own, but I open up the private chat that's been dormant for the past ten days.

Just wanted to let you know, I'm up to the s3 finale. Think I've finally got my head around the plot better too now. Will let you know my thoughts after . . .

I leave it with a "dot dot dot," though I debate for a good long minute about that or a question mark; an exclamation mark feels too happy-go-lucky after the long gap between this and his last message. At least *not* using a question mark means I don't have to worry about a lack of response, and can double-message without it being so weird. And I *hate* that I'm thinking so hard about these tiny things, when it's always been so easy to talk to Jake—and I've never had to think twice about anything I've messaged him over Discord before, even less so than I do via text, where I try to be a little more flirty.

I hate that things have changed.

It's not even about The Fangirl Project anymore, or feeling annoyed and sorry for myself that Jake can't see what a good match we are or how much I like him—I'd give up on The Fangirl Project altogether if I could just get my best friend back.

It's not very long before I'm double-messaging @runicrascal, then triple-messaging, and then basically sending a live feed of my thoughts throughout the entire episode. I've heard that this is a big one, with a dramatic twist for Roach, Rogdan, and the rest of the Rascals, a main character death, Daxys confronting some of his former brothers-in-arms who are still guards for the evil royal family, and—the part I've most been looking forward to—Lady di Silver and Devon sneaking into a masquerade ball at the palace. Sir Grayson, the Moonwalker, is at the ball in disguise, too, and it's the first time in the entire series that they meet.

I watch, gripped, phone in hand ready to pester Jake with my reactions—whether he replies or not.

"I've heard much about you, Lady Adanna."

"How did you—?"

"You give yourself away." The Moonwalker spins her across the dance floor, and when he draws her back in, he ensnares her in his arms with a smirk, his finger tapping her bracelet, the one with the di Silver crest. *"And is that a dagger you're smuggling beneath your dress, or are you just happy to see me?"*

"Careful, sir; I thought knights were supposed to be noble, and you are being very ignoble right now." She spins again, and this time when they come back together she gives him an arch look, and the Moonwalker's eyes flash behind his mask. *"Now I believe our interests are aligned, are they not, Sir Grayson? Perhaps you should tell me what you know, and we might stop wasting our time squabbling instead of seeking answers. That is what you are here to do, isn't it?"*

"They warned me you'd take no prisoners." He grins, though it's sharp as a knife, and the pair watch each other as if weighing an opponent; then Lady di Silver smiles, like she's relishing the challenge. The song ends, and the Moonwalker bows deeply. She watches him go.

I betray myself, because I kind of like the dynamic they have going on, and I can see why people ship it.

@mythicwitch
UGH as if the Moonwalker and Lady di Silver had THAT MUCH chemistry. I'm offended that I enjoyed that scene so much

WAIT THAT'S IT? She's just going to interrogate the prince?

WE HAVE BEEN ROBBED

WHAT THE HELL

YOU'RE TELLING ME she mentions dancing with Devon but WE NEVER SAW IT????

THE SHOWRUNNERS ARE BIASED

THIS IS SILVERSMITH SLANDER

NOOOO THEY CUT AWAY TO DAXYS. I mean. I know, plot, more important, etc., but!!!! We could have had them DANCING TOGETHER! I needed an entire episode just for the ball!

@runicrascal
I am just catching up on all of this but wow. Wow. Someone's deeply invested . . .

> **@mythicwitch**
> Someone's deeply upset and stunned rn that's for sure
>
> Also, hi. It's been a while x
>
> **@runicrascal**
> Okay, you finish the episode (there can't be very long left), I'll catch up on the 87 messages you've sent about it, and then we'll talk
>
> Also, hi back

I'm a mess. A puddle. Jelly. Totally wrecked.

My whole body is buzzing with adrenaline from the excitement and immediate letdown of the masquerade ball, and it spikes my heart rate all over again when I finally get a response in the Discord—and a promise to talk.

I don't know if I'm relieved or nervous or what. I also don't know if my heightened emotions are more down to the show or the chat.

I don't bother pausing to try and puzzle it out, because there's only sixteen minutes left in the episode—in the season—and it feels like way too many character arcs and plotlines to try to contend with in such little time.

And no offense to Jake, but if he's kept me waiting for him to feel like talking for almost two weeks, he can bloody well wait another sixteen minutes for me to focus on something else. Something I only even *started* watching because of him.

I'm not surprised when, sixteen minutes later, the finale ends and leaves me feeling irked and unsatisfied, and eager to dive straight into the start of season four—which only aired last year and is the most recent.

But season four will have to wait.

@runicrascal
Wow okay so you had a LOT of feelings about s3 haha (and yes, Daxys being persuaded back to the royal guard was . . . a lot. A moment for Roach getting arrested and sacrificing himself for the rest of the Rascals though! That's a GREAT scene)

@mythicwitch
A Silversmith dance >>> Roach's moral quandary, pls

@runicrascal
Haha

It's a shame we didn't end up having a watch party for this one

@mythicwitch
Yeah . . . Where've you been lately? You've been quiet

@runicrascal
So have you

You never messaged last week, and after Comic Con I thought

Well you just seemed kind of off, when we left

I figured you weren't very interested in talking much

@mythicwitch
I figured YOU weren't very interested in talking much

@mythicwitch
To tell you the truth I thought *you* were off with me after Comic Con. I don't know. Maybe that was all in my head lol. I'm sorry if I did something to upset you, though, and made you feel like I didn't want to talk

@runicrascal
How come you didn't end up wearing the costume?

@mythicwitch
Is that what this is about?

@runicrascal
It's just a question

@runicrascal
You seemed really excited about it. I could tell you were lying when you said it "didn't work out"

@mythicwitch
The honest truth? No judgment?

@runicrascal
Rascal's honor

@mythicwitch
I don't know that I can be the kind of person who makes being a fan of something their whole personality. Or at least, shows so much of it, so openly. It just felt really weird, and I feel icky saying that, and I'm not trying to dunk on the people who do cosplay

@mythicwitch
But it's still . . . niche? Weird? Generally very very very far outside of my comfort zone

@mythicwitch
I know that sounds really silly because, if anything, I should be cool with cosplaying so that I fit in better. I basically do that anyway with my friends, matching my style to theirs and trying to just do what everyone else is doing so that I "belong" or whatever, but . . .

@mythicwitch
Sorry, I think I accidentally turned this into a therapy session. The short answer is, I was too much of a coward to be seen in public like that

@runicrascal
Putting on my best, most amateur therapist hat, sounds like you spend a hell of a lot of time worrying about what other people think

@mythicwitch
Don't you?

@runicrascal
Why should I?

@mythicwitch
Doesn't it . . . I don't know, narrow the pool for finding friends? Generally make you less respected by others? Make you kind of an outcast? Not YOU personally, obviously, but . . . in general

@runicrascal
Who cares? If someone's going to write me off or disown me as a friend for liking something different than them, or wanting to spend my free time doing something they don't care about, they're not worth my friendship anyway. I don't want to surround myself with people who are going to make my life smaller just so I can say I fit in

@runicrascal
I like the things I like, I have friends who matter to me, and, frankly, idgaf what anyone else thinks of that

Even if sometimes that does make me . . . defensive

@mythicwitch
Defensive?

@runicrascal
Sometimes I can be on my guard when I think someone's trying to belittle the stuff I'm into. Like with OWAR. I know people think it's just "some stupid fantasy series" but it's not, it's so much more than that. It's finding characters you relate to and people you connect with and new perspectives. New inspiration for artwork . . .

@mythicwitch
Yeah, I'm starting to understand that now

So is that why you've been off with me? You thought I was belittling your love of OWAR?

@runicrascal
The 87 messages I missed earlier would suggest I was wrong. I'm sorry

@mythicwitch
I'm sorry, too. It's been sort of an adjustment for me to try to move from "some stupid fantasy series" to "this is becoming part of my personality"

@runicrascal
Truce?

@mythicwitch
Truce!

@runicrascal

And I saw you've tracked down another irl OWAR friend! Anissa?

@mythicwitch
Yes! She clocked my Téiglin fanart in class haha

@runicrascal
What're you working on now?

@mythicwitch sent 3 photos

@runicrascal
Holy shit. That's AMAZING. Cerys, that's really beautiful

@mythicwitch
Thanks! I'm really proud of this one. Also, peep the dandelions near the bottom left . . . Some may say they're "just dandy" ;)

@runicrascal
Oh, God

. . . It's me, I'm some.

Very dandy though haha

So aside from you making new fandom friends and creating magickal artwork, what else have I missed? Things still rough with your parents?

@mythicwitch

UGH don't even go there. Feels like any day they're going to turn around and tell me the divorce is off, and I'm dreading it. I think I almost preferred it when they were fighting compared to this weird truce they've got going on . . . At least I knew where I stood then. Thanks for asking though, I appreciate it 🙂 Kinda needed someone to talk to about it lately. But we can get back to that later lol. How about you?

@runicrascal

Ugh, the usual. Bogged down with coursework, stressing about uni applications and exams even though they're still ages off. We're doing well in the local league for soccer though, so that's something! Got another match on Sunday

@mythicwitch

Oh, good luck!

@runicrascal

Should be a good one!

Worried about my dad. He's been really focused on me getting into a good uni and stuff, but I think once I'm actually gone, he's going to find the whole empty nest thing really tough. My sister was meant to be coming home soon for reading week but she said she might just stay there with some friends, and he was pretty upset

@mythicwitch

Oh no! That must be hard for him—and stressful for you

@runicrascal
Eh, could be worse. Preaching to the choir here

@mythicwitch
Haha, don't I know it

I'm glad we're talking again 😊 I missed these chats x

@runicrascal
Me too, Cerys x

The world feels like it's been tipped back into balance; I have plans with the girls to keep me busy, I'm on top of all my schoolwork, there's no weirdness with Anissa in the school hallways and we chat often online, and Jake is *finally* texting me back properly a bit more.

And, most important, the Discord chat between us hardly stops.

So, on Sunday, I do the unthinkable, and I show up to watch my crush's soccer match.

Daphne thought it might be a bit needy (her own recent attempt with the rugby match was totally fruitless and now they're sort of *not* talking anymore), but Chloe and Nikita agreed that it was a worthwhile move; Evie said that knowing Jake, he'd need the extra push anyway.

It didn't used to be weird, when I'd go to watch Jake play soccer. One of the other boys in our group was on the same local team, and we'd all go along to cheer them on for an important match, or just to hang out on the sidelines when the weather was good. We'd do it for the girls' hockey matches, too.

Except now, when I show up, I'm very aware that I'm here *alone* and that most of the other girls shivering on the sidelines in the wet, late October drizzle are clearly girlfriends of some of the players. There are parents and friends around, too, but not so many that I can just melt into the crowd.

The teams are both doing warm-ups, and Max spots me first.

He's stretching his hamstring, but stands up straight when he notices me, staring and staring and *God,* is he for real? It's like he's seen a ghost. Do I have something on my face? Do I really look so out of place? I'm in a navy raincoat and I've brought my umbrella, and I'm even wearing some sensible boots because it's so wet and muddy. It's not as if I've come dressed for maximum "ask me on a date already, Jake!" seduction—for a change.

You'd think I'd shown up in my own set of elf ears, for all he's staring.

Determined to one-up him at his own standoffish game, I give him a cheery smile and a wave so overenthusiastic it must be blatantly obvious that I'm being facetious.

Then Jake says something to Max and straightens out of his own stretch, turning to follow his gaze—and spotting me, doing my stupid wave and goofy smile.

I drop it, but Jake's already jogging over, laughing, and pulls me into a hug so tight he practically lifts me off my feet. I laugh, too, my umbrella falling out of the way, Jake's damp soccer shirt turning my cheek wet. Over his shoulder, I see Max coming toward us, too, his dark eyebrows drawn low.

I've seen Jake in his soccer uniform a hundred times. Not these colors, but it's all the same thing. His narrow shoulders and lean frame, all sharp angles beneath his blue jersey, with matching socks pulled up high over his shin guards.

But my gaze snags on Max before I can help it, and I find myself doing a double take.

Does he . . . does he look . . . *good*?

His legs are thicker than Jake's, corded with muscle and dusted with dark hair, and even with his long hair pulled back from his face in a silly man bun, *it looks good*. It makes his cheekbones look higher, his jawline more defined without his hair hiding it. Stockier than Jake, Max somehow makes him look *boyish* by comparison, softer and younger, while he looks more . . .

More . . .

More *something*, anyway, and it triggers a flurry of butterflies in my stomach that I point-blank refuse to acknowledge.

They're just because of Jake, because he's giving me a hug, that's all.

And definitely *not* because of how good Max looks in his soccer uniform.

Besides, no matter how flattering the uniform is, it *cannot* make up for such a heinous personality.

"Cerys!" Jake exclaims, setting me back down. "What're you doing here?"

"Oh, you know. I thought I'd come see the match. A little like old times."

I bump my shoulder to his and give him a smile that—I hope—

borders between cheeky and flirtatious. By now, though, Max has joined us, with his *impeccable* timing as always.

My smile turns rigid, but I face him anyway. "Hi."

"This is . . . a surprise," he says.

Oh, I'm sorry, Max, do you think I'm intruding on your quality time with your best friend? Tough luck, pal. This is what it feels like.

Not, of course, that I'm here to spite Max. I really am here for Jake. But it's an unexpectedly good side effect, which might be vindictive of me, but I can't bring myself to care too much. Max just has a way of bringing out that side of me.

"I just thought it's been ages since I saw you," I say, which is half in response to Max, though I direct it to Jake. "I've missed you."

Jake sighs, rubbing the back of his neck. "Yeah, sorry, Cer. Things have just been . . . intense, lately. And I'm sorry about skipping out on the Wednesday watch parties, but sounds like you're enjoying the show?"

Max gives a short breath of laughter, shooting me a pointed look I can't distinguish. It doesn't feel like his usual judgment and accusation, but whatever it is, I'm not getting it. Aware that I'm staring back at him now, I say, "Thanks for putting me onto the audiobooks, by the way."

"Sure thing." He nods once, then scuffs the toe of his cleat against the grass.

God, am I *really* that awful to talk to? Is it *such* a chore for him to be halfway polite?

Fine. Whatever.

Jake is as oblivious as ever to the tension between the two of us, and clasps Max's arm before saying to me, "Hey, actually, now that you're here—I've been meaning to tell you! One of the guys at school is throwing a house party for Bonfire Night next week. You should come!"

"Are . . . Bonfire Night parties a thing now? Are we not doing Halloween parties anymore?" I ask, glancing between the pair of them, feeling like I've missed something. Is this a guy thing? A Jake's school thing? Have Halloween parties looped back around from being cool to childish once more?

They both share a look; Max scoffs, and Jake rolls his eyes.

"We tried," Max says. "But most people decided they couldn't be bothered with costumes. Nobody cared enough."

Costumes. I bet he was going to show up in his *OWAR* cosplay.

Thank God it's *not* a dress-up party, I think suddenly. They might've expected me to wear my Lady di Silver outfit. I don't know how I would've explained that to a group of total strangers.

Jake tells me, "The guy's parents are away that weekend, and some of the year above are coming, too; they're old enough to buy fireworks, and they're going to bring some drinks."

"Right. Yeah! Sounds . . ."

Oh God. This changes things. A *proper* no-adults, boozy house party.

I mean, it's not like we haven't had a few drinks at a party before. Ginny was always great about slipping us a bottle of wine to share around, and someone had usually gotten their hands on a few ciders, but never enough for things to get *properly* messy. And whoever was hosting usually had their parents down the road at the pub or shut away upstairs out of the way, so it wasn't like things were completely unsupervised . . .

This sounds like a *real* house party.

My mind suddenly fills with images from American teen rom-coms: red Solo cups and beer pong at dining tables, couples kissing on sofas and in bedrooms, maybe doing *more* than kissing in bedrooms, vodka shots and rowdy games of Truth or Dare and Never Have I Ever . . .

Could this be what Jake and I need, to break the ice and move our relationship from friendly to romantic at last? A kiss in a game of Spin the Bottle, stepping away from the party to get a quiet moment of fresh air together, sitting on a stoop outside a door, huddled close against the cold?

"Sounds brilliant," I say, my voice cracking only a little. I force my smile wider to make up for it.

"You could stay in Gin's room, if you want. She's not coming home for reading week, so it'll be empty."

"Oh! Um . . ."

A sleepover at Jake's? Yes! No? Yes. I don't . . .

"Maybe! I'll see."

"And you could bring some of the girls from St. David's, if you wanted? The more the merrier! It'll be a lot of Colleg Carreg lads anyway . . . And I mean, I sort of already know Evie, so that wouldn't be weird, would it?"

Immediately, I'm torn. I'd love for the girls to meet Jake and really get the measure of us together, tell me if they think we *do* have chemistry or if it's all in my head, and I think it'd earn me some brownie points as a friend to be inviting them to a party, which definitely can't hurt.

But if they meet Jake, they'll meet Max, and Max is . . .

Well, he wears his fandom on his sleeve.

Or around his neck . . . *literally*. Even under his soccer jersey, he has on that rope-chain necklace he wears with his Moonwalker cosplay. With Max, there'd be no escaping the boys' love for *Of Wrath and Rune*—or mine.

And I'm just still not ready for that to be a firm, cemented part of my personality. The girls were kind of judgmental about Comic Con—would they cut me out altogether if they found out I was one of the nerds who had a fun time there? And didn't just go for a guy's sake?

Jake smiles at me, expectant, *waiting*, and I glance past him to Max, who's watching me closely like I'm bound to say the wrong thing, and—

Then it hits me.

"You know what?" I tell Jake smoothly. "I know *exactly* who to invite."

On Monday at lunchtime, I find Anissa in our art classroom.

She's wearing earphones, but her eyes flicker toward the door when I come in, and she brightens, smiling as she takes one out. "Hi."

"Hey." I head straight for her, my preplanned speech forgotten when I notice what she's working on. It's a charcoal scene of a stormy coastline, and even though it's not quite finished yet, it's *visceral*. The rage of howling winds and lashing rain is so strong that it hits me like a punch in the gut.

"Whoa. That's . . . that's . . ."

Anissa waits for my verdict, and a trickle of shame slides down my spine, making me squirm.

Art is a way for me to express my emotions, sometimes; an outlet, a way to help me process something I can't quite put into words even to myself yet. Seeing the emotion Anissa's poured into her drawing—and how pleasantly surprised she looked to see me just now . . .

I feel bad. I feel so, so terrible.

"That's really good," I manage at last, and she beams. Her smile makes her *glow*, like Jake's does, but this time instead of making me want to smile back, I just want the ground to swallow me whole.

I don't think I've ever been mean to Anissa. We've never talked enough for that, and certainly never spent enough time together for me to have actively shunned her or anything.

But I also realize in this moment that I've never been *nice* to her, either, and I've been as judgmental toward her over the years as Max has been of me since I first met him. We talk daily in the Discord since I introduced her to it, and I enjoy those conversations; but I know that I haven't been a good friend to her.

That's also when I realize: Anissa *is* my friend.

Maybe she might have been all along, if I had ever given her a chance. Jake would've gotten on with her really well if they'd ever hung out at school, especially with their shared love for *OWAR*.

I think about how alone she always is—how lonely that must be. I wonder if *anybody's* ever given her much of a chance.

Maybe I'd know these things, if I were a better friend.

Anissa doesn't seem to be aware that I'm wildly psychoanalyzing her, or feeling like a totally wretched excuse for a person, because she's already leaped out of her chair to pull out a canvas from the back of the room and plops it down on a table nearby before adding her sketchbook beside it.

"I'm doing a storm series, for my nature-inspired pieces. So this one"—she jerks her head behind her at the charcoal piece, already busy flipping through her sketchbook for the right pages—"is your miserable, moody, British countryside weather. And then this one's obviously more tropical storm—I need to touch it up, I know, everything's half finished right now . . . And then I thought I'd do more of a woodland theme one . . ."

The canvas painting is the total opposite of her angry charcoal: richly colored palm trees bending in the wind, the waves off the sea crashing into each other almost playfully, a messy sandcastle with a red bucket half buried beside it. The woodland one is all vibrant wildflowers, petals heavy with raindrops, and evokes something calmer and gentler.

The guilt that's taken root in my gut eases a little, as I realize that not *all* her work is as angry and sad as the one in progress on the easel; for a few minutes we lose ourselves talking about her plans for the different pieces and the feedback we've both had from our teacher so far, and the conversation flows as quickly and easily as it does in the Discord, our voices overlapping occasionally like we can't get the words out fast enough.

It's such a contrast from her usual reserved self. Almost the whole of lunch break passes with neither of us making any progress on our art coursework, and instead talking nonstop.

It's only when a text pings through from Jake, making me check my phone and notice the time, that I remember why I came here in the first place.

I say, "We'll have to pack up, lunch is nearly over—and I cannot be late for media again. Anyway, I was looking for you before to see if you wanted to come to a house party this weekend."

"A *party*?" Anissa repeats, with such open disbelief written all over her face that it must be the first time she's been invited to one.

I am a horrible, horrible person, and an even worse friend.

But my intentions aren't . . . malicious. Are they? I'm not doing this to be *nasty* to anyone. I'm just . . .

Thinking ahead. Big picture. Trying to . . .

I swallow the lump in my throat and forge ahead. It's too late now. I've mentioned the party, I've *invited her,* I can't take that back.

"Yeah. You know my friend Jake? Jake Wandsworth, from school. Well, he said some guy at his school is having a house party, and he said I could bring a friend along. So I just thought . . ." I take a breath, Anissa's wide, wide eyes and gaping mouth making me skirt as close to the truth as possible. "Because he's an *OWAR* fan too, and his friend Max—the guy who does the Sir Grayson/Moonwalker cosplay, he'll be there as well, so I thought maybe you'd . . . want to come? Hang out with them a bit? You could come and get ready at my house, and—"

Anissa's eyes remain wide, but now there's a gleam in them, and her open mouth splits into a broad smile. "Are you serious?"

"Yeah. I mean . . . yes. Why not? There's going to be alcohol there, and no parents, and I have no idea what any of the Colleg Carreg lot are *really* like, but Jake wouldn't be friends with anyone that horrible—"

Except moody, judgy Max . . .

"And . . . and like I said, I thought maybe you'd get on all right with him. And Max."

Very much *and Max.*

I am a bad friend.

Or a good one? Maybe they'll hit it off. Maybe *they'll* be besties right off the bat, and I'll get Jake back, and we'll all be friends and everyone will be happy.

And I really *would* like to spend time with Anissa. The party could be fun. Maybe around some new people and with some common ground, she'll open up a bit and be more like she is in the Discord, like she's been this lunchtime. Bubbly and unfiltered and funny and engaging.

Is it *really* that bad if I'm also hoping she might take Max off my hands?

Anissa's still quiet, so I carry on. "I don't know if it's exactly your scene, but—well, you could stay over at my house as well after, if you wanted. My mom won't mind. And if it's that bad, we can just leave early and watch some episodes of *OWAR*. Or—"

"Cerys," she interrupts. How long have I been rambling and babbling? It's mostly down to guilt, but also I've never invited someone to a party and a sleepover before. This whole "making friends" lark is a *lot* less straightforward when you can't just match your outfit to theirs and bump into them at a coffee shop before school.

God, imagine asking someone on a *date*. This is bad enough.

No amount of rom-coms could prepare me for that.

So I shut up, and Anissa smiles at me like *I'm* the one who needs reassuring, and says, "That sounds awesome. I'd love to go."

I breathe a sigh of relief, and promise to message her all the details later, and we can sort out timing for her coming by on Saturday.

This *will* be awesome. We'll have fun hanging out, she'll get on fine with Jake, I don't doubt that she and Max will end up in some deep discussion about their favorite fan theories, and while they're keeping each other busy, Jake and I will have the perfect opportunity to grab some alone time.

The Fangirl Project is officially back on track.

So why do I feel like I'm doing everything wrong?

OWAR Discord #324
#Fanfictions!

@mythicwitch
So . . . I did something 👀

@thesebootsweremadeformoonwalking
Why do I feel like the only appropriate responses are "uh-oh" or "do you need help hiding the body?"

@mythicwitch
Haha, very funny. No it's . . . a good something! A weird something? And I just feel really excited about it and want to share it with someone who'll get it haha (which I feel like is this channel!)

@silversmithhh
OMG YOU DIDN'T?!?? PLS SAY YOU DID

@mythicwitch
I maaaay have . . . had a go at writing some Silversmith fanfiction 😬 (don't judge me @ladyanissadishipper!!!)

@ladyanissadishipper
dw girl I am JUDGING. #moonsilversupremacy #iwillgodownwiththisship

@runicrascal
What! Cerys that's awesome! Can we read it?

@silversmithhh
SEND. US. THE. LINK.

One More Dance Before the Dawn by mythicwitch

Lady Adanna di Silver/Devon Smith, Lady Adanna di Silver,
Devon Smith, Sir Grayson "the Moonwalker," One Shot, Fluff

When Devon sees Lady di Silver dancing with the infamous knight
at the masquerade ball, he can't help but feel jealous.

Words: 461   Chapters: 1/1   Hits: 7

As the Moonwalker melted into the shadows at the edge of
the ballroom, Lady di Silver let out a breath she didn't realize
she'd been holding, and steeled herself. Finally meeting an
adversary—ally—oh, whatever he was—wasn't going to deter
her from the mission at hand.

But before she could leave the dance floor, a hand took hers,
and an arm slid around her waist, sweeping her back into the
midst of the crowd. Adanna gasped, an indignant remark ready
on her painted lips, but found she recognized the masked man
before her.

She recognized him so very well indeed. She knew him in her
marrow. She knew those calloused hands which had helped lift
her out of the dirt during their sword practice, she knew that
scent, like leather and pine, and she knew the curve of that chin
and those lips. She had imagined the feel of them against her
own, sometimes, even if she had never been bold enough to
try it.

She would know her dancing partner *anywhere*.

"Devon," she said, "what are you . . . ?"

"I am dancing, my lady." His mouth curved into a smile, one that felt like a secret he was sharing with her, and Adanna's heart leaped. "I would have thought that was obvious."

"I didn't realize common soldiers were so familiar with the waltz," she teased, and gasped when he spun her quickly, gracefully, before she was standing in the cocoon of his arms once more. It was hardly the first time they had been close—sometimes they were even closer when sparring and training—but this felt *different*. Charged, electric, like the air before a lightning storm.

He was close enough to kiss.

Adanna liked to think of herself as brave in a lot of ways, but she wasn't sure she was brave enough to lean in and risk his rejection. Devon was so dear to her, and they had been through so much. What would she do without him?

When the song ended, he dipped her low, and she could taste the chocolate cake from the feast on his breath, sweet and intoxicating. Through his mask, his shining emerald orbs were fixed on her.

"Devon . . ." she breathed.

He set her back upright, his usual mask of the respectful, faithful guard slipping back into place. "We ought to—"

"No." She caught his hand within hers. "Stay. Just one more dance?"

He took her in his arms once more. "Anything for you, my lady."

They could not dance the entire night away, she knew that, and from the shadows of the ballroom she was sure she could feel the watchful gaze of the Moonwalker upon them.

But this dance with Devon was hers; just as she was his, until the end.

"*Be nice,*" I hiss to Mom and Dad, who are seated at opposite ends of the living room. The TV is on—a cheesy crime drama, one of the few things they've always enjoyed together—though Mom's also reading articles on her iPad and Dad has his laptop open, browsing for some new sneakers. I'm acting like an old biddy twitching anxiously at the blinds, waiting for Anissa to get here.

"Of course we'll be nice!" Mom clicks her tongue in admonishment. "Honestly, Cerys."

"I mean *don't embarrass me.*"

"When have we *ever* embarrassed you?" Dad drawls, and Mom laughs, and why, WHY have they chosen now, of all days, to band together and act all pally? This is definitely weirder than the fighting.

Why is Dad even here?

Oh God, I hope they're not having a *date night.* Gross.

"I think it's nice," Mom says, "that you've made all these lovely new friends. And that you've gotten friendly with Anissa, even though you didn't know each other well at school. Didn't you invite the other girls to this party, too?"

"I . . . well, it's not someone I know hosting, is it?" I point out. "I didn't want to show up with the whole gang in tow, that might've been a little rude."

It's not untrue. Just . . . not exactly *the* truth. She hums in agreement, though, so I'm off the hook.

"Mind you don't go drinking too much," Dad says.

"Yes," Mom agrees, and I swear to God, I am going to riot. They argued over my bloody birthday presents, but this? A party? Oh, *now* they're a united front. "You know the drill, Cerys, don't go drinking anything you haven't poured yourself, keep hold of your drink—"

"We'd tell you not to drink *at all*," Dad says, then laughs, "but we're not so old and decrepit that we don't remember what it's like being sixteen and going to a house party."

"Who are you calling old!" Mom cries, but even *that* makes them both laugh, and I really will scream if they keep on. "Jake'll look after you, though, I'm sure."

"Mind you look after *him*, too," Dad jokes, and again they both laugh.

I am spared spontaneous combustion at the total personality transplant both my parents seem to have had, because a car has pulled up outside, and Anissa is climbing out of the passenger seat with an overnight bag slung over her shoulder, calling, "Bye, Mom!" as she closes the door behind her.

"Omigod she's here!" I jump away from the blinds and run halfway across the room, then stop, remembering I have to wait for her to ring the doorbell. It's just been *ages* since I had anybody over who wasn't Jake, and I haven't had a sleepover since someone's birthday party when we were about twelve years old. I hope my parents don't embarrass me, and I hope Anissa doesn't, either, by mentioning any of the fandom stuff, and—

She rings the bell.

Mom pulls a face at me, making a show of setting aside her iPad. "Shall I get that, then, Cerys?"

"Oh shut up," I mutter, and dart out into the hallway. Behind me, Mom whispers to Dad in mock-outrage, pretending to be the grandma in *Princess Diaries*, and the two of them muffle their laughter.

I guess at least they might seem halfway normal to Anissa, like this.

Not normal for *them*, of course, but . . .

I undo the latch and hold the door open for Anissa to come in. "Hi!"

Her mom has idled on the curb, and gives me a wave through the car window before rolling it down. "You girls have fun tonight!"

"We will!" Anissa shouts back. As the car pulls away, she whispers to me, "My mom mixed us some gin and lemonade. And she took me shopping for a new outfit. I think she's more excited about this than I am."

I grin, although something about the admission brings that shame crawling back up inside me, that Anissa's been so left out of things before. I tamp it down, though, and wave for her to follow me inside. We both stick our heads in through the living room door. "Mom, Dad, this is Anissa."

"Hello, Anissa! Lovely to meet you," Mom chirps.

"Yes, hello," Dad says, and then *goes to stand up,* like this is some bloody business meeting and he's going to shake her hand. He used to shake Jake's hand whenever he saw him, and they'd both make a joke of it. I glare at him and he catches on, sitting back down. He and Mom exchange another look with raised eyebrows. Instead, he says, "We picked up some pizzas for you girls, in case there's no food at the party. Shall I get them in the oven?"

"Yes, go on," Mom says for us. "Can we get you anything to drink, Anissa? Some pop?"

"Oh! Um . . . If you've got any Diet Coke or something, please?"

"Coming right up!" They both stand in unison, and Mom ushers us away to my room to get ready, saying she'll bring everything up. Dad's *whistling* to himself, and Mom doesn't even snap at him to be quiet.

Anissa and I go up to my room, and I cringe. "Sorry about them. They're not normally . . . that weird."

She laughs. "Don't worry, my parents are a little like that, too."

Anissa sets her bag down at the end of my bed. There's a blow-up mattress squashed into the corner that Mom will sort out later. Unzipping the bag, Anissa pulls out a dress and scrunches her face up.

"So I know you said you were wearing a dress, but . . ."

"That is *so* cute, omigosh!" I take it from her to hold it up; it's a pink wrap dress with a tie in the front and long sleeves. I'm sure I have a lipstick that matches it she could borrow, but Anissa is already pulling some other clothes out of her bag.

"Mom got *really* carried away. I'd never normally wear this sort of thing, but I didn't have the heart to tell her that. She was just so excited, you know? I don't . . ." Anissa blushes, and bites the inside of her cheek, then looks down at the floor as she blurts, "I mean, I don't need to tell *you*, I don't really get invited to stuff like this. I think she was just happy I was finally being included in something."

I set the dress down next to her bag, and because I'm not sure there'll ever be the right time to ask, I say, "I always thought you just . . . preferred to keep to yourself? You never seemed very bothered."

She shrugs one shoulder, still not lifting her eyes from her feet, in a way that says she very much *was* bothered.

"Oh. I . . . I don't . . ."

"It's okay." She gives a thin, fleeting smile, hardly glancing up at all, and sits on the edge of the bed smoothing out the fabric of the other dress bunched in her hands. Her shoulders are slumped, but there's something relaxed about her posture that's more accepting than self-pitying. "It's one of those things, right? I just . . . haven't found my people yet."

Now Anissa smiles up at me, and it's hopeful, like she's not worried about making friends—just finding the right ones.

Like maybe *I'm* one of the right ones.

Not, you know, a heinous traitor with an ulterior motive.

"The Discord's been really fab, though," she gushes. "My parents aren't really into any of the fandom stuff and I didn't know anybody at school who was, so it's nice to finally have some people to talk to about it, and you're right—they are a really nice bunch, and so easy to chat with. I just wish I'd known about it sooner!

I wish I'd known *you* were a fan sooner, too. You wouldn't have seemed so intimidating to try to talk to, then."

She laughs, but all I can do is stare.

"Intimidating? *Me?*"

"Well, yeah! I mean you always just seem so . . . so cool, and like you always know what to do and what to wear and what to say, and you never seem to have any trouble making friends or—"

I burst out laughing so hard that she looks miffed at the interruption.

Mom chooses that moment to appear with a glass of Diet Coke for us each. "Pizza won't be too long! I'll bring some snacks up with it, too. Don't want you drinking on an empty stomach! Are you going to be having alcohol, Anissa? Does your mom know? I'd rather you girls be sensible about it, is all."

"*Please* don't do the *Mean Girls* 'cool mom' speech," I groan, and Mom immediately starts pretending to hold out a video camera and do the "Jingle Bell Rock" dance like in the original movie. Anissa is giggling behind me, and I can't decide whether to laugh, too, or wish the ground would swallow me whole.

"I might have a little bit, and my parents know," Anissa says, though she doesn't mention the gin she's been supplied with.

Mom nods, and I usher her out before she can repeat her whole "safe partying" spiel. Anissa meets my eye with another giggle and I just roll mine, and we start discussing outfits. While she's leaning toward jeans and a T-shirt, I've got a dress Nikita lent me that the other girls all approved, and I try to persuade Anissa to wear her dress, too. I don't want to look out of place; I don't want *her* to feel out of place, either.

She seems to have bundled half her wardrobe into her duffel bag, though, so we have plenty to choose from, and by the time we're snacking on pizza and potato chips, she's happily settled on a long-sleeved black tube dress. It's knee length and a little plain, but by the time she adds some makeup and a pair of hoops, it'll be perfect, I think—but then I'm forced to bite my tongue when she layers on a necklace with a misshapen jade pendant and clips on a gold ear cuff that looks like a snake.

She's still wearing the evil eye bracelet, too. None of it matches, and with the black dress, she *does* look very witchy. Maybe that's the vibe she's going for, though . . . ?

I guess if she feels comfortable, that's what matters?

I think of Max, so confident in his cosplay out in public, and every time I've fussed and fidgeted with my carefully curated *ordinary* outfits. It's inconceivable, but . . . I could kind of do with a little of his confidence right now, or Anissa's.

Nikita's dress fits me mostly okay; it's a little big in the boobs, and shorter than I was expecting, but I'm determined to wear it. Short-sleeved and bright red, Chloe called it a "showstopper."

(Evie joked that I wasn't going on *Bake Off,* and Daphne did a whole bit pretending to be Paul Hollywood and shake my hand, which makes me want to laugh again just thinking about it.)

I tug at the dress in front of the mirror, trying to make it sit right.

It makes my boobs look even smaller than normal, despite the fact I'm wearing my best bra; and it gapes open around the neck, but Jake won't notice something like that. And it's the perfect color—passionate, romantic, sexy. That's what's important.

"Wow," Anissa says, glancing over from where she's doing her eyeliner. "You look fab."

"D'you think so? It's not . . . ?"

I turn this way and that, scrutinizing my reflection, but Anissa shakes her head vehemently. "Definitely not!"

I breathe a sigh of relief; even if we have quite (okay, *very*) different taste in partywear, the reassurance is a big help. I sit down on the floor, pulling my makeup bag to me, rooting through for my lip gloss.

As I pull it out, I remember Daphne painting my lips for me in the school bathroom and how it didn't feel like me, more like I was putting on a mask, and I say to Anissa, "Do you really think I'm intimidating?"

"Maybe that came out wrong," she replies softly, and lowers her hands from doing her makeup. "It's more like . . . you seem so sure of yourself. Who you are, where you belong. Does that make sense?"

Again, bizarrely, I think of Max.

And I tell Anissa honestly, "I always thought *you* seemed like that."

"*What?* Yeah, pull the other one, Cerys."

"No, I mean it. You never seemed to care if you were on your own or . . . or if people were bitching about your dodgy haircut in Costa when you could hear."

We lock eyes in the mirror.

"It *was* pretty dodgy," she admits, and cracks a smile that takes a weight off my shoulders.

"I'm . . . not, for the record. Sure of myself, I mean. And I definitely don't feel like I always say or wear or do all the right things. I *try* to, because I want to fit in, rather than—"

Be like you.

I catch myself before I say it out loud, but Anissa seems to hear it anyway. She fidgets with her eyeliner.

"I don't blame you," she says. "Sometimes I think I'd rather fit in than just be myself, too."

"No, that's not . . ."

It's . . . not what I'm doing. Is it?

I'm not trying to pretend to be someone else. I mean, everyone knows you have to get the right school bag or water bottle and follow the right influencers and style your clothes just so, and show up at a coffee shop at the right time before classes start so you're not left behind. But that's not changing who you *are,* it's not . . .

It's not like delving deep into a fandom you don't care about, just so a boy will like you.

Just because I want to fit in, or fit a mold (like "perfect future girlfriend right here, Jake, hello!"), doesn't mean I'm not being *myself,* though. I'm myself in the Discord—there's a safety and comfort in being on the other side of the screen where nobody is being judgmental. And I'm myself with Jake. Sort of. Mostly. I *used* to be, anyway.

But . . .

I guess I don't feel very much like me when I'm walking on eggshells around Mom and Dad at home; and sometimes, at school, it feels like I'm reading off a script. Holding pieces of myself back because they don't fit the part. Like the outfits I wear—after consulting OOTD posts on the girls' Instagram Stories—are the cosplay I've picked out for the day.

But—*everyone* does that.

Don't they?

I'm quiet for long enough that Anissa shuffles uncomfortably, looking like she wants to apologize, even though she didn't say anything wrong, so I do the only thing I can think of, and ask:

"Do you want me to do your lipstick for you?"

22

Dad drops us off at the party and I promise, for the ump-teenth time, that I'll see him at half-past midnight, and yes, I'll call if we want to come home earlier.

The party is in a detached house at the end of a cul-de-sac. The blinds and curtains are all open, the lights all on, and Anissa and I hurry to the door, shivering without coats in the frigid eve-ning air.

I knock, but the door's already cracked open, so we step inside and find the party in full swing. Charli XCX blasts out of a speaker somewhere, and there's the stench of beer in the air. There's a living room off to the left and I spot a couple of boys from Jake's new soc-cer team in there, playing on the Xbox. Three girls are huddled on the staircase in front of us, the one in the middle crying, her friends alternating between soothing her and hyping her up—"He didn't bloody deserve you anyway!"

"Shall we, er . . . ," Anissa wavers. "Find the kitchen?"

"Good idea."

There's a lot of noise coming from the end of the hall; on the right is a dining room and sunroom filled with people. On the left, the kitchen looks quieter, with only three guys and a girl standing around with drinks in hand.

They glance over at us, and one of the boys frowns, confused, not recognizing us, and I feel like we might as well have flashing neon signs over our heads saying WE DON'T GO TO YOUR SCHOOL. He says, "Uh, hi?"

Anissa shrinks behind me.

Guess it's up to me to take the lead. Intimidating, cool, knows-what-she's-doing me.

Apparently.

"Hi," I reply. "We're friends with Jake . . . Jake Wandsworth? He invited us."

"Oh!" The boy clicks his tongue, grinning now. "Wandy, yeah! He mentioned a couple of girls from St. David's were coming. I'm Raf."

"Hi," I say again, assuming this is his house and his party, and deciding I'll tease Jake later about his nickname. "I'm Cerys. This is Anissa."

She waves, still half hidden behind me.

"Think he's out in sunroom, if you're looking for him. He's with that guy, uh . . . the one with the hair?" Raf glances at his friends, and the blank look on the girl's face tells me that my suspicions that Max is a far cry from Mr. Popular are confirmed.

"Matt?" one of the other guys suggests.

"Do you mean Max?" I ask, and Raf snaps his fingers.

"That's the one! Yeah, him."

"Cool. Well, we'll, uh . . ." I gesture to the bottle of lemonade Anissa's holding, and Raf waves us in the direction of some glasses. The four of them resume their conversation, having to talk loudly to be heard over all the music and noise, which somehow helps give me and Anissa a little breathing space.

I'm glad I brought her with me; this would've been terrifying to walk into alone, and I can only imagine what the other girls would have to say about Max.

Anissa pours us each some of the spiked lemonade, and we cheers before taking a sip.

I pull a face, looking at her quizzically.

Anissa lowers her glass, licking her lips thoughtfully and frowning before she says, "You know, I don't think my mom *actually* put any gin in this."

"I don't think she did, either."

"I think she was hoping I wouldn't know well enough to notice."

"Probably."

We lock eyes for a beat before we erupt into giggles, toasting our not-so-spiked-after-all drinks once more. Anissa shakes her head, muttering under her breath in a way that makes me laugh all over again.

"I'm just going to use the bathroom," Anissa says. "Will you wait here for me? Then we can go find the boys."

"Yes! Sure." I don't love the idea of being stuck by myself, but I don't want to abandon Anissa, and this place is so packed it might be ages before we find each other again. I take her glass of lemonade, and am trying to decide whether to go talk to Raf and his friends or if I can lean against the kitchen counter looking cool, when someone sweeps into the kitchen from the living room and my heart plummets.

Her hair is down for once, in carefully styled black curls around her shoulders, and she's wearing a pale blue minidress, cheeks flushed and eyes bright, an empty glass in her hand.

And even though she hasn't noticed me immediately, even though I want to run in the opposite direction before she can see *me*, I blurt, "*Daphne?* What are you doing here?"

What *is* she doing here? I never told the girls any details about the party, and I made it sound like I was going with Jake, rather than as this little group including Max and Anissa, and—and *oh my God*, Max and Anissa are here, and Daphne is here, and . . .

Why is she here?!

She breaks into a grin, dashing over to throw her arms around me. I can smell the alcohol on her breath, sweet and potent, and her palms are clammy as she holds my arm.

"Oh my gosh, Cerys! This is *such* a small world! You should've said it was Raf's party you were coming to!"

"Do you . . . know . . . Raf?" My head is swimming. This cannot be happening.

"Not really. We're friends on Insta. Do you remember that guy I told you about, in the year above at school? Daniel?"

"The rugby guy? But I thought that fizzled out?"

"It did, but then he messaged me the other day totally out of the blue. Well, he fire-emoji reacted to my outfit of the day, so I messaged him, which, I *know,* I know we said I shouldn't and I should be done with him because he was so flaky, but then he invited me tonight because he plays rugby with a bunch of the Colleg Carreg guys and . . . Oh my gosh, *please* don't be mad, Cerys, I swear I was totally going to tell you all! I was just embarrassed it wouldn't work out, but he's been *so* flirty all night, and it's going really well!"

I'm too overwhelmed to say much beyond "That's . . . Wow, Daphne."

Relief washes over me. *She's here for a boy. Of course she is. This has nothing to do with me.*

Tipsy, she leans in, swaying slightly, and babbling, "And I thought, well, I couldn't bring you lot *with* me, like backup. Nikita would've shown up in a trench coat and a fake mustache, haha! And it would've been weird. Like, *you* were coming to a party for a boy, and *we* weren't all tagging along. It's sort of a date! But I don't know anyone else here, and it's a bit . . . I mean, everyone's lovely, obviously, and I'm with Daniel, so."

"Right. Yeah." I'm not sure what her point is, and if she's just drunk or if she's genuinely worried I'm about to tell the girls she went somewhere without us and *she'll* be ousted from the group.

Mostly, I'm thinking: I have to get out of here before Anissa comes back from the bathroom and Daphne sees her.

"Should you be getting back to Daniel, then?" I ask, and my stomach knots even as she beams.

"Yes! And you should be getting back to Jake." She nods at

the second lemonade I'm holding, and I don't correct her. Daphne grabs a bottle of white wine off the counter, splashing some into her glass, then she winks at me. "Come find me later, though—I want you to introduce me properly! I can interrogate him about why he hasn't kissed your face off already, LOL!"

"Ha. Yeah. Great."

Okay, add to list of people Daphne cannot interact with tonight: Anissa, Max, and Jake.

She's out of the kitchen, though, and Anissa is back—they miss each other by mere seconds. The relief makes me dizzy, but I rush forward to Anissa, who is smiling, none the wiser, and say, "Come on—let's go find Jake."

We find him in the sunroom as promised. There's a TV that's not turned on, the doors are open to the garden, and most of the room is taken up by worn brown leather sofas. Jake is squashed into one with about five other people, telling a story. He's got a whole crowd hanging off his every word, his infectious smile matched on their rapt faces.

Lurking by the side of the sofa, shoulder leaning against the doorframe and arms crossed, his usual bored and irritably aloof expression in place, is Max.

His eyes snap to mine in the same second I notice him, and it almost stops me in my tracks. He drops his arms slightly, stands a little straighter.

He looks *good*.

And not just "boy in soccer uniform" good, but . . .

I sigh internally, because *sexy* is not a word I would *ever* want to associate with Max, and yet. And *YET.*

He's wearing dark-wash jeans and a black sweatshirt that manages to strike the perfect balance between casual and flattering, the long sleeves pushed up near his elbows. His hair is in that stupid some-up-some-down bun again, except right now I really have to (and hate to) admit to myself that it looks very much the *opposite* of stupid; his hair looks shiny and wavy in a way I almost envy.

Someone leaves the room, and Anissa bumps into me as she moves to let them past, reminding me exactly what motivated me to invite her here in the first place. Jake, playing up to his audience, still hasn't noticed us.

"Come on," I say to Anissa, and we pick our way across the room. When we get close to Max, she steps to my side instead of huddling behind me, and I say, "Anissa, this is the guy I was telling you about—"

But I don't get much further, because then Jake suddenly cries, "Cerys! You're here!" and leaps out of the sofa with surprising agility considering he was rather hemmed in by all the people piled on with him, and I'm engulfed in a hug while Anissa and Max are left to make their own introductions. I'm relieved to hear them both speaking quietly behind me.

Jake wiggles me side to side, and I laugh, realizing he's already tipsy. I can smell the cider on his breath, matching the almost-empty bottle in his hand. When he finally releases me, I notice he's in his usual partywear of a blue shirt I once told him brings out his eyes, and his favorite brown chinos.

He looks good, too.

Just not quite as—

Nope. NOPE. We are not even entertaining that thought, Cerys, shut up.

Jake takes in my dress, and says, "That's new. Does it fit? It looks a little big here." He gestures to his own chest, and even though it stings, even though *of course* he would notice, I was stupid to think he wouldn't, I remember The Fangirl Project and swipe lightly, playfully at his arm.

"Is this another display of the famous Wandsworth charm, Jake? You staring at my boobs within three seconds of seeing me?"

He laughs, holding his hands up, and pulling an "oops" sort of face. I suppose a bit like that misguided attempt with Daphne's lip gloss, at least he *is* noticing me, and that's a step in the right direction.

"You look very nice, Cerys," he says sincerely, and the smile he gives me—the way he looks me right in the eyes, all soft and lovely and familiar—makes me feel warm and fuzzy in a way no amount of gin-spiked lemonade ever could.

"Thank you." I let my eyes flick slowly up and down his outfit, too, and I let him notice. "You don't look so bad yourself, Jake."

"Scrub up all right, don't I?" He winks, then slings his arm around me as he turns me to face Max and Anissa. "All right, Anissa? Good to see you!"

"Y-yeah, um, you too."

"Wish we'd known sooner you were so into *Of Wrath and Rune.*

You could've come to Comic Con with us! Next time, though, yeah? It'll be sick."

"I'd love that! I was telling Cerys earlier, I've never really had anybody to share the fandom stuff with, and Comic Con seemed way too intense to go to on my own. I didn't even realize they did them outside of London."

Excitable, animated, the words spill out of her, and she misses the stunned double take Jake does that says, *Really? Anissa, a chatterbox?*

The look I give him in response says, *Tell me about it!* And I bump my hip to his to make sure he's paying attention to her.

"I looked into going to a Dungeons and Dragons night at one of the board game cafés in town before," she's saying now. "There's a couple of podcasts I listen to about it, like *The Adventure Zone* and *Critical Role* and stuff, and it seems *so* cool. I even made a whole character sheet! It said it was for new players, but I sort of chickened out . . ."

"Shut *up*. No, dude, *yes*, right." Jake is so swept up that he can hardly form a sentence, and I laugh—until he drops his arm from around me to grab Anissa. "I would totally go to that with you! I play with my brother and some of his friends, and it's mostly over video chat and stuff now, but we haven't done that in *ages*. I play a bard, obviously, I'm a nat-twenty charisma through and through, like I was ever going to play anything else . . ."

And just like that, they're gone, falling onto a vacant chair, Anissa with her feet propped up on the seat and Jake with his legs straddling the arm, hands waving wildly as he speaks and Anissa's own enthused gestures no less passionate, both talking a mile a minute.

I blink. What just happened?

Have I . . .

Have I just been usurped *again*, and given Jake his ideal fandom-loving girlfriend in Anissa, instead of showing him that *I'm* that girl?

This isn't . . . that wasn't . . .

She was supposed to bond with *Max*, not Jake!

A fingertip brushes lightly under my chin, pushing my gaping mouth closed where my jaw has plummeted to the floor. I jump at the touch, mouth snapping shut, and turn to see Max smirking at me, eyes glittering.

"Think he's found a new best friend," he says.

"Again."

I don't mind that it comes out sounding sharp or bitter, and Max just inclines his head, taking the dig annoyingly gracefully.

"I take it you weren't expecting that to happen."

"He knew her at school! They've barely ever said hello! I thought they'd get on all right, but . . ."

Max gives a breath of laughter. "The power of fandom, huh? Cursed be ye who try to get between two nerds once they get going about their D&D campaigns."

"Yeah, apparently."

Brilliant.

Now I've lost *two* friends, the *only* people I know at this god-forsaken party except for Daphne, who I need to avoid for obvious reasons, and I'm stuck. With Max.

I gulp down the rest of my lemonade, forgetting for a moment that it's not something stronger.

He pushes away from where he's leaning against the edge of the patio doors, casting another bemused look at Jake and Anissa before looking back to me. "Do you want to get a drink?"

"I thought you'd never ask."

Max supplies me with a raspberry hard cider from a case stashed inside the washing machine.

I look around for a bottle opener, but when I don't see one, he smoothly takes the bottle out of my hand, angles it just so against the kitchen counter, and gives the top a whack. The lid pops right off, and I'm impressed enough that I have to make an effort not to gawk as I take the bottle back.

I clear my throat, trying to shake it off. "So, um . . ."

Great work, Cerys. A conversational superstar.

It's not my fault, though. Max makes it so hard to talk to him.

He's all stoic and serious and superior and downright *annoying,* and it's not as if he's here throwing out "Hey look at me, I'm Mr. Approachable, small talk is my forte" vibes, is he?

Thankfully—God, this is what my life has come to, that I'm stuck alone at a party with Max and *grateful* when he has something to say—he finds something for us to talk about.

"Anissa seems cool."

"Huh? Oh yeah. Yeah, she's . . ." The exact opposite, but maybe in Max's books she's the height of cool? She definitely is where Jake is concerned, it seems . . .

"You went to the same school, right? Jake mentioned you guys were never really friends, though."

"We weren't."

I don't have much else to say—the truth is I'm still uncomfortable with being seen hanging out with Anissa in case I'm judged and exiled for it, but she *does* seem really great, and I regret not getting to know her sooner. I feel a whole mess of shame when I think about any of that, and I'm realizing it has less to do with her and a *lot* to do with me, but that's really scary to confront. The very last person I want to open up to about any of that is *Max*.

He takes my brusque response as some kind of invitation to pry, though, saying, "So what changed? Don't tell me all it took was a mutual appreciation for *OWAR*." He quirks an eyebrow, apparently skeptical as ever about my own investment in this fandom.

I bristle. Not because he's *right,* but because I *am* invested. Genuinely, deeply. I've written fanfiction, for God's sake! Not— *NOT*—that I am about to prove that to him by sending Max my lovey-dovey one-shot of a ballroom dance. I'd rather set myself on fire.

But I'm backed into a corner: I don't want to stand here elaborating on my fangirl status to make a point, and I don't want to reveal just how shady my motivations for inviting Anissa to the party tonight were. I don't want that getting back to Jake—or worse, to Anissa.

"I didn't realize my friendships were any of your business," I snap.

Max scoffs.

"What? What's that supposed to mean?"

"Nothing."

"Clearly, it meant *something.*"

His jaw works for a minute before he shakes his head and mutters, "Forget it," and sets about finding himself a drink. He doesn't bother with the washing machine ciders, but yanks open a cupboard to find a glass, and pours himself some Coke.

That ever-present tension between us is back, amped up, crackling and angry, making me grit my teeth as I wonder who the hell he thinks he is to try to pick apart my newly forged bond with Anissa, and what the hell that scoff was all about. It takes every ounce of my willpower to try to let it go.

Fine. Let him think what he wants. Let him hate me. See if I care.

But I am *not* going to let him spoil my night any more than Jake and Anissa and even *Daphne* already have. Eventually, they'll run out of steam and come hang out with us again, and I don't want to be in a foul mood when they do.

For now I'm stuck with him. I guess I have no choice but to *try* to be civil, if I want to salvage this night.

Max, it seems, has the same idea, because although he leans against the counter a safe distance from me, his frown looks more perturbed than annoyed now, and I get the sense he's trying to think of small talk that's safer ground.

If that even exists; I don't think we've managed to have anything resembling a normal conversation since we met.

This time, it's me who breaks the ice.

"You're not drinking?" I ask, nodding at his own glass.

Max shakes his head. "I drew the short straw." Reaching into his pocket, he pulls out his car keys, gives them a little jangle, then puts them away. Then he tilts his head in the direction of a few other people clustered in the kitchen. "Just wait till later, I'll suddenly be everybody's best friend, even if they don't remember my name and call me 'Matt' half the time."

"Doesn't that bother you?"

He locks eyes with me, and it's so piercing that I almost flinch. "Should it?"

I think about Anissa, about my conversation with Jake in the Discord channel, about how desperately hard *I've* tried to fit in.

It's definitely a lot easier to chat behind the safety of a screen with the *OWAR* fandom as a shield, but I swallow, my mouth dry, and dare myself to ask, "I get that 'finding your people' is important, but . . . you don't think it gets lonely, alienating yourself like that? Being . . ."

Max waits for me to finish that sentence, and I cringe.

Altering course slightly, I say, "Don't you ever get lonely?"

His lips curve into a wry smile. "I do okay. Why? Do you get lonely, *not* alienating yourself all the time?"

Yes. That's why I can't afford to lose what I do have.

I take a fortifying sip of cider and fight back a grimace at the sickly sweet taste. Gross. How does Jake enjoy this stuff? I wish Ginny had made it home for reading week; she would've given us some of that cheap rosé I actually *do* like. I don't much fancy minesweeping any of the open wine bottles scattered around the kitchen.

I tell Max, "Sure, when my best friend is replacing me. But I do okay, too."

Mostly. Sort of.

At least, I thought I did.

Max, as if knowing there's a lot more I'm not really saying, huffs a small laugh and clinks his drink to mine. "Here's to doing okay."

Drinks in hand, we leave the kitchen and go to the living room. I check that there's no sign of Daphne before deciding to stay. There's a big group involved in a noisy card game at a coffee table, with even more people clustered around to watch. There's a vile-looking mixture in a pint glass in the middle of the table, and as we find a spot behind a sofa at the edge of the crowd to watch, someone pulls a card that makes everyone howl and jeer, and they slosh some of their own drinks into the pint.

I wrinkle my nose, watching the liquid turn an almost purplish shade of brown. Even just *looking* at it threatens to turn my stomach. Surely nobody has to drink it?

I don't realize I've said that last part out loud until Max says, "You've never played Ring of Fire before?"

"What?" Then I blink. "And *you* have?"

"Like I said—I do okay. This isn't my first house party." He lifts his Coke slightly. "And I'm not always the one driving."

"But . . ."

But *who* invites him anywhere? He said himself, most of these people don't even get his name right. Who does he have parties with, playing drinking games like this? I have so many questions, but I'm aware how not-civil they all sound, so I keep my mouth shut.

Max must be secretly cooler than I give him credit for.

As we watch and people take turns pulling cards from the pile surrounding the gross pint glass, Max explains the rules to me. He's standing close—my shoulder grazing his chest, his mouth near enough to my ear that he doesn't have to raise his voice to be heard over the shouting and the music. His breath tickles at loose strands of my hair and the edge of my neck, and a shiver threatens to roll down my spine. Someone bumps me and makes me spill some cider over my hand and shoes, and my mind goes completely blank at the sensation of Max putting his arm around me—wrapping it solidly around my lower back, his hand resting on the back of the sofa just by my hip, like a shield between me and stumbling partygoers. The heat of his arm seems to burn right through the thin fabric of my borrowed dress, my attention zeroing in on my shoulder against his solid chest, his breath skating across my skin and just *how* close his face is to mine.

I don't catch all the rules, and blame that on the noise. It's not like I'm distracted. It's not like *he's* distracting me.

Unthinkable. Impossible.

I think he asked me something, because from the corner of my eye I notice that he tilts his head, looking at me as if he's waiting for my response. I'm biting my lip and staring a little too hard at the gameplay—seeing none of it.

"Uh-huh," I manage, a noncommittal mumble.

The arm isn't *around* me, obviously, he's just trying to balance himself, that's all.

Whatever comment or question I've just responded to, though, Max chuffs a breath of laughter and faces back to the game again. Did I insult him? Ignore him? I don't quite have the brain capacity to care.

Someone draws a card and there's a cacophony, voices hollering and howling, and the boy who drew the card—Alfie, the goalkeeper who flaked on games to be with his on-off girlfriend—buries his head in his hands with a loud curse before lurching to his feet, throwing his card, a king, down on the table, and reaching for the pint from hell.

"He's not!" I gasp.

"He is," Max says.

There are chants around the room—*"Chug, chug, chug!"* and "Weeeee like to drink with Alfie, 'cause Alfie is our mate, and when we drink with Alfie . . ."—and I watch in horror as he downs the entire horrible concoction, gagging only a little halfway through, and belching when he slams the empty glass back down on the table.

Grim.

A fresh game of Ring of Fire is set up, with the players shifting as some spectators and participants swap places, and the scummy glass is set back on the table for everyone to pour a little of their drinks in anew, laughing and looking excited.

Raf is in the group playing now, and sits cross-legged on the floor opposite us. He notices me, and waves me over with a grin.

"Wandy's gal! You wanna join? We can make room for one more."

I eye the dubious foam floating on the top of the mixed pint, as people who don't even know me are smiling, calling me over, making space to include me. "Er, I don't think . . ."

Isn't this what I wanted, though? Isn't this what *everybody* wants, when they think about going to house parties? Isn't this the teenage dream, the stuff of rom-coms? This is how I become the cool girl, popular and well loved and oozing "fun" from every pore, and Jake will wander in and see me getting on with all his new friends, see me being the life and soul, and he will sit down next to me to join in, hating to be left out, and . . .

If it was all the girls playing, if it was Daphne asking me, would I join in? If it was Jake asking me to play, would I hesitate?

I can't even summon up any excitement about being referred to as Jake's "gal." My stomach is too busy churning.

"We were just gonna go get some air," comes a reply for me, and I'm being steered out of the room to a disappointed chorus that ends before I'm even through the living room door, and my brain doesn't catch up until we're in the hallway.

I twist around, shoving Max's arm off me.

"What the hell was that?"

He rolls his eyes, head facing more toward the living room than to me. "I know, Raf means well but—"

"Not *him*. You!"

"What?" Max turns now, looking at me properly, his eyes searching mine as a frown begins to crumple his forehead.

"I didn't need you to step in for me, you know. This is real life, Max. I'm not some damsel, and you're *not* Sir Grayson."

"That wasn't—"

"And it's not up to you whether I join in a drinking game or not; I didn't ask you to interfere. Maybe I wanted to—"

There it is. That *scoff.*

Again.

As if he knows better. As if he's so high and mighty, and . . .

It boils my blood. It really, really does.

I sneer right back at him. "Please. You don't know me, you don't—"

"I know you better than you're giving me credit for. And *any-one* could see that you were looking for any excuse not to join in that game. But let me guess—you're worried what they'll be saying about you, that you didn't *fit in* well enough."

"It's not a bad thing to want to fit in! Just because you don't give two shits what people are saying behind your back—"

"You're right. I don't. If it's that important, they'll say it to my face."

"Well, consider this me saying it to your face, Max—nobody likes a self-centered prick who spends all their time looking down on everybody else, *especially* those of us who actually *want* to fit in, who want people to like us, who *care*. Being lonely doesn't make you better than the rest of us—it just makes you an asshole."

With nowhere else to go because he's blocking my path to the living room and the rest of the hallway, I tromp up the stairs. The three girls are still there, though they've acquired some fresh drinks and nobody's crying anymore.

"Yes, bish!" one of them yells to me as I clamber over them. Another says, "You tell him!"

At the top of the landing, I almost collide with Daphne. Her eyes are wide, her cheeks still flushed, but she doesn't look like she's having such a fun time anymore. If anything she looks annoyed, her glossy lips in a pout. Her curls are limp, and there's a sheen of sweat around her forehead, some of her eye makeup smudged.

But when her eyes light on me, she lunges for me, grabbing my wrist with a smile. "*There* you are! Omigod, Cerys, so Daniel totally kissed me—and then he said he was going to get a drink, and he's just *vanished*. I thought maybe it was code for 'meet him upstairs,' but obviously not. Haha! God, how embarrassing . . . I was actually thinking I might just leave. Anyway, I'm *so* glad I found you. Shall we go back down to the party? How's things going with Jake? You can tell me everything—"

And it's all too much. Anissa and Jake, Max with his chivalry and Raf with his drinking games and Daphne wanting to ask about it all like I could even *tell her*. It's too much, and I want to scream.

I wrench away from her, breathing hard, and snap, "*Omigod, Daphne, I don't *want* to talk about Jake. Or Daniel, or . . ." *Or Max. Especially not Max.* "Do you even hear yourself? I don't want to talk about your shitty boy drama!"

"But . . . I wasn't . . ." She blinks at me, her face blank, and for once she doesn't look like the polished icon of put-togetherness that I've envied for the past couple of months. She looks young. She looks *hurt*.

And then her face contorts into a scowl that probably matches my own. "Well, screw you, Cerys! As if *you're* not the one who's *constantly* whining about this boy who doesn't fancy you back, as if it's the *only* interesting thing going on in your life! Forgive *me* for the fact that a guy actually *is* interested in me, and you can't handle that!"

I don't stop her as she storms off. I know—a tiny part of me knows—I should go after her. That I've been callous and cruel and she's upset, and I didn't mean any of that, but she's *right,* I do only talk about Jake, and I should fix this . . .

But it's such a small voice in the back of my mind, crushed quickly by the raging thought of: *good riddance.* At least now all my horrible secrets can stay buried.

By some miracle the bathroom is empty, and I shut myself in, being sure to slam the door to give myself that satisfaction of finality. Fight with Daphne aside, I've finally put Max in his place after *weeks* of putting up with his attitude. I should feel on top of the world.

But instead, I'm standing in the middle of a bathroom clutching a drink I don't even want, feeling more wretched than ever.

Nobody comes to knock and tell me to hurry up because they need to use the bathroom, so I don't feel too guilty for hunkering down with my back against the door. Jake and Anissa are probably still downstairs realizing they're soulmates, Daphne's probably gone home early like she said, and Max is . . .

Well, who cares about him anyway?

Me, I do. Just a little.

Not because of the arm around me and the breath on my neck or any of that, but—because I know I shouldn't have said that stuff. That I was out of line. That, even if there is some truth in it, I had no right to say any of it.

My first proper house party is turning into a right royal shit show. My new friend has abandoned me, my best friend has replaced me, Daphne's definitely going to kick me out of the group, I've yelled at the *one* other person I know, the host and his friends will think I'm boring for not joining in their game—

—and now I'm shut up in a bathroom, in the dark because I couldn't find the light switch.

Brilliant.

Stellar work, Cerys, this is exactly how it always goes in the movies. Gold star, kid. You're nailing it.

I unlock my phone. There are some notifications waiting for me—a few things in the group chat, the other girls telling me to have a good night and let them know how it goes with Jake, demanding outfit pics I forgot to send earlier. There are some from Instagram I ignore, and a few Discord ones I'm about to click on when I see an email. It's from the website I posted my fanfic on. Someone's left a comment.

UGH, THE SCENE WE NEEDED! THE SCENE WE DESERVED! LOVE ITTTT. Are you writing any more fics???

My heart gives a funny somersault, and I cradle my phone for a moment, smiling at the screen, this random internet stranger making me feel a little better. I grab a screenshot to send to @silversmithhh, aka Heather, who I know will freak out with excitement on my behalf. Someone liked that silly little thing I made! Someone else feels like we were robbed of a ballroom dance between Lady di Silver and Devon! They get me!

Heather isn't online and doesn't see my message, though, so I spend a couple of minutes scrolling through the latest messages in the main chat when I notice one that's like a punch in the gut.

It's from Anissa, a few hours ago. I hadn't checked the chat while I was waiting for her to arrive, and then we were too busy getting ready. There's a reply, too. I stare at them for a while.

> **@ladyanissadishipper**
> Ooh, sounds like fun
> **@thesebootsweremadeformoonwalking** And good luck with that birthday party from hell **@fauningforhim**, hope your gluten-free cupcakes turn out okay. I'm off to my first proper party tonight (erk, talk about scary!) but at least I'll get to meet **@runicrascal** properly!
>
> **@runicrascal**
> Excited to hang out with you! Glad Cerys was able to introduce us! Been nice having another book fan to debate with haha

Have Anissa and Jake been . . . talking, in the Discord? Privately? Have they been messaging before meeting in person today?

He wants someone to talk about the books with, which obviously isn't me.

Ironically, The Fangirl Project has worked.

Just not for me.

A knock on the bathroom door startles me and I fumble my phone, turning off the screen even though nobody can see it—or see me spiraling.

"Just a sec," I call.

"It's me," the voice on the other side replies.

Max.

Why is it Max?

Surely I'm the last person he wants to talk to? Is he here to demand an apology? It doesn't . . . it doesn't *sound* like it. I mean, it's not as if he hammered down the door, and his "It's me" sounded quiet, not pissed off.

He must need the bathroom. It's the only explanation.

But as I start to drag myself to my feet, there's a sound on the other side of the door like he's . . . sitting down. The light spilling in beneath the door is sliced with a shadow, and I realize he *has* sat down. We're back to back, with just the door in between us.

The noise of the party is muted up here.

"I'm sorry," Max says. "I thought I was helping you out."

"You did," I mumble. It's a little easier to admit that in the dark, without him *right there*. It's a little like talking to Jake over Discord, actually. That same sense of detachment and distance, allowing for a little more vulnerability. "I'm sorry, too. I shouldn't have said any of that stuff."

There's a beat before he says, "That's really how you see me, huh?"

The fact that I hesitate is all the answer he needs, because I hear a mirthless chuckle on the other side of the door. The wood creaks slightly, shifts behind me, as if he's leaning farther into it. I hear a muffled, soft *thump* like he tips his head back against it.

"Is this the part where you try to tell me you *haven't* been judging the hell out of me since the first moment you met me?" I ask, even if my heart is a nervous hummingbird beating against my ribs, and my fingers preoccupy themselves by picking at the label on my bottle of cider.

"Can you blame me? You didn't exactly do a good job of pretending like you cared about anything at the Worlds Beyond con except for Jake. You were obviously just there to hang out with him, not because you had any interest in *OWAR*."

"Um, excuse you, but I've *watched the show*. I started listening to the audiobooks. I—I made fanart, and . . . and stuff. And you still—"

"Got defensive," he interrupts me, but it's matter-of-fact, not argumentative, and I'm shocked by both the evenness of his tone and how much his words remind me of what Jake said in our Discord chat the other week. No wonder they're such good friends; they have so much in common. Max goes on, "I didn't think you were serious about it, and . . . *Of Wrath And Rune* means a lot to me."

"It's more than just 'some stupid fantasy series,'" I say, echoing what Jake said online. What I said I was starting to understand. But I can't resist biting back at Max. "I didn't realize being *deadly serious* was a requirement for being a fan—even if you do a very good job of embodying that. People can like something in a different way than you do, you know." Now I'm thinking of another Discord chat—and what Heather/@silversmithhh told me after I admitted I couldn't bring myself to wear the cosplay.

"I think I just thought it was . . ." He sighs. "Kind of *performative*. You just seemed . . ."

I raise my eyebrows, even though he can't see it, daring him to finish that sentence.

He does, saying, "Clearly, other people's opinions of you matter a lot more than what *you* think."

"If this is your way of trying to convince me you're *not* a self-centered prick . . ."

"I don't think it's self-centered to want to live my life on my terms, not some . . . prescribed, conventional rubbish that I don't care about, or doesn't make me happy. Cosplaying and being into this nerdy fantasy series isn't hurting anybody. I don't see why I should have to push it aside or pretend it doesn't matter to me just so other people accept me better."

When he puts it like that . . .

"It—" he starts, and falters, and my ears perk up. I turn my face toward him—or toward the door, rather. Straining, I hear the stilted, ragged breath he draws. I imagine him running his hand over his hair.

I wonder if it feels as soft as it looks.

Finally, he says, "You were right. It *does* get lonely sometimes. D'you think I didn't get bullied for being such a nerd? For—I don't know, for *everything*. For wearing my hair too long, for reading too many books, daring to be a decent left wing and earn a place on the soccer team when I was supposed to fit this mold everyone else designated for me, for being *interested* in stuff at school, for . . . And I . . . I tried, once. For a while. I cut my hair, I stopped trying in class so much, I did all the things everyone else told me I was supposed to be doing."

Wore the right clothes. Got the right school bag.

Got off the bus at the right stop before school to bump into the right classmates.

Max must be finding it easier to talk without having to *fully* confront me, too, because this is more than I ever would've imagined him saying to me otherwise. Half the time, he talks around me and won't even look at me. Normally, that would annoy the hell out of me, but right now, it feels . . . different.

Like we're on level ground.

And I want him to keep talking.

"What happened?" I ask.

I imagine him shrugging. After a beat, Max lets out another of those curt, dry barks of laughter. "I was miserable as sin, what do you think happened?"

"Oh."

"I still got bullied, but at some point I just thought, fuck it, why am I even bothering?" His voice rises, gets heated, but it's still not angry. It's something else, something that makes me wish the door wasn't between us and I could see the look in his eyes. "Why should I make my life—make *myself*—smaller for their sake, when it didn't change anything anyway? If they were going to pick on me, I might as well enjoy myself. My dad would say, 'They're just jealous,' or that they're dissatisfied with their own lives, but I don't know how true that really is. I just figured that I didn't want to waste my life pretending I didn't care about the things I *do* care about."

He falls quiet, and I'm too frozen to do what I really want to, which is reach for the handle and open the door. His words bounce around inside my head, and I remember the way he walked around the cons in full cosplay, how unbothered he was. I thought he was being superior and all up himself, but . . . maybe it's not that after all.

Defensive, he'd said, which checks out, but also maybe he's just . . .
Confident. Himself.

I wish I could be more like that.

"You're right," I tell Max. "That's not so self-centered."

"Sorry if I made a dick of myself by judging you."

"Sorry if I did that to you, too."

"Truce?" he says, and there's a smile in his voice.

"Truce," I agree. Then I say, "It wasn't . . . I mean, I don't think
I've been totally fair to you, either. To be honest, I've been . . . really
jealous of you." The words taste like ash, and I press the cold glass
of my cider to my forehead, hunching over my knees. But I've said
it now, I've put it out there, I might as well carry on. "Because you
and Jake got so close so fast, and I thought we were best friends, so
I felt really pushed out. Maybe I *did* go a little harder on the *OWAR*
stuff at the beginning when I wasn't actually that into it, to try and
make up for that."

"You don't say."

"But I think I was . . . maybe a little harsh to you, because it
was hard for me."

After a moment, Max says, "Like at Comic Con."

"Yeah. Yeah, like then."

"Cerys," he says, and his voice pulls all consonants in my name
into something soft and enticing. "I wasn't trying to *steal* him from
you. I mean . . . you do realize that, right?"

"Yeah. Obviously."

Ish. Sort of. Not really.

I must not sound very convincing, because he laughs again.

"You're impossible," he informs me.

"I do my best."

"D'you wanna come out of there yet?"

I shrug, debating it. I *should* get myself together, go downstairs, join in with the party, try to find Jake and Anissa, maybe even Daphne if she's still here somewhere . . .

But I also know that the second I open the door, I'll end up face-to-face with Max, and that suddenly seems . . . like a lot. Like too much.

There are goose bumps all along my arms, and I hug my legs tighter into my body.

No, I decide. I am not ready to leave yet.

Rather than answer him, I say, "Can I ask you something?"

"Sure."

"What's the deal with the necklace? The one you always wear. Is it part of your cosplay?"

"It's . . . I mean, yes? No. Both? I got inspired to make it because of *OWAR,* and it fit my Moonwalker cosplay, but it's . . ."

There's something raw in the edge of his voice that prompts me to say, "You don't have to tell me."

"Nah, it's okay. It just sounds kind of stupid." He laughs, self-deprecating, in a way that makes me think it's the very opposite of stupid. "So they don't make it as obvious in the show, and I don't know if you've gotten to this part in the books, but the Moon-walker wears this pendant to remind him about his mission—"

"An arrowhead from the attack that killed his family, yeah."

"Right. And—well, my dad's always wanted us to do well with school, worked hard to make sure we have the opportunities he didn't. I remember when me and my big sister were little, he took

247

us to the zoo one time, and obviously we wanted to go mad in the gift shop—"

"The best part of any day out," I agree somberly.

"But things were kind of tight, so he took us over to one of those pressed penny souvenir machines. He got us to make a wish while we turned the crank, and this tiny, crappy piece of copper felt like *magic,* you know? Way beyond anything else we'd have found in the gift shop. It turned into a tradition whenever we went anywhere, or what we'd come back with from a school trip, and we thought they were so cool. Me and my sister had this whole collection. I kind of forgot about them until a couple of years ago, and found this box full of them, and I realized this really fun memory we had with our dad was . . . you know, his way of trying to make the best of things when they were tough. So I drilled a hole in one, to wear. It's . . . I don't know. It feels like a good luck charm, or something . . ."

He trails off quietly, awkwardly, a *lot* uncomfortably.

My hand shifts, even though I can't reach for him from here. It lands next to my side on the floor, empty and cold.

"That's not stupid. That's really sweet, Max."

It makes me wish things were different with my parents. It makes me wish *I* were different—that I could have some mature, inspired, grown-up take on why they act the way they do, like Max had about his dad and those pressed pennies.

I inhale deeply through my nose, but it ends up sounding like a sniffle, and when I bring my hands up, my cheeks are wet.

I don't even know why I'm crying. Tonight has just been a *lot,* and it's not even over yet.

"Cerys? You okay?"

"Yeah." It comes out a little shaky, but I stand up, and sound steadier when I add, "I'm just gonna use the bathroom. I'll come find you and the others downstairs in a sec, okay?"

He pauses, and I think about that arm around me after someone bumped into me, and close my eyes. As if I'm not frazzled enough right now without adding *that* whole weirdness to the mix. But Max says, "Okay," and I hear him leave.

I dump my mostly untouched cider down the sink. I don't need to add "drunken mess" to the state I'm in. I've already got the "mess" part down pat.

Just when I think I've got it together and am totally, absolutely, most *definitely* equipped to handle whatever the rest of the night has to throw at me, I hop down the last of the stairs and come face to face with Jake and Anissa huddled in the kitchen doorway, arms tangled together, both sipping drinks, heads bent near as they giggle about something.

It's another gut punch. It's worse. It's someone spiking my heart on my favorite stiletto shoe and smiling while it bleeds out slowly.

Not that they're kissing, or anything close to it, but—what if they did, earlier? What if they do?

It's not like Anissa owes me anything. Sure, there's girl code, but it's not like I ever *told* her that I liked Jake. It's not like she knows I only brought her here to distract Max. And as for Jake—

As for Jake . . .

God, he really doesn't see me that way, does he? Not if he can ditch me at a party *he invited me to,* too busy canoodling with

Anissa to even know I've been hiding in the bathroom crying, to even care.

He's supposed to be The One.

He's *supposed* to be my best friend.

I catch sight of Max coming through the kitchen door, and decide I really cannot deal with any of this. It's all too much. I just want to call Dad and ask for a lift home, even if it's too early to leave yet.

But as I whirl away I find myself caught in a sudden tide of movement, bodies pressing out of rooms in all directions and heading to the sunroom—to the back garden. I just about make out Raf calling, "Come on, gang, time for the fireworks! Ozzy, mate, you all set? Where's Dez? Oi, Alfie, give us a hand setting these up, will you?"

Of course—the fireworks display. The reason we're here.

I notice Jake and Anissa swept along in the crush, too—I pick out Jake's sandy hair, slightly disheveled from its usual style, and see the flash of Anissa's snake-cuff earring. Part of me wants to do what I thought Max had been doing to me these last few weeks: insert myself between them, be an annoying third wheel who ruins the sweet, flirty moments they're sharing, destroy any and all hope of taking things further. And don't I *want* to hang out with them anyway? Would it be so horrible if I pushed through the crowd until I found them, and we all watched the fireworks together? I'm sure Max would find us, too.

But I really, really don't have the energy right now.

Let them have the fireworks, I think, dragging myself out of the way and latching onto a quiet corner in the sunroom where I can stay put. Let them have a kiss if they want one. It's too late anyway.

I'm too late.

The last stragglers pour through the sunroom doors, out into the pitch-dark night. There are phone flashlights swinging around and boys shouting instructions as all the fireworks are set up, ready to be lit. I stay inside as the frigid air rushes in, leaving me without an alcohol jacket—or a real jacket—for protection.

I draw a breath. Let it back out.

I'm too late, I think again. And maybe I never stood a chance in the first place.

"You're not going out to see the fireworks?"

"Jesus!" I jump, clutching my chest.

"Nope, just me."

I cut Max a glare, not impressed by the joke—or by his lurking. Now that we're face-to-face, I'm embarrassed by the fact that I had a bit of a meltdown, and by all the things I said to him. I'm embarrassed that *he* had to come and check if I was okay, because my so-called bestie was too preoccupied to notice. And that he's caught me hiding from the party *again*—when I should be the one throwing myself into it, when he's the one whose name people get wrong, when . . .

When he's looking at me like that, unflinching, seeing too much, and I bristle, hugging my arms tighter to me.

"Just because Jake—"

"Drop it, Max."

He doesn't, though; he steps into the room, closing the distance between us inch by inch. "Just because he's getting on with Anissa, or because he's friends with me, doesn't mean—"

"I don't want to hear it." I don't. It's bad enough I have to reassure myself that Jake isn't trying to get rid of me; I don't need Max's pity, too. "I told you, my friendships are none of your business. Jake and Anissa can—they can do what they like. And Anissa—"

Anissa isn't even my friend anyway, except . . . I'd really like her to be, but I feel like I've already screwed that up because of how I've approached it, even if she's none the wiser.

"It is my business, if it's upsetting you," Max says. "I thought we were—"

"Just because we called a truce—"

He scowls. "Cerys, I don't know how many ways I have to explain it for you to understand. I thought we were on the same page here."

"Oh yeah? And what page is that?" I snap, but it's a serious question. Just because I understand where he was coming from being all judgmental, and he knows I was jealous of his friendship with Jake, just because we *talked* . . .

I'm shivering, teeth gritted and beginning to chatter, and he's near enough that he angles himself between me and the draft from the open doors, his hand on my arm, rubbing it up and down.

It takes me back to the Worlds Beyond con, how I didn't bring a jacket because I wanted Jake to offer me his.

"Listen," he tells me. "Jake is not going to—"

"Why do you care so much, if something upsets me?" I bite out.

I want to know, *need* to know all of a sudden, but I also really need to not hear the end of that sentence. Jake is not going to—what, ditch me, forget about me, ever be interested in dating me?

"Because," Max says, visibly frustrated, shifting a little closer. The hand on my arm has stilled, holding me rather than warming me up, although the heat of his palm is searing, sending prickles all through my body. His jaw is clenched, his breathing heavy and shallow. Mine is, too. Has been for . . . I don't know how long. "Because—"

I never get to hear the end of that sentence either.

I think I realize what's happening the split second before it actually happens, because my chin ticks upward and I inhale his exhale sharply, lips parting, before his mouth crashes down on to mine.

My mind eddies, void of everything but the sensation of being kissed, of kissing, of the body against mine and the silk-soft hair between my fingers when I drag my hands up to anchor him closer. My nostrils fill with a sharp, clean scent like pine; the hand on my arm slips to settle between my shoulder blades and the other rests on my hip, the grip tight and trembling, just like my arms around his shoulders are.

I've kissed boys before. Three, to be exact. One at a party when I got a little tipsy—sloppy and only half remembered the day after; one behind the bike sheds at school when I was fourteen and we were supposed to be on litter-picking duty—not worth remembering; and one fleeting peck on the lips on a date when I was thirteen that might as well not really count.

I have never been kissed like this before. I have never *kissed* like this before.

I always assumed I would have to think so intently about every part of a kiss like this: how our lips fit together, careful not to knock teeth, hyperconscious of where I put my hands and where his are and if our noses are in the way and how to move my lips and to remember to breathe (do I always breathe this loudly and weirdly?) . . . And trying to figure out the right pressure, or if it's appropriate to add tongue and *when* to add tongue, and a million other things the movies never quite explain.

But this isn't like that. At all.

It just *happens.*

Max's mouth is soft and urgent against mine, and when his teeth catch my lower lip ever so slightly I gasp, and test how he responds when I drag the tip of my tongue just a little over *his* lip.

I knot my fingers tighter in his hair, vaguely aware of the fact I've stumbled—*stumbled,* like my knees have actually, genuinely gone weak. The foot-pop moment in *The Princess Diaries* is suddenly making total sense to me. The wall is now at my back, and I'm very content to be pressed between it and Max if it means this kiss.

We break apart to catch our breath. His pupils are blown wide, his eyes as dark as his hair. I've messed up his bun, he's all disheveled now, and his lips are full and bright and his cheeks are flushed and I wonder if I look like that, too. I bet I do.

I want to kiss him again.

"Cerys," he murmurs, "I—"

I drag one of my hands through the silken waves of his hair, bringing it to settle against his shoulder, and that's when I notice them.

Him.

All thoughts of resuming our kiss (and *oh my GOD, that KISS!* And also, *oh my God, I kissed MAX!*) go up in smoke because Jake is standing in the open doorway, face ashen, mouth hanging open as he stares at us.

There are tears in his eyes.

He doesn't look like he just caught some of his friends kissing at a party; he looks like he's been stabbed in the back.

No no no, this is *not* happening.

Max clocks me looking over his shoulder—my expression must shift, but I don't know what he finds there. Guilt? Horror? Regret? All of the above, probably—and he starts to turn around, too.

Anissa is just behind Jake in the doorway. She stares at me and Max with wide eyes, but there's only ordinary surprise on her face.

Not like on Jake's.

And oh, God, *Jake.*

A firework booms in the sky, a hollow sound I feel inside my chest, and I flinch.

"I—" I start, but have nothing to say for myself.

I kissed Max. *Max!* One single stupid truce and suddenly—this happens? What was I thinking?

Why did it have to be such a *wonderful* kiss?

And, also, WHY AM I STILL CLINGING TO HIM?

I snatch my arms from around Max's neck, as if that's going to make any difference right now. His hands fall away from holding me, too.

"How could you?" Jake whispers, staring at me.

"Jake—" I don't know what to say to him, I don't know how to deal with this. I don't know why he cares when—

Oh, no.

How could I—because I had that same thought seeing him with Anissa: how could *he*?

Because it wasn't that I'd lost my chance, wasn't that I never had one . . .

How could I—because Jake is in love with me like I've been in love with him for so long, and must have been too scared to risk our friendship just like I was.

Why else would he be so upset over me kissing someone else?

Oh God, I've ruined everything, for one reckless, foot-pop-worthy kiss.

My heart hammers in my chest, and all I can do is stare because Jake's in love with me, too, and this is the best news and the worst news and I have to fix it, I have to . . .

Jake bolts past us, into the house, and I peel out from between Max and the wall to follow him, only pausing to snap, "*Don't* follow me," at Max. I can't undo the kiss, I know that, but I do know that he can only make things worse right now.

I catch Jake's arm in the hallway, tugging him to a halt.

"I'm sorry," I say. "I don't know what happened, I—"

"You don't even *like* him!"

"I—"

Oh shit, I'm really not as subtle as I think, am I? He knows, he's probably known all along, he probably thought that inviting us both to watch *OWAR* was a good way to help me get along with his new mate . . . No wonder he cut me out of things like their cosplay-crafting for Comic Con when he knew I didn't like Max!

"It's not that I *don't* like him, Jake, I—"

"You never talk to him! Both of you! You never even talk to each other! You act like you can't bear to be around each other, *all the time*! Is this why? Is this . . . Have you both been . . . How long—" His face crumples, and he presses his fingers to his eyes before his tears can fall. They leave smudges on the inside of his glasses when I draw his arm away, but he pulls back, like he can't bear for me to touch him. He hiccups, and I bite my lip, not sure how much of this is real and how much of it is just close to the surface because he's been drinking. I don't suppose it matters either way.

"Jake, it's not like that, I promise, it's—it was—"

"How could you?" he asks again, with another hiccup, and this time a couple of tears spill over. "You're supposed to be my friend, Cerys, my *best* friend, but—"

A laugh cuts out of me before I can stop it. It's a short, barking sound that is nothing like me, so much so that Jake startles, pausing whatever tirade he's got brewing. I laugh again, another horrible, hollow sound, but somehow it feels *so good* to let it out.

So I let some of the rest out, too. All the dark, anxious, nasty thoughts I kept pushing down and pretending there was a good excuse for. I let it all come spilling out.

"Best friend?" I sneer. "Is that what you call it? When you hardly talk to me, or tell me anything anymore? Half the time I feel like you're ghosting me, trying to cut me out of your life like you did everyone from school, and when we *do* talk it's only because of this stupid fandom—"

"What, you mean the *stupid fandom* you only got into because I told you about it? I didn't *make* you get involved, Cerys. I thought you'd like it, and I thought it'd be a cool thing for us to enjoy together, but I didn't *make you* watch the show."

"If I didn't, we'd never talk! I'd never see you!"

"That's not true—"

"Yes it is, and you know it. If we're supposed to be best friends, then why haven't you been there for me? You *know* how much shit I've had going on at home with my parents, but you only seem to bother asking when it's convenient. I *needed* you, Jake. I needed my best friend and you were—you were too busy geeking out over *OWAR* with your *new* friend—"

"So what, this is your idea of revenge? This is how you're getting back at me for having a life outside of you? By going after Max?"

"I'm not *going after* him, Jake, I'm—that's . . ." This whole thing feels like it's gotten so wildly off track; I try to wrangle it back. "I'm not *mad* at you for having other friends, I'm mad at you for—"

"Yes, you are!" he scoffs, then hiccups again and shifts his weight from one foot to the other. Even if he is tipsy, this fight seems to be sobering him up by the second. Every word thrown seems to make him steadier on his feet; it makes me feel wobbly and queasy. He scowls at me, and brushes another rogue tear off his cheek. "You *never* let me have anything of my own, Cerys. You're always— you're always *tagging along.*"

"I'm *what?*"

"You are!" he bursts out, nodding sharply, even as his breath shudders. "You tagged along at school, and you tagged along to the Worlds Beyond con, and now you're tagging along with *OWAR* and Max just like you tag along with the girls at school and wear whatever they wear and do whatever they do—"

"Oh, like you were *so* into the idea of cosplay before Max—"

"At least Max *cares* about stuff! At least he knows who he is!"

"What, unlike me, you mean?"

"Yeah! Yeah, unlike *you*. And you're so shallow about it—"

"You want to talk about *shallow*, Jake? How about your soccer drama, and Ginny being annoyed that you're borrowing her car to learn to drive, and every time you crack the same joke about being late with your homework? All you ever talk about is what's going on with *you*. You barely ever *ask* how I'm doing, Jake, and when you do—"

I break off, trembling, sick to my stomach. When he does, it's hidden under layers of conversation about *OWAR* in the Discord. Like he's . . . ashamed of me. Squashing me down, pushing me out, tucking me out of the way of his "real" life.

My eyes search Jake's, and cold settles into my bones. My best friend feels like a stranger to me.

"It's like I don't even know who you are anymore," I tell him. "And you know what? If this is how you're going to be, I'm not sure I want to."

He staggers back, the words slicing between us like a guillotine, and the fight drains out of him in a shuddering exhale. Jake's whole body slumps, his face growing taut around the edges and eyes shining with more tears, but he doesn't let them fall.

Instead, he spins on his heel and storms out of the house, slamming the front door behind him.

I watch him go, feeling all at once numb and agonized. Jane Austen's Captain Wentworth eat your heart out: I am *all* in agony now, and it's definitely worse than when there was still half hope.

I've destroyed it. Not just the hope of a potential romance, but the hope of salvaging our friendship. It's gone. I did that.

The fireworks keep going outside. *BOOM* and *crack!* and *fizzzzz*, and the oohs and aahs of an appreciative, tipsy crowd watching them all.

Behind me, I'm aware of Max and Anissa standing silently, having watched the whole fight.

Max can't meet my eye.

That hurts almost as much as Jake storming out on me. I feel so *stupid* for thinking Max was more than this superior, judgmental ass.

I feel so stupid for thinking maybe he meant it, when he acted like he cared about me, and that's why he kissed me.

Anissa gives his elbow a quick squeeze, saying something to him that I don't catch, before coming over and slipping an arm around me. "Do you want to go home?"

I nod.

We don't ask Max for a lift. He makes himself scarce. Anissa and I wait at the foot of the stairs until my dad texts to say that he's outside.

"How was the party, girls?" he asks brightly.

"Yeah, great. Really good. We're just tired," I say, and if he thinks our mood is subdued, he understands now is not the time to ask about it.

We're halfway home when Anissa waves her phone at me. "Jake went back to the party. He's going to get a lift home with some of the others."

Right. Of course. They've been chatting in the Discord. She's someone he likes chatting with about the books.

Mom tries to give us more of the third degree when we get home, and I offer up a few half-hearted responses. Anissa fills in for me with a bit more enthusiasm, and a huge yawn that has Mom sending us both off to bed to get some sleep.

Anissa and I change quickly and in silence, and I don't think this is how sleepovers are really supposed to go. I'm not being a good host.

Then again, we're not twelve, and my life has just imploded because of a kiss.

I roll over to face Anissa down on the air bed.

"I didn't mean to hurt him," I whisper into the dark. I don't think she's asleep yet. "I didn't even really mean to kiss Max, it just . . . happened."

"I thought you and Runic . . . I mean—"

"Yeah," I say. "I thought so, too. I don't know. It's all a mess, and . . . God, the look on his *face* . . . I've never seen Jake like that. He was devastated. The things I said to him . . . I really didn't mean . . ."

Anissa props herself up on one elbow, the air bed making a plasticky rustle. "He said some pretty harsh things, too, Cerys."

"It's nothing I didn't deserve. He's right, I do . . . tag along, I'm—"

"He was out of order," she reiterates, so sternly that I let myself believe her. At least for the moment. "And anyway, he'd really been putting those hard ciders away, plus a few vodka Jell-O shots . . . Give him a couple of days to get his head straight, he'll see things differently. You can both apologize and go back to normal. It won't all seem so horrible then."

"Do you think?"

She nods; I see her silhouetted head bobbing as my eyes adjust to the dark.

Weirdly, I trust her judgment. If she's been chatting with Jake for a while—and she knows him from school and spent all night at the party with him . . . At the very least, I trust her judgment *far* more than mine right now.

Can I blame Jake, for being so hurt? He caught me kissing his best friend. He wouldn't have reacted like that if he didn't feel the way about me as I do about him. Isn't that a good thing? Isn't this what I wanted?

So why is it *Max* that my mind keeps circling back to—putting his arm around me, keeping me warm from the chill, coming after me when I got upset, then *not looking at me after the kiss*? Why is that the part that seems to hurt so much more right now?

Is this how Jake felt when he saw me kissing another boy? This overwhelming ache in the pit of my chest that feels like it'll drag me down, drowning me?

A couple of minutes pass in silence, though neither of us falls asleep. Instead of processing anything, my brain just feels full of raging white noise I can't decipher. My lips are still tingling from the aftermath of the kiss, and I touch a finger to them.

I really don't know what I was thinking. I don't even know

how we got to a point where we were kissing! I thought Max hated me. I thought *I* hated *him*. That can't all change in the span of one conversation on opposite sides of a bathroom door, can it?

Is this what the whole fuss is with the enemies-to-lovers trope? I kind of understand it if that's the sort of kiss it leads to.

One very quiet but very clear thought swims to the surface: *I wish we hadn't been interrupted.*

I risk saying out loud, "It was a really good kiss, though."

Anissa giggles. "I'll say! We only caught the tail end but you two looked *very* steamy."

"And his hair's really soft."

"Mm-hmm." She makes the sound through closed lips, like she's trying not to laugh. I throw a spare pillow down, smacking her square in the face, and a giggle bursts out of her.

And because she's proving to be a good listener—a good friend—I say, "For a minute when I saw you and Jake together, I thought . . ."

Anissa snorts. "As *if.*"

"Oh. Well . . . okay." *Good.* Bad? I don't know anymore. "Thanks for, um, coming with me tonight. And for coming home early with me. I know you were having a good time . . ."

"Of course!" she says. "I did have fun. It's sad we didn't get to hang out more, though. You totally vanished after we got there. I thought . . ." She gives a small laugh. "Well, after I saw you and Max all over each other, I thought maybe that was why you'd invited me. So you could both ditch Jake without it being weird. Fourth-wheel me. It's okay if you were," she adds in a rush. "I just—"

"No, Anissa, I—" *Rumbled,* but not quite. I feel truly, properly heinous for having used her at all—even if it backfired wildly, and even if I do genuinely like spending time with her. More sincerely, I tell her, "I'm sad we didn't get to hang out more, too. Honestly, I thought you and Max would get on really well. I'm sorry."

"Maybe . . . ," she starts, and then falls quiet, never finishing her sentence.

I try to finish it for her. I don't know her like I do Jake, but I think I'm starting to. I know I'd like to. "Maybe we could hang out again soon? Outside of school or the Discord chat, I mean, and without boys getting in the way."

"Yeah." I can hear the grin in her voice. "I'd like that."

GIRLIE POPS! ✦

Nikita

@Cerys we are on TENTERHOOKS girl, how did the party go????

Chloe

DID YOU GUYS KISS?

Me

The party was okay, no kiss with Jake though. Nothing to report sorry gang

Evie

Oh boooo! That sucks babe

Nikita

But it was so promising!
Did he get too drunk?

Chloe

Maybe he didn't know how to get a moment alone with you to make a move, and it was just too intimidating with everyone else there?

Evie

That's gotta be it!

Nikita

I see you reading these messages **@Daphne**, any thoughts/sorrows/prayers for poor Cerys over here?

Me

It's okay, the whole thing was just a bust. I'd rather not talk about it tbh

Daphne

Kind of busy right now sorry. Will catch up later

Evie

Our resident yappers going quiet? I never thought I'd see the day!

Chloe

Okay well we can just catch up at Costa this week? Morning debrief? 😚

Me

Not sure if I'll make it sorry

Daphne

Me either. Super busy with coursework rn

Nikita

What?! You two better make time! I sense DRAMA! Can't wait to hear all about it

Private chat with @runicrascal

@runicrascal
Hey, can we talk about the other night?

@mythicwitch
Maybe that's not such a good idea. I'm sorry.
Maybe . . . Can we just forget about it?

Try to go back to normal a little with us?

I really am sorry

● ● ● *@runicrascal is typing . . .*
● ● ● *@runicrascal is typing . . .*
● ● ● *@runicrascal is typing . . .*

@mythicwitch
Please

@runicrascal
Is that what you really want?

@mythicwitch
I just hate the idea that it'll change things between us,
so yes

@runicrascal
Okay

@mythicwitch
☺ friends?

● ● ● *@runicrascal is typing . . .*
● ● ● *@runicrascal is typing . . .*

@runicrascal
Yeah. Friends.

Mistakes by mythicwitch

Lady Adanna di Silver/Devon Smith, Lady Adanna di Silver/
Sir Grayson "the Moonwalker," Lady Adanna di Silver, Devon
Smith, Sir Grayson "the Moonwalker," One Shot, Angst, Lady
di Silver can unalive a man in the blink of an eye but kiss one
and she turns into a wreck

Words: 533 Chapters: 1/1 Hits: 12

Stalking through the palace corridors in search of her prey, Lady
di Silver removed her mask and felt for the dagger beneath her
ball gown. The prince's study should be down here somewhere,
and once she found him . . .

But someone else found her first.

A figure slipped out of the shadows between the torches,
forcing her to an abrupt halt. He, too, had removed his mask
since their dance in the ballroom a short while ago, and without
it she could make out every plane of his cheekbones and
aquiline nose. He *was* a striking figure, there was no doubt
about that. His elfin blood gave him a grace that few humans
possessed.

"What are you doing here, Sir Grayson? Not interfering with my
mission, I hope."

"I rather thought I would help with it."

Lady di Silver scoffed. "I do *not* require your help, sir. I am no
damsel in distress."

He held up his gloved hands in surrender. "I did not say 'take over.' But if you'd prefer *not* to have my assistance . . ."

"I thought you had business of your own in the castle tonight."

"I did," he said in a low voice, stepping closer.

"What changed?"

He held her gaze. "Our dance."

Oh.

Oh.

Lady di Silver wasn't sure which of them had moved first, only that they were upon each other before she could blink, the frustration of their earlier meeting on the dance floor melting in a hungry kiss, their tongues battling for dominance as her fingers carded through his long, white-blond hair, skimming over the tips of his pointed ears. It ignited a fire in her belly—not unlike the sort she normally only felt in the heat of battle when swinging a sword, but more intense. It consumed her, and every thought in her mind.

She couldn't say which of them broke the kiss, but when they parted, she was catching her breath—and trying to understand exactly *how* this had happened, where these feelings had sprung from out of their earlier animosity—when the Moonwalker's eyes slid over the top of her head, and his lip curled.

"Ah," he said. "I forgot that you're never alone."

Lady di Silver spun on her heel and found Devon some distance away, his head bowed, hand resting on the hilt of his sword, not quite looking at either of them, but noticing her gaze on him. He bowed slightly. "My lady."

Lady di Silver gasped, bringing a hand to her throat. Her lips felt swollen, the ghost of Sir Grayson's kiss still imprinted there, but guilt squirmed in her stomach to see her faithful, steadfast friend looking wholly uncomfortable and put out by the impassioned display—and she didn't think that was anything to do with the kiss itself, but more to do with *her*.

"Devon," she whispered, but when she glanced behind, the Moonwalker had vanished, silent as the shadows, and she steeled herself. One kiss—one reckless, impulsive moment—could not derail her mission. She could not afford to let it.

"Come, Devon," she said, squaring her shoulders. "We have a prince to interrogate, and I shall need your help."

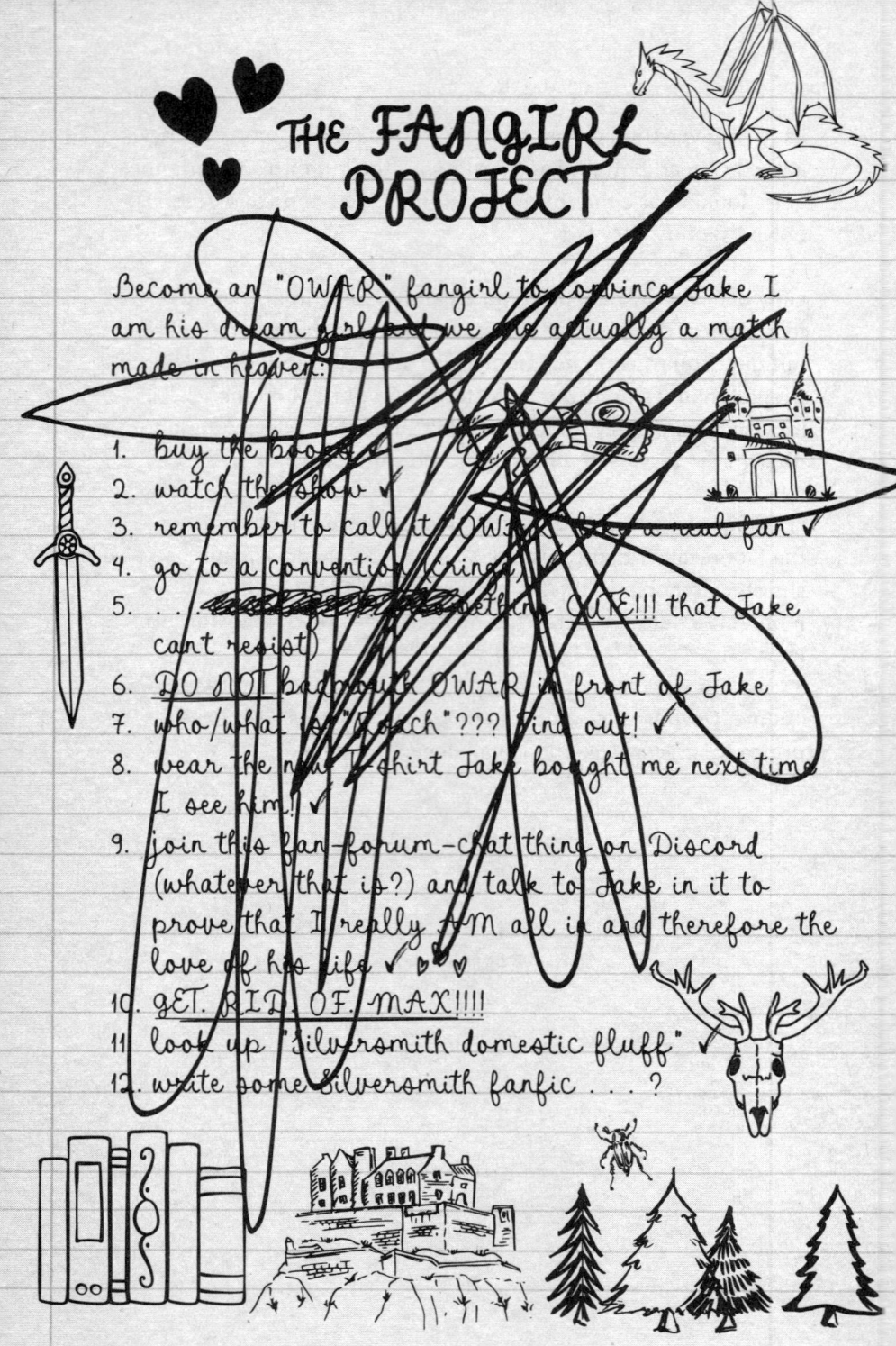

THE FANGIRL PROJECT

Become an "OWAR" fangirl to convince Jake I am his dream girl and we are actually a match made in heaven:

1. buy the books ✓
2. watch the show ✓
3. remember to call it "OWAR" like a real fan ✓
4. go to a convention (cringe)
5. . . . ~~something~~ CUTE!!! that Jake can't resist)
6. DO NOT badmouth OWAR in front of Jake
7. who/what is "Roach"??? Find out! ✓
8. wear the new T-shirt Jake bought me next time I see him! ✓
9. join this fan-forum-chat thing on Discord (whatever that is?) and talk to Jake in it to prove that I really AM all in and therefore the love of his life ✓ ♥ ♥
10. GET. RID. OF. MAX!!!!
11. look up "Silversmith domestic fluff" ✓
12. write some Silversmith fanfic . . . ?

I hardly hear from Jake in the weeks following our last Discord chat. I send him a few texts asking if he's okay and if he's free to hang out, and try to break the ice by sending him a couple of funny Instagram posts or TikToks I think he'll like, but the most I get is the thumbs-up emoji.

It's worse than if he just left me on read.

I don't know how to fix it. I don't know if I *can* fix it.

I thought finding out that Jake had feelings for me and I didn't have some enormously unrequited crush would be the best thing in the world, that I'd be over the moon, but I'm left with this hollow ache in my chest, and whenever I think about it, it's hard to breathe.

Is this what heartbreak feels like?

Except . . . I'm not sure that's what it is.

I keep picturing his face and the tears in his eyes, the betrayal that cracked his voice, and it just feels *lonely*. And then I keep thinking about Max shielding me from the chill and saying, "Because—because—" and feeling the ghost of his lips on mine.

Max hasn't tried to reach out to me, either. We never swapped numbers, but it's not as if I'm hard to find on social media the way he is. He could DM me if he wanted to.

Which, clearly, he doesn't.

His radio silence doesn't hurt as much as Jake's does, but it still stings. I can only assume that he's keeping a distance from me for Jake's sake, for their friendship. It's harder for them to avoid each other when they have classes together and are on the same soccer team, I suppose, and I can't really blame him. I'd do the same in his shoes, wouldn't I?

It was just a kiss, though. *One* conversation and *one* kiss, and it doesn't matter if it's all I keep thinking about, because Jake and I have a foundation so much stronger than that. I keep scrolling back through the Discord to prove that to myself, every time I'm tempted to reach out to Max on his latent Instagram account.

I *cannot* throw it all away for a boy who barely even speaks to me.

I know Anissa talks to Jake; sometimes, I see messages from @runicrascal flash up on her phone screen when we're hanging out in the art rooms at lunch. And two weeks after the party, Jake uploads an Instagram photo of him and Anissa at the Argonauta concert, the one Max told me about that time he drove me home.

Max isn't in the photo. He and Jake must not have patched things up too well, if Anissa's taken his place.

I can't bring myself to hold it against Anissa the way I did with Max. Max felt like an interloper; the fact Anissa and Jake even interacted at all is my doing. And she's so *nice,* so warm, I don't begrudge her the friendship—even if it does feel like it's at the cost of my own.

My friendship with the other girls is on thin ice, too. Every message in the group chat feels stilted, I keep avoiding the morning Costa runs, and Daphne and I still aren't talking.

Chloe corners me one day to ask, "What's going on with you two? Did you have a fight?"

Daphne clearly hasn't told them how awful I was to her, which makes no sense to me, so I settle for shrugging and saying, "Nothing. We're fine." Which we both know is a blatant lie, but it's the only way I can think to get out of it.

I'm the one in the wrong, though, so I do Daphne the favor of withdrawing from the group as much as I can, even if I have classes with Nikita and Evie I can't avoid. In media lessons, Daphne has taken to sitting at an empty desk at the back of the room—as far away from me as she can get.

And if the girls notice I'm spending more time with Anissa instead of them, they don't confront me about it. Nikita sees the Instagram photo from the Argonauta concert and asks if I want her to *hex the man-stealing witch,* but the laugh I give in response is high and false, and we don't talk about it again.

I don't talk about much of anything with them these days, actually.

In the end, I retreat into the Discord. I have eighteen tabs open on my phone with different fanfictions I'm reading, and upload a couple more one-shots myself. Mostly they're about Lady di Silver trying to muddle through conflicting attraction to the Moonwalker and her long-standing bond with Devon.

I, obviously, can't relate at all.

I do venture to the dark side, though, and read some of the Moonsilver ship fics that I find linked in the Discord.

I start painting more, too, feeling consumed by the need to actually finish the pieces I'm working on. Dark, moody scenes of Lady di Silver and Devon standing on opposite sides of the horse they shared in season one, unable to look at each other. A busy ball-room in a more fuzzy style with too-bright colors where she twirls across the floor, caught between the Moonwalker and Devon. Her abandoned vanity strewn with weapons and jewels in a place that never really felt like home anyway.

It's *cathartic*. So much so I'm almost annoyed at how well the fandom, the artwork, all of it, is helping my messy emotions feel a little less overwhelming. Even if I can't make sense of them yet, it's helpful to process it through this medium, to express it without having to make it so personal. I get a weird sense of satisfaction from the paint splotches staining my hands and fingernails, a sense of real triumph when I finish a piece. I finally see why those girls wrote that eight-hundred-thousand-word *OWAR* fanfic, why Max devotes so much time to perfecting his Moonwalker cosplay. Art has always been a fun outlet, a distraction, but *this* is . . .

It's the equivalent of a kiss that makes you weak in the knees and too dizzy to think straight. It feels like finally being able to *breathe*.

It's so silly, because it's obviously not going to *fix* anything.

But . . . it does make me feel a little less at sea.

I don't watch much more of the show, instead rewatching old episodes. The new content feels tainted and leaves me with an ashy taste in my mouth now that I can't share it with Jake. I don't want to annoy him, and he obviously isn't interested in talking to me—even in the Discord. Our chat's been dead since we agreed to be friends.

Which is the greatest goddamn irony of all.

I'd give up The Fangirl Project and my crush and even—*especially*—that kiss, if it just meant I got my friends back.

That's when I realize that I even miss Max. Putting the kiss aside, he was . . . I mean, he was *there* for me at the party, wasn't he? And he drove me home that time. He put me on to the audiobooks, and Argonauta has become a firm fixture in my Spotify listens since he introduced me to them. And after our conversation through the bathroom door, I realize that I misjudged him a lot, too.

I keep replaying what he said about being himself and not living his life for other people. His cosplay doesn't seem so mortifyingly cringeworthy, in that light.

I think about it every time I debate over what to wear to school and trawl Instagram to see if the girls have posted a fit check yet that morning—it's habit, at this point, even if I'm avoiding our morning Costa trips for now.

Jake's voice rings in my head, shouting at me for being so shallow.

But I guess I don't know how to be otherwise, and I keep

picking outfits based on what the others are wearing. At least, I figure, it'll help me fade into the background.

November slips past with the weather as gray and dismal as my mood, and then I'm kept blessedly distracted by extra shifts at H&M and heavy loads of schoolwork. The girls start making plans to go ice-skating or watch the new Lindsay Lohan Netflix Christmas movie, and I make excuses to get out of all of it.

Which works, until it doesn't.

"Because you're taller than me! Cerys, *please*," Evie wheedles. "I can't be bothered to go find the stepladder. Just grab me the box of chalk on the top shelf, will you? It'll take *two seconds*."

She's being weirdly annoying about such a small favor, dragging me to the art room after school finishes to help her get some supplies, badgering me at my shoulder even though I've already agreed.

She undoes the latch on the supply room door—

And shoves me inside, slamming it shut behind her. I'm pushed right into someone; the light is on, and it's Daphne—pink-cheeked and seething, her arms crossed tightly.

The latch flips back into place on the other side of the door, and I rattle the handle uselessly.

"Evie! What the hell?"

"You two need to sort this out! We're all sick of you both doing the whole cold-shoulder thing."

"But—"

And then Chloe's voice joins in from the other side of the door, too, shouting, "Whatever's gone on, you two need to talk through it and hear each other out. Then you can either make up or decide you're not friends anymore. We're going to get coffees; we'll be back in half an hour."

Nikita calls, "Try not to kill each other!" Then her voice drops, but I can still hear her through the door. "Wait, Evie, are there scalpels in there? Should we have checked?"

"We're not going to kill each other!" Daphne and I both shout back, and share a look. Her mouth purses, and I swallow a huff. There's the sound of the other girls walking away, though, leaving us stuck in here until they let us out.

Daphne sighs, moving to the corner to sit on a stack of boxes. She doesn't quite look at me as she asks, "Did Evie tell you she needed help reaching the top shelf, too?"

"We're not even that much taller than her. Why did we fall for it?"

She rolls her eyes, but it feels good-natured. "Because she's Evie."

I hesitate before taking a seat, too. I get stuck sitting on the floor, since there aren't any other boxes to perch on, and I wrap my arms around my knees. "They sound like the couples' counselor my parents see. *Talk through your problems, hear where the other person is coming from.*"

"How's that working for them?"

I snort.

"Oh. You . . . um, you never . . . mentioned anything."

"I didn't want to bring the mood down." I shrug, then meet her eye. "Talking about my shitty boy drama with Jake felt like a better way to get you all to like me than complaining that my parents' divorce is a living hell."

Daphne's eyes go wide, her face falling into something sympathetic and gentle, full of her usual earnestness. But she seems to check herself, because she sniffs and says nothing.

I sit up straighter. "I shouldn't . . . Look, I'm not saying you should hear me out, and I get it if you don't want to be my friend anymore. But I shouldn't have said that stuff at the party. I shouldn't have brushed you off like that. I'm sorry."

Daphne scoffs. "You're *sorry*?"

But before I can tell her I am—that I really, *honestly* am, she's burying her face in her hands and laughing shakily.

"Why are *you* sorry?" she exclaims. "Cerys, *I'm* the one who was a total bitch! Like you were jealous and boy-crazy, when . . . I mean, come *on*, like we don't all ask you what the latest is with Jake and dissect it a hundred times over! I was just—I was . . . Oh God." She sighs, another wobbly laugh catching on her words, and she slumps, pulling her hands away from her face to look at me. "It was so stupid. It's so embarrassing."

"What?"

"I basically invited myself, that night. Daniel didn't invite me. You went to Jake's soccer match and it worked out so well, and Daniel had already told me about the party, so I thought—I thought I'd try to be more like you . . ."

"Like *me*? But . . ." But *Daphne's* the one *I* look up to. The one I take cues and guidance from!

"You just always seem so . . . Well, you get stuck into things, you'll give anything a go, and you're sort of fearless! I mean, I could *never* have just gone up to a group of girls I didn't know and tried to be friends with them like you did! I had to drag you all along to that rugby match with me because I was too much of a coward to go on my own, and even *then* I was too scared to actually go up to the guy and talk to him! But you—you go to Comic Con, for God's sake!"

I'm stunned that she sees me that way. Stunned because it's like how Anissa said she saw me. Stunned because . . . it's how I've started to see Max, and I admire that about him a lot, actually. And it's sort of nice to hear that Daphne, of all people, thinks it about *me*.

"Anyway," Daphne carries on, "I thought I'd just *do* it, you know, bite the bullet, be more Cerys, so I went to the party, and— oh, I just didn't know anybody there, and Daniel wasn't actually all that bothered to see me. After we kissed, he went to get a drink, then when he didn't come back, I found him kissing *another* girl in the sunroom! I'd just shut myself in the bathroom upstairs to have a little cry and try to decide whether he was worth it or whether to just go home when I ran into you, and I was too mortified to say anything. But of course you thought the same as Daniel, obviously, that I'd made a drunk mess of myself and was being all annoying and clingy—"

"No! Oh my God, no, Daphne . . ."

I can't believe she thought *I* was the one judging *her* for how she acted at that party. I feel so awful she's been stuck feeling embarrassed all this time, when I should've just talked to her.

This time, it's my turn to confess all.

Well—at least some.

"I was upset, and I shouldn't have taken it out on you. You were just asking me about Jake, and things with him were such a mess and going *so* badly, I couldn't face it. And I'd just had this fight with Max—"

"What! Third-wheel Max?" she exclaims, and it's like nothing ever happened for a moment—like we haven't been dodging each other for weeks, like it's a regular Thursday morning debrief about boys over coffee. Her eyes are bright, scandalized, her hand over her gaping mouth. "What did you two even fight about? Did you call him out?"

"Sort of . . . But I was really mean about it. Like I was to you, and . . . Honestly, Daph, the whole night was a total shit show. It's not an excuse, but I'm sorry I took that out on you. And I'm sorry I didn't tell you that sooner."

"No! Oh gosh, no, babe, *I'm* sorry! I thought for sure you must hate me—"

"I thought *you* hated *me*—"

And just like that, it doesn't even matter, because she's throwing herself off the makeshift stool to give me a hug, and we're both laughing, and I'm cussing out Daniel for treating her so rubbish and she's tutting about boys being not worth all the hassle anyway.

She's right, they're not.

I'm just . . . sad that my friendship with Jake had to get destroyed in the process. That all still hurts too much to go into right now, though, and the main thing is that Daphne and I are patching things up. My shitty boy drama can wait.

By the time the girls are back from their coffees, we're giggling over how stupid the two of us have been, and when Evie unlocks the door, the five of us pile into a group hug.

Maybe I am shallow and tag along, or maybe I am fearless and get stuck into anything, but whatever I am, it feels good to have friends who accept it and fight for me.

Even if those friends aren't Jake.

It's Christmas before I know it, and all I can think about is how Jake and I should be hanging out watching *Elf* and feasting on the biscuit casualties left over from his family's annual attempt to make a gingerbread village. When Ginny uploads a photo of this year's wonky spectacular, I have to swipe away before I start crying.

Should I reach out to Jake now? 'Tis the season, and all that, and maybe he's missing me, too? Giving him space seemed like the right thing to do, even if it meant letting him get over *his* crush on *me*, but I don't care about that anymore. I just want my friend back. Daphne and I patched things up; couldn't Jake and I? Then again, there were no broken hearts and betrayals involved there . . .

In the end, I decide not to.

It's Christmas, he's busy, he's having fun with Ginny being home, and his older brother, Thomas, has finally moved to Cardiff, so they'll be playing D&D campaigns and whatever, and I don't want to spoil the holidays for him. I've already been selfish enough when it comes to our friendship.

He's been hanging out a lot with Anissa, so I try to ask her advice about it, but she only cringes whenever I bring it up.

"Jake's just . . . he's got some stuff going on, and he's working through some things," she says, in what feels like a very rigid and prepared answer. "*Please* don't bring me into the middle of it, Cerys. I don't want to get stuck between you."

"Well, you kind of are."

"I know, and it's *rubbish,* believe me. It's not very nice when he asks me how you're doing, either, you know, and I've told him he should just *talk* to you. You both feel so bloody awful, I almost . . ."

"Want to lock us in a storeroom closet until we're friends again?"

Anissa laughs; she got a real kick out of that story. "Don't tempt me. But you're both moping around, missing each other, and . . ." She lets out a big sigh. "I really don't want to get involved, Cerys, it's not my place. Jake will come around. He'll talk to you properly soon, I'm sure of it. Just . . . give him some time, okay? Maybe after Christmas?"

"But it's already been *ages.* Nearly two months."

"I know. I know, but . . ." She looks so sad, so conflicted, I wonder what really *is* going on with Jake. Is he more heartbroken than I realize?

More heartbroken than . . . I have been?

When I try to ask Anissa about that, though, she refuses to get into it. "This is for the two of *you* to sort out. Now come on—I thought I came over so we could read the new update on that Moonsilver fic. It's *six thousand* words about the ballroom scene, Cerys, and I don't think they even kiss yet . . ."

Maybe I haven't known Anissa that long, but the shared love of

OWAR has helped us forge a strong bond—and I trust her. Enough, at least, to promise myself that I'll carry on giving Jake space until at least the new year.

My own Christmas is as strange as it is chaotic. Mom and Dad are back to being frosty with each other, and every conversation they have is in clipped tones. We have my Aunty Jude's party on the 23rd with my dad's side of the family; we spend Christmas morning with Dad's parents, and the afternoon with my maternal grandma, plus a bunch of my younger cousins with their noisy new games and food we're too full from lunch to really eat. Then it's a drive up to Bangor on Boxing Day to see my granddad and step-nan, with only one argument over the route Mom takes. I put on the third *OWAR* audiobook and pretend to sleep for most of the journey.

See? I want to tell them. *I knew this would happen.* The whole "happy families" act was never going to last.

At least for New Year's Eve, Chloe's invited us all over. It'll be a welcome escape from all the family time I've been subjected to.

Like tonight, with rain lashing against the windows, and all three of us sitting around the kitchen table, the mood eerily calm. *Pleasant,* almost. Mom and Dad are holding an actual conversation, and there are a few smiles and laughs between them that make me wary.

After they've hashed over all the usual chatter—my New Year's plans with the girls, how work and school have been, if I've had any more thoughts about uni yet ahead of next year's applications—Mom broaches the one subject I was hoping they'd been too pre-occupied to notice.

"You haven't mentioned Jake very much lately. What's going on there?"

I freeze. "Um . . ."

"Have you two had a falling-out?" Dad asks—and, *brilliant*, now they're both doing the kind, concerned parent act, teaming up again like they did when Anissa came over.

"Not really. Just . . . um . . . you know." I shrug. "We've both been busy."

It's a pathetic excuse, and I'm sure they both hear the lie in my voice based on the glance they exchange.

"It's such a shame," Mom sighs. "He was always such a lovely boy, and a good friend."

"He's not *dead*, Mom."

They both laugh. She waves her fork at me. "I know that, silly. I only meant it's a shame you two haven't managed to stay close."

"We—"

We would've, if not for Max. If not for the kiss.

If not for The Fangirl Project, and my determination to see it through ruining everything.

"We're fine," I end up saying. "Just, you know. Christmas. School. Stuff."

Mercifully, they let it drop, and I'm left to scroll on my phone at the table while the two of them work in tandem to load the dishwasher and pack away leftovers. Dad says something that makes Mom laugh—a tinkly, mirthful sound—and she swats him lightly with the tea towel.

It's so disgustingly cozy and domestic, the words finally come spilling out of me.

"You're not getting back together, are you?"

"What?" says Dad, and they both turn, confused, processing what I just said. I clamp my mouth shut, horrified that I even said it at all, hoping maybe I can pass it off as them mishearing or me saying it at something on my phone, but then they exchange a look and Mom sighs, coming back over to the dining table. Dad clips a lid onto the tub of leftovers and joins us.

They both drag out chairs, the noise like nails on a chalkboard, and my heart is in my throat.

Fab work, Cerys, they're sitting down for A Talk. Last time they did this, it was because you got a week's worth of detentions for cutting PE class with Jake and the others. What fresh hell have you unleashed now?

Mom sighs again, folding her hands on the table, but not before I see them shaking. Dad reaches over and places one of his hands over hers, giving them a reassuring squeeze.

And again, I blurt, "You are, aren't you? You're getting back together. You're not going through with the divorce. You're—"

"Cerys," Dad interrupts. "We're *not* getting back together."

In a voice that's so timid it hardly sounds like Mom at all, she says, "We've just been trying to make more of an effort for . . . well, for you. This hasn't been easy for us, and we know that we get a little . . . carried away, sometimes. That can't be very easy for you, either. And it's Christmas."

"So?"

"So we—we just . . ."

"What next, you'll tell me Santa Claus isn't real?" I snap, scowling. "I'm not a child. I'm not *stupid*. I'm—"

"You *are* a child," Dad says. "That's . . . That's . . ."

"What? The problem?" Great, amazing, first Jake, now my parents.

Mom cuts him a look filled with more of their old animosity before saying to me, "This whole thing has been difficult and drawn out, and there's still things we're trying to sort through with the lawyers, but we wanted that to impact you as little as possible. There's been so much upheaval for *you*, we were . . ."

"Trying to keep the ship steady," Dad fills in, with what I'm willing to bet is some metaphor provided by their couples' counselor. I give him a deadpan look—as if this ship has *ever* been steady. He raises an eyebrow, clearly agreeing, but only says, "What with me moving out—"

"And you off to a new school . . . ," Mom adds.

"And uni on the horizon . . ."

"And . . . well, and with things getting serious with . . . with Jeremy."

"With—what?" I interrupt. "Wait. Who's *Jeremy*?"

Mom *blushes*.

Oh my God. Oh my *God*, I'm such an idiot! Of course she's not out with friends *that* often—of course her book club didn't suddenly go from once a month to every few days. I was so busy worrying that Dad might be moving back in that I never stopped to consider why Mom was going *out*.

I can't believe my mom, the bitter divorcée, has a more successful love life than I do.

"You have a *boyfriend*?" I blurt, and look at Dad and say, "Are *you* dating someone, too? Are you both—?"

Mom cringes. "It's very early days. He's divorced as well, and he's got two kids—younger than you. We're . . . taking things very slowly."

"Right." Right, except—wrong, so wrong. Since when did my mom lead this double life where I potentially have future stepsiblings?! She starts trying to reassure me that she's not moving a whole new family into our house and that's not what this is about . . .

I'm stunned speechless, and her words wash over me.

They're still getting a divorce. This new civility isn't them trying to make it work, it's them . . . *moving on.* Or trying to, anyway. The relief is so immense I feel like my chest might cave in, and I think about how I can't wait to pour all of this in a long, rambly Discord message to Jake. He'll never believe it, he'll . . .

Not answer, because he's not talking to me.

My face must fall because Mom pauses to say, "Cerys? Are you all right? I'm sorry, darling, I know this is a lot. I didn't want to spring it on you quite like this."

"I *told* you it was too soon," Dad mutters, and she glares at him.

"No, it's not . . . it's not that, it's . . ." I really don't fancy getting into the whole Jake drama right now; this conversation has been emotionally exhausting enough already. And saying it out loud will make it real. I'm not ready for that.

I think about the *Of Wrath and Rune* episode I was rewatching earlier. Lady di Silver's family had allied with the evil usurpers in the palace, even issued a warrant for her safe arrest, and faithful Devon had tried to comfort her now that they were on opposing sides—enemies. I think about the earnest look she gave him in response.

"We are not on opposing sides, Devon. We are all making our choices for the good of the kingdom, the good of our people, because it is our duty. We are all trying to do the right thing for those who matter most to us. I cannot blame them that their path looks different than mine."

The whole duty thing and the fact they're talking about quests for long-lost magickal beings aside, she had a point.

I take a deep breath, and the smile I give my parents feels more sincere than any of the brush-offs and hasty side steps I've gotten away with for the past few months.

"I'm not upset. I'm . . . I'm glad you told me about all this. But don't feel like you have to do the whole 'forced family fun time' thing for me. Seriously. I mean, that's not exactly been *normal* for us, even before you were getting the divorce," I point out, and they pull faces, abashed. "It's . . . it's okay with me if us spending time together looks . . . different, I guess is what I'm trying to say."

In fact, I'd welcome it.

They swap another look, both visibly relaxing. Mom gets up to come and give me a hug while Dad says, "That's really mature of you, Cerys."

"All that therapy you guys have been doing must've rubbed off on me," I say, smothered in Mom's embrace, and we all laugh. She drops a kiss on my forehead.

"I'm sorry we didn't talk to you about it properly, love. We'll be more upfront and honest going forward, yes?"

I nod, and as she starts to peel away, I hug her a little tighter.

"Actually . . . actually," I repeat, then haul down a deep breath. "In the spirit of being *honest,* I've . . . well, I've been thinking lately.

About uni. About what I want to study. And I think maybe . . . maybe I'd like to do art, instead of business and media."

"You would?" Dad says, surprised. "But I thought you weren't that interested in it these days?"

Meanwhile, Mom says excitedly, "You do? Oh, Cerys, that's lovely! You've always had such a talent!"

I pull back now, staring between them. "Wait. You're . . . not mad?"

Mom laughs. "Why would we be?"

"Well, because . . . I mean, Dad always . . . I thought you both . . ."

Am I missing something? Did I imagine all those arguments between them about it?

Catching on, Mom sighs, and Dad tells me, "Cerys, just because I made decisions about *my* career doesn't mean you'll be in the same boat. We were young, we had a kid and a mortgage. I had to think about more than just what *I* wanted to do."

"We never meant for *you* to stop pursuing it, if it's something you're passionate about," Mom adds. "I think it's safe to say we both assumed you were good at it, but not necessarily *passionate* about it."

Dad raises his eyebrows at me. "Are you?"

"Y-yeah. I am. A lot."

"Right!" He stands up, clapping his hands. "Where are all those uni prospectuses? We'd better start having a proper look at their art courses."

Mom gives me a squeeze. "Have you got some finished pieces you can show us? I'd love to see them."

Omigod, *no*. As if I need to get into all the fandom stuff, too . . . But maybe that wouldn't be such a bad thing?

I've been so worried about keeping the ship steady, like Dad put it. Not making a fuss about my artwork, not wanting to lose Jake, not wanting to be too openly friendly with Anissa in case it cost me the girls, even trying to force Max out to salvage my own friendship with Jake at the cost of his . . . And where's that gotten me?

Where has it gotten any of us?

A little change might be nice.

28

"All right, spill."

"What? Where?"

I look around, horrified that I've just stained the fluffy white rug in Chloe's humungous bedroom with barely-alcoholic mimosas, but there's no mark on the rug, or on me, and I look back at her, confused.

Evie rolls her eyes, before leaning back on her hand and tossing her hair. "Not the drink, you gumball. *You.* What's up with you lately? You've been acting super weird."

The "weird" accusation hits hard, even if that's not how she meant it, but I'm spared a moment to recover by Nikita letting out a noisy cackle and echoing, *"Gumball?* What the hell kind of insult is that?"

Evie grunts. "Ugh. Don't even. It's off this show my little brothers watch. I guess they can't call anyone a 'dickhead' on TV for six-year-olds. It's on *constantly,* there is literally no escape. I keep singing the theme song all the time, too."

She gives us a little rendition, cracking everyone up, but soon enough the attention turns back to me. Daphne gives me a look that I can only describe as "mumsy"—gentle but firm, and full of concern.

"Come on, *gumball*," she says. "She's right; even after we patched things up, you've been really quiet lately and not like yourself."

"I—"

Crap. First Max, then Jake, and even Anissa figured out why I'd wanted to invite her to the Bonfire Night party. And now this! I need to take acting classes, or something. Practice my expressions in front of the mirror.

Right now, it's New Year's Eve, it's eight o'clock, and we're all piled into Chloe's bedroom for a much more low-key affair than Raf's house party. We're armed with a good playlist and mimosas that are more orange juice than prosecco, and they're all looking at me like this is a very nice, obviously premeditated interrogation.

Then Daphne raises her eyebrows and jokes, "Not to keep rehashing the shitty boy drama, but . . . is it about Jake? You haven't mentioned him at all lately. Did something happen?"

And that's the question that finally makes me dissolve into tears. Daphne cries out wordlessly while Nikita says, "Oh, babe, no! What is it?" and Chloe, next to me, pulls me into such a big hug that *she* spills half my drink over her lap.

It all comes pouring out of me in huge, gasping sobs. I work my way through half a dozen tissues before I have enough breath in my lungs to tell them the whole story.

And this time, I don't hold back.

I tell them about The Fangirl Project, about the convention in

September and Max showing up in cosplay, and the *OWAR* watch parties he crashed and how, actually, I'd come to really *like* the show, Anissa, and all the friends I've made in the Discord, but I've ruined everything.

I tell them about my parents dragging a divorce out for ages and how I'm sick to the back teeth of it.

And now I've lost Jake *and* Max *and* it almost cost me my friendship with Daphne after the party, and it's—

Nikita whistles, long and low. "You're right, babe, that is a *lot*."

Daphne smacks her in the arm.

"Ow! It is! That's not a bad thing to say, is it?"

"You should've just talked to us," Evie tells me. "Especially to me. You know my mom and dad split ages ago, after he ran off with his mistress from the office. I've done the whole 'family falling apart' thing—*ow*, Daphne! Stop hitting us!"

I sniffle; I'd forgotten that whole drama around Evie at our old school years ago, but now I remember some boys teasing her about it and how she'd show up to school with bloodshot puffy eyes. She's right, I could've talked to her about it—she probably would've understood.

"I never thought about it," I admit.

"So all those times you've been busy *working on your art course-work*," Nikita asks, "you were ditching us to hang out with Anissa?"

"I haven't been *ditching* you . . ." Hmm. "Okay, maybe I was a little bit. But we *were* working on our coursework, too. It's just, you know, Anissa isn't exactly . . ."

"Normal?" Nikita snorts.

"That's mean, Nik," Chloe tells her, but Nikita only shrugs.

"I was going to say 'your kind of person.' And—" Something bubbles up in my chest, and I swallow the lump in my throat. "And Chloe's right, that *was* mean. Anissa's great. She's funny, and kind . . . She's just shy, that's all."

"And a total *weirdo*," Nikita presses.

"Why? Because she likes different stuff than you?" My cheeks feel warm, and Nikita does a double take, but none of the girls are looking at *me* like I'm in the wrong for calling her out, and I remember my conversation with Max through the bathroom door. "Why does it matter to you if she likes different stuff? It's not hurting anyone. It makes her happy. Why is that such a problem?"

You could hear a pin drop, and I'm surprised to realize that the others are all waiting for Nikita to answer.

"I—I don't . . . Well, I just . . ." She blinks a few times before saying, "Yeah. Okay."

I blink back at her. We are in a blinking match of epic proportions. I have no idea who's winning.

"Okay?"

"Okay," she repeats. "Yeah, you're right. It . . . shouldn't matter? I *was* mean?" Even though she phrases them as questions, she looks sincere; just awkward.

"*And?*" says Daphne.

Nikita rolls her eyes, but says, "And . . . if you want to bring Anissa along to Thursday morning Costa debriefs, I won't make digs at her or . . . be mean. I'm not saying I *get it,* and she *is* kind of weird, but . . . yeah, whatever. If you're cool with her, I am."

Chloe makes a funny squeaking sound.

Evie says, "Me too. I'm okay if she wants to hang out. As long as it's not all fandom stuff."

"It's not."

"Is she a witch?" Daphne whispers, wide-eyed and deadly serious.

"I don't know! Well . . . I never asked. No? That's not *really* a thing, is it?"

"That's not really a thing," Nikita says.

"It totally is. Her nan—the Irish one—is a psychic," Evie says knowledgeably. "I remember her saying in primary school. Her nan's still got a website and stuff, she does readings online and seances."

Nikita snorts, but her skepticism seems a little shakier now. She tells me, more softly, "Hey, you do you, Cerys. If Anissa doesn't want to hang out with us, no worries, that's up to her. It's not like you have to pick and choose, or anybody's giving you an ultimatum."

I must look surprised, because all four of them laugh.

"Yes, God forbid you have *other friends*," Evie deadpans. She waggles her fingers at me. "It's us or nothing, or I'll curse you."

This time, it's Nikita who gives her a light backhanded swipe on the arm, while Daphne shudders. "Don't even joke about that sort of stuff, it creeps me out!"

"I actually think it's pretty cool," Chloe mumbles. She gives me a squeeze, her arms still wrapped around me from earlier. "And Anissa's hair looks *much* better these days. Good for her."

"Listen," Daphne says. "I swear, any time I bring up boy drama, I *hear it*, I do, but . . . can we just go back to the Jake stuff for a second? It was a *big deal*! This is your best friend we're talking about, the love of your life, who *apparently* fancies you back based on his wild overreaction to you kissing another guy . . . although frankly, if he's that pissed off, you're better off without him. What a jealous, sad little *boy*. I can't believe he's just cut you out of his life like that! He never seemed like that kind of guy when you talked about him. Even if he *is* butthurt about you kissing his friend—"

"Did you *really* kiss the cosplay guy?" Evie interrupts. "Have you got pictures?"

I nod and reach for my phone. As much as I appreciate where Daphne's coming from with the Jake slander, I am—for once—more comfortable talking about Max instead. I still want to hope that maybe, somehow, there's a chance to repair what Jake and I had.

This is just our act three conflict before the end of the movie. All good rom-com heroines need to think they've lost the man before they get the grand gesture, don't they? And this is *Jake*. We've been too close for too long to let this go.

I find the Brayden Brown selfie from Comic Con and point Max out, explaining, "Except obviously he doesn't have long white-blond hair like that. Although his hair is a *little* long. And—"

"Is this him?"

Daphne's shoving her phone in my face now, and I realize it's a photo of the soccer team Max plays on, a shot of him kicking the ball. When I just stare, she says, "Jake tagged the team in his profile."

Before I can confirm or deny, Evie's snatched it, and pokes her tongue out over her teeth as her jaw drops.

"Cerys, you've been holding out on us! Look at his *legs*! Look at his butt!"

"I can't say I've ever noticed his butt . . ."

"Too busy ogling his pointy ears," she teases, and I flush—not because she's right this time, but because that's *exactly* the sort of thing I was worried about them saying.

But the general consensus is that, yes, Max *is* hot in that edgy, interesting, Adam Driver–esque way, even if they also find the cosplay thing strange, and stare at me too hard when I say things like "pauldrons" and "bandolier."

"So is it like . . ." Chloe's eyes go wide, suggestive, and she's blushing when she whispers, *"Role play?"*

"Oh, no, that's LARPing. Live action role play."

Again, they stare at me, and I realize I've become someone who knows what LARPing is.

"Kinky," Nikita deadpans.

"Omigod not *that* kind of role play!" I cry, laughing, realizing I've misunderstood. "I thought you meant like when people go to those renaissance fairs and get dressed up and pretend they're actually an elf warrior or something. Not like *that*."

"Hmm, I don't know," Daphne murmurs, taking my phone to look again at the Brayden Brown selfie. "The wig's kind of hot."

Now it's her turn to feel the full force of everyone's stare.

"What! I've seen a lot of TikToks of Henry Cavill in *The Witcher*. It *is* hot."

"Are you a secret nerd, too?" Chloe teases her.

Daphne rolls her eyes and hands my phone back. "Nope, just a sucker for a good jawline. Not, obviously, that there's anything wrong with being a nerd and liking that stuff, Cerys, it's just, um, it's not for me, I don't think."

"R-right, yeah, th-thanks."

They're not going to cut me loose or mock me. They're not going to shun me. They don't necessarily *get* it, but . . .

Max was right; I don't have to pretend the things I like don't matter to me just for other people's sake. I don't have to make my life smaller to accommodate what *they* think is right, just because it's "the done thing."

I'm still reeling, waiting for the other shoe to drop with bated breath, when Chloe bursts out with—

"I'm a Twitch streamer!"

"You're what?" Nikita says. "Like, video games?"

She nods, and bites her lip before saying, "I fell into an internet hole during lockdown and got really into collecting Pokémon, and then I started playing the video games, and now I have twenty-three thousand followers."

"And you didn't tell us . . . *why*?" Daphne cries, outrage written all over her face. I wince on Chloe's behalf, and Chloe stammers while Daphne barrels on, ignoring her. "I cannot believe we've been friends for eight years and you've *never,* not once, mentioned this! I could've been throwing you *Pokémon*-themed birthday parties! Buying you socks covered in Pikachu for Christmas, instead of ones with horses!"

"I still like horses," she says. "But, um, sometimes I'm not at show-jumping classes. I'm streaming."

"This is *madness.*" Daphne snatches her phone up and narrows her eyes at Chloe. "Now tell me where to find your channel so you can have twenty-three thousand and one followers. Also, Cerys, should I block Jake on Instagram? That seems appropriate."

"I think we should get drunk and DM him to call him out on being such a gumball," Nikita says, making Evie groan and mutter into her hands, "I'm never going to live that down, am I?"

I shake my head, smiling. "You don't need to block him. And I don't want to call him out. I'll . . . I need to deal with it. He's avoiding me, but we've been friends for too long to just *fizzle out* like this. If he doesn't want me around anymore, I want him to tell me. And not over a drunk text."

"Fair," Nikita says, and that's all we say of Jake before we make Twitch accounts to follow Chloe's channel, and then after enough pestering I cave and let them read some of my fanfictions, which gives us all a good giggle.

Later, I text Anissa to wish her a happy New Year, and then ring in midnight with a shouted countdown and Buck's Fizz with the girls, feeling light and giddy in a way that has nothing to do with the drinks.

It feels like a good way to put the past year to rest, even if something is still missing.

OWAR Discord #324
#general

@wizeguy
Happy New Year, everybody! Hope the hangovers aren't too bad today! Any resolutions?

@ladyanissadishipper
Lol no hangover here! Quiet one in with my parents and the Big Fat Quiz of the Year 😊 Happy New Year all! I'm so glad I found you guys, this Discord is such a special place. My resolution is to be braver and try joining in with some more things like this!

@fauningforhim
The hangover here is BAD. Dry January sounds very appealing right now . . . Happy New Year, everyone!

@sirmoonypants
Happy NY! Resolution: actually upload the 342,000-word OWAR fic I've been working on!

@fauningforhim
I'm happy to beta-read if you need!

@thesebootsweremadeformoonwalking
Ditto! Happy New Year's, gang!

@silversmithhh
Hangover? Pfft. Ya girl's still dronk. And also down to beta-read fics, just sayin

Private chat with @runicrascal

@mythicwitch
My resolution is to try to fix things between us. I'm sorry. I miss you. I miss our chats, but I understand if you still need space. Hope you had a lovely Christmas and New Year x

@runicrascal
Happy New Year, Cerys

I've missed this too x

I mean, who else is going to spam me with 87 messages about the OWAR episode finale?

@mythicwitch
Nobody in this forum, that's for sure #fakefans

I really wasn't sure if you were going to reply. Thanks for giving us another chance

@runicrascal
For you? Of course

Until the end

THE NEW
& IMPROVED
FANGIRL PROJECT

1. Fix things with Jake (APOLOGIZE! But also he should too?). This may require a grand gesture. (Borrow a horse from Chloe? Ride to Jake's house in full Lady di Silver cosplay???)
2. Invite Anissa to Thursday morning debriefs.
3. Invite the girls to half-term art showcase with my OWAR fanart coursework (invite Mom and Dad!??).
4. Tell Jake about Chloe's Pokémon videos ~~if~~ WHEN you fix things (he'll love it).
5. See Max. Apologize. Actually be friends, this time, maybe. (~~Maybe more??~~)
6. Be more fearless.
7. Watch the final season of OWAR! With or without the boys!

January is as much a blur as December: I end up taking on extra shifts at work, school feels more hectic than ever, and now that I'm not avoiding the girls or trying to keep my friendship with Anissa so secret, I make more time to see them all. Anissa even joins us for a few Thursday morning trips to Costa before class; it's awkward at first, with Nikita being guarded, Daphne working too hard to carry the conversation, and Anissa being overwhelmed and shy—but she and Chloe bond quickly, and she has the same dry sense of humor as Nikita, a fact that seems to surprise them both. They're not all instant besties, but nobody expected that. It's kind of nice to see them all opening up, though—and to feel like I'm doing the same thing.

It's nice to feel like after all the years I spent taking Jake's lead when it came to friendships, I can finally return the favor for someone else.

Jake is still quiet over text, even if I do get a couple of *actual* replies every so often, but at least the Discord chat is nonstop. Things still feel off-kilter because we aren't hanging out in person (though he is spending time with Anissa), and because I haven't seen Max since our kiss, but it doesn't make me spiral and panic the way it did before.

Maybe Jake had a point about me tagging along: I *do* feel more independent these days. And I feel happier, too. This must be how Max feels all the time, I think. Wholly, unashamedly himself.

The true weirdness isn't in me mentioning some fanart I'm working on to the girls, or Anissa boldly swapping seats in history to sit by me and Nikita, but at home—which is actually *good,* for once.

The forced friendliness between my parents has worn away into something more comfortable. Dad still comes by, but it's usually—as I now know—when Mom is on a date with her new boyfriend, Jeremy. I even go visit Dad's new flat. We pick out paint for my bedroom there, and I notice there's an easel set up in the living room, and a box of shiny new acrylic paints.

"Working on something?" I ask him.

"Not yet . . . I'm out of practice. I've signed up for an evening class, though. You inspired me to try to get back into it, and actually your mom encouraged me, too."

"She did? Seriously?"

Dad puts an arm around my shoulders. "And here we thought we did such a good job of shielding you from our problems. I know things have been tough, kiddo, but it's going to get better for all of us from here on out, I promise."

Then one morning, when I'm pouring cereal before school and Mom is waiting for the bagel in the toaster to pop, she says, "Jeremy and I have been talking, and I wondered if you might like to meet him, soon. Maybe he could come over for dinner one night? Or we could go out for lunch somewhere."

She says it totally offhandedly, like she's asked me to pass the butter out of the fridge, but I can feel the tension radiating off her.

I think about it for a minute. My brain can't quite wrap around the idea of Mom with someone who's *not* Dad, but equally, the idea of them as a couple has been so toxic the past few years, this might be a breath of fresh air. And I guess it's nice that she's found someone?

I remember my chat with @runicrascal when he mentioned his dad being upset about the reality of an empty nest after he goes off to uni, and I decide this will be a good thing for Mom. For Dad, too, who's apparently not dating anyone right now but is "open to the idea if he meets the right person," proving that my "soppy romantic" trait isn't something I only inherited from Mom.

"Yeah," I say, and the nervous lines in Mom's face relax away into a tentative smile. "I'd like that."

Also file under things I'd like: to finally, FINALLY, get through season four of *OWAR*. Now the chat with Jake (via Discord, at least) is well and truly back to normal, and as February slides in with sleet and pale skies and long nights and more time to myself, I spend a few evenings settling in to watch it properly. I have to try not to hurl my laptop at the wall or scream when Lady di Silver and the Moonwalker cross paths again and have *the* best sexual chemistry and tension I've ever seen onscreen, or when Daxys, now a palace guard again, comes across Roach being interrogated in the dungeons about the rebellious Rascals.

Jake obviously receives my every thought and reaction about the show via Discord. I wait for him to suggest a proper watch party again, so we can sit down and share the experience together, but he never does, and I'm not quite brave enough to ask him. I still have a lot of making up to do, and I don't want to fracture the friendship we've begun to rebuild too soon. Especially with him being so *meh* over text. It's hard to know where the line is now, and I can't risk it.

Plus, those watch parties might involve Max, and . . . I'm not sure how I feel about that. Beyond the flicker of *something* akin to the warm fuzzies that I try not to think too hard about.

One boy drama at a time, please.

Saturday night rolls around and I'm up to the finale of the show. It's pretty much caught up to the books at this point, and from what I've gleaned in the Discord threads, this episode is another "doozy."

Still, I'm in *no way* braced for what unfolds.

At last, the main cast has assembled. Daxys broke Roach out of the dungeons and they stumbled across the Moonwalker; Téiglin has banded together with Rogdan and the Rascals, along with a couple of his fellow forest creatures from the Gilded Glade; Lady di Silver and Devon have been traveling with a trio of goblins and a blind, aged blacksmith dwarf who forged the Eldritch King's crown. Everyone has met up and joined forces, shared theories and legends and answers, and put their magick together, and now they've found the Eldritch King at last.

I can't help but hold my breath, laptop balanced on my stomach and phone poised, half forgotten, in my hands. Wasn't the whole point of this convoluted plot to *find* the Eldritch King so he can be restored to his throne and save the realm? What more story can there possibly be after this, to warrant at *least* another season and what's rumored to be three more books? There's only seven minutes left. Maybe they'll end it on a cliffhanger of everyone walking into this hidden cavern in the woods, but they won't actually *find* him yet?

Even as I think it, the cast spill into what can only be described as a sort of throne room, bowing and dropping to one knee before a throne made of white birch with roots tangling into the ground and branches weaving high. The pale, wizened man upon it seems like he could be made of the same bark; the makeup department have really knocked that look out of the park.

"*O King*," says the Moonwalker, and Lady di Silver cuts him a look, irritated he beat her to the punch. "*Long have we searched for you, and finally destiny has led us all here, to restore you to your rightful place.*"

Téiglin whispers to Rogdan, "*He's even older than you are. I didn't think that was possible.*" It earns a few snickers from the Rascals, and a long-suffering but fond eye roll from the grizzled man with his broken glasses.

Lady di Silver pitches in, "*The realm is dying, my liege, and a new age is upon us—one of bloodshed and anarchy—if we do not stop it. You are the only one who can save us all.*"

There are similar weighty comments from some of the other

characters, and the Eldritch King's pale, milky eyes sweep over them all. He finally opens his mouth, and I wait for the inevitable *Of course I will help,* or whatever, but instead all that comes out is a bone-chilling laugh that makes the hairs on the back of my neck stand up. His eyes turn black, his mouth gapes open too widely, and the flesh seems to rot from his skin, the birch-tree throne creaking and snapping around him.

@mythicwitch
WHAT

WHAT DID I JUST WATCH

WHAT DID I JUST WITNESS

THEY SPENT FOUR SEASONS TRACKING THIS GUY DOWN JUST FOR HIM TO BE A TRAP???? WJAT

ASJSDKFJFK

HE JUST TURNS INTO MOTHS? THE CAVERN COLLAPSED? HE TOOK LADY DI SILVER?!??? IS ROGDAN DEAD? WHHAT IS THIWS

@runicrascal
And thus the newbie becomes a full convert

@mythicwitch
I don't like it, take it back, this show has ruined my life

@runicrascal
Brilliant, isn't it?

@mythicwitch
I am actually genuinely literally shaking. That was incredible

Wait so is the Eldritch King even real???

Omigod Devon and the Moonwalker are going to have to team up to save my gal Lady di Silver aren't they aren't they yesss

@runicrascal
Haha bet you're already writing the fanfic for it! And that IS the question. We still don't know for sure. Is he a rumor planted by someone? Is he a myth? Is he actually real and just somewhere else? Is it less a person and more a title/fate and, like, Roach will end up being crowned the Eldritch King and saving the realm?

Lmk when you're ready to hear ALL my thoughts on *that* theory. I have many

@mythicwitch
I am in shock. Wtaf. I'm just staring at myself in the laptop screen wondering what to do until the next season airs in September. Is this fandom life?? How do you cope? I am NOT OKAY

@runicrascal
I think you've achieved full fangirl level status. Congrats/condolences

@mythicwitch
So tell me more about this Roach is the Eldritch King theory, I am ready to SPIRAL

@runicrascal
How long you got? (I mean that, I could talk about this for hours, and it's already pretty late)

@mythicwitch
How long have I got?

Until the end 😊

@runicrascal

@mythicwitch
OMG just finished that fic you sent last week! The one where Lady di Silver's a vampire, Devon is her familiar, and the Moonwalker is a vampire hunter—what a roller coaster! Can't say the amount of angst and plot twists didn't absolutely DESTROY me though, I'm still a wreck from the s4 finale

@silversmithhh
Looooool sorry about that! (Which is to say, not sorry in the slightest hehehe)

@mythicwitch
I was talking to Anissa (@ladyanissadishipper) the other day btw, and I know you're at Cardiff uni, so we're not far at all—we thought maybe it'd be fun to meet up for coffee or something? If you wanted? @fauningforhim might be around too, we could maybe make a thing of it?

@silversmithhh
Are you kidding? I'd love that! Would be fab to meet you guys irl! Fauning's a gem, you'll love her

It's been WAY too long since we've had a meetup, we tried organizing last summer but things just got in the way and we never got around to sorting something out again lol

Have you met any of the rest of the group yet?

@mythicwitch
Just @runicrascal . . .

> **@silversmithhh**
> Fear not, my friend. Consider me your big sister in fandom, your fairy godmother of nerdiness

#general

> **@silversmithhh**
> MEETUP ALERT! Who's down next Sunday (Valentine's weekend) for a hangout in Cardiff? Coffee and cake and a conversation sans screen? 2pm, location TBD

> **@fauningforhim**
> Oooh, yes please! Sunday afternoon's perfect, the kids are at a party so I can put hubby on duty for pickup/dropoff!

> **@wizeguy**
> I am ALWAYS down for cake.

> **@sirmoonypants**
> I might be able to make it! Will let you all know asap

> **@thesebootsweremadeformoonwalking**
> I should be free! Maybe if there's enough of us we could look at booking a room in one of the board game cafes? There's a place one of my friends uses for D&D nights

> **@ladyanissadishipper**
> YES PLEASE I WOULD LOVE THAT
>
> I NEED SOMEONE TO PLAY CATAN WITH
>
> My parents are absolutely rubbish at it lol, it's boring always winning!

@wizeguy
Bloody love Catan. I'm in!

@runicrascal
Sunday 2pm, sounds like a plan. See you all there!

30

"Where did you say you're going again?" Dad asks, loitering in my bedroom doorway, car keys in hand, while I hurtle about my room grabbing my jacket, my shoes—no, not *those*, what am I thinking?—and being generally very, very late.

We were supposed to leave eight minutes ago. I'll miss the train!

And I really don't want to be late to my first proper fan-meet with the local *Of Wrath and Rune* Discord, and Anissa's already waiting at the station for me. She doesn't want to walk in on her own, I know.

"Board game café," I respond. "Have you seen—? Never mind, there they are. And where's . . ." I cast about for the postcards I made—personalized fanart of everyone's favorite characters. It's kind of like the Taylor Swift friendship bracelets, I figure, only nerdier.

They *were* on the desk, but I see Dad's picked them up to look at.

"Did you say it was with some *internet friends*?" he asks. He frowns at me. "Your mother mentioned Anissa's going too, but is this . . . safe?"

"It's not just Anissa. Jake's going, as well. There's a few of us."

And Max, too, according to Anissa . . . My heart squeezes, thinking about actually *seeing* him again. At least we'll be surrounded by other people, so maybe it won't be so awkward? Maybe he'll be the haughty, annoying guy from those early watch parties, and I won't even *mind* that he never reached out to me after our kiss.

If he's the guy from the party . . . open, and vulnerable, earnest and confident, and *sweet* . . .

I am *not* prepared for that.

I shove all thoughts of Max aside. I can't afford to get distracted by him today; it's too important.

"And it's for this . . . fantasy show." Dad holds up the postcards, and I snatch them to shove in my bag. "I thought that stuff was always more Jake's thing."

"It was. But it's mine now, too."

On my own terms.

"Are those pictures for your internet friends?"

"They're just *friends*, Dad, you don't have to call them *internet friends*. Besides, Chloe does stuff like this all the time with other Twitch streamers." A thought strikes me, and I look at him in horror. "Oh God, you don't think it's totally dorky for me to bring them paintings of their favorite characters, do you? Is that really weird?"

He laughs. "It sounds just weird enough, if you ask me. And

those are really bloody good, Cerys. Now *come on*. You're late enough as it is!"

I really am, and we make it to the train station with three minutes to spare. Dad spends the whole car ride asking me with great interest about the show that's inspired my recent artwork and helped me forge new friendships. I wouldn't be surprised if he starts watching it when he gets home.

Anissa's waiting nervously between the platform and the parking lot, and I swear I hear her sigh of relief through the car window when she spots me and waves.

"Thanks for the lift!" I say, already hurtling out of the car.

"Of course. Have a nice time with your not-internet friends. And—Cerys."

I pause, not quite shutting the door, agitated because he sounds serious, and I really don't have the time for some lecture. Mom already did that. I ended up having to swap numbers with Heather/@silversmithhh so we could FaceTime and Mom could see she was a perfectly normal nineteen-year-old woman. Still, I try not to sound too annoyed when I say to Dad, "Yeah?"

He grins. "Those paintings are *really* good. Maybe you can show me and your mom some more of your work properly sometime? And show us what we're missing with this series, if it's inspired you so much."

"Er . . . yeah. Yeah, okay. I actually have a showcase coming up with school in a couple of weeks for the Eisteddfod . . . Maybe you guys could come to that?"

"Cerys!" Anissa yells. "The train!"

I shout a last goodbye to Dad and hustle over the bridge with her to the other platform. As we collapse into some seats, my heart is thundering, but I think that has more to do with the adrenaline rush of what today is about than the dash for the train.

I'll get to meet everyone, this odd collection of friends I've come to know and cherish over the past six months and never would've met without *OWAR;* and, more important, it's the first time I'll be seeing Jake since the fireworks party.

And Max. But I'm not thinking about Max. *I am not— thinking—about—Max!*

My stomach in knots, I unlock my phone to look again at the last few texts with Jake to try to reassure myself.

Me

> Hey, I just wanted to say I can't wait to see you tomorrow at the meet-up, Anissa mentioned you were definitely going. I've missed hanging out with you x

Jake

> Me too. I'm sorry Cer, my head's just been all over the place. Everything after the party was just . . . I dunno, it's a lot to explain?

Me

> I really never meant to hurt you

I know. Me either. I'm sorry. See you tomorrow? X

The texts might be short, but they feel honest and *weighty* in a way his other texts lately haven't, and ever since, I've been toying with an idea I can't quite shake. A grand gesture, per The *New and Improved* Fangirl Project.

Something I know I'll regret if I don't do.

Because, really, there's only so long we can do the constant messaging and flirty banter over Discord while pretending like we're keeping each other at arm's length, isn't there? I know it feels safer and less scary when we use *OWAR* as a front, but that doesn't make it any less *real*.

I thought I didn't want to ruin the friendship we'd salvaged, but—it's so much *more* than that, isn't it? My longtime crush. The endless late-night conversations. His reaction to the kiss with Max. That's not just *friendship,* is it?

"Are you okay?" Anissa asks me. Her leg hasn't stopped jiggling, but she's nervous for different reasons.

I turn my phone screen off, and take a deep breath before smiling. "I'm perfect. *Today* is going to be perfect. I think . . . Anissa, I think I'm going to tell him how I feel."

She beams at me, showing the gap in her teeth, and gives an excited wriggle in her seat. "About time!"

I laugh. "Is it that obvious?"

"You *both* are. Never mind Moonsilver, I'm shipping Mythic-rascal these days."

"You really think he'll take it well? That he . . . he feels the same way?"

The level gaze she gives me reminds me that she might even know Jake better than I do currently.

I swallow a shriek, trying to contain myself.

I'm on my way to meet up with my fandom friends, with Anissa, and I'm finally going to tell the boy I like that I love him.

It really is all coming together.

When Anissa and I enter the back room of the board game café just before 2 p.m., the place is already packed. It's not a very large space, but it's full with about fifteen people—faces and voices I don't instantly recognize, even if I've known these people for months.

A blond girl who's five foot nothing comes barreling toward us, enveloping me and Anissa in the same hug. "Mythic! Lady di Shipper! You came!"

When she pulls back, I realize I saw her on FaceTime just two days ago. "Heather?"

She grins. "That's me!"

"I thought you'd be taller!" I blurt, then feel my cheeks flame as I stammer, "I—I mean I thought—in my head, you were like five foot ten, or something. You just—not that you're—"

She laughs, not offended. "I totally get you. It's definitely the weirdest part of meeting someone IRL—finding out how tall they actually are! I thought you'd be more my height, but that's probably 'cause of the angle of that Brayden Brown selfie . . . Anyway, come meet the others!"

Heather grabs us both, introducing people by their screen names and *then* their actual names, which is actually really helpful. @fauningforhim is Fiona, a willowy brunette with thick-framed glasses and a shy demeanor; @wizeguy, aka Andreas, is a stocky guy not much taller than me or Anissa, with a broad, wonky smile, who gives everyone big bear hugs. Sam, @sirmoonypants, turns out to be a beefy bearded guy and looks more like he belongs in a punk rock band than studying economics, while @thesebootsweremadeformoonwalking is a waify woman in her fifties named Theresa—with her nose ring, pinstripe trousers, and matching waistcoat, she's also not at all who I imagined.

Mostly everyone's from the Discord, but some people brought their partners, and it turns out Anissa and I are the last to arrive. A waiter comes in to take our drink orders, and as the group starts splitting up to grab tables and board games, I see two people talking in the corner.

My heart leaps. Contracts. Falls to the pit of my stomach. Does somersaults.

Generally, goes a little haywire.

My mouth is dry and my palms sweat, but I'm suddenly laser-focused. Maybe it's not the perfect time—but when is? It never is! I should just do it. Shouldn't I?

I'm already walking over, so I guess I really *am* doing this.

Jake is standing with his back to me, and Max is distracted by the rules on a card game box, so they don't notice me until I'm right there.

It's Max who sees me first, doing a double take and then opening his mouth like he's about to say my name, although he never quite does. He just ends up staring at me, which, really, is fair enough, because I'm stuck doing the same thing. Staring at his parted lips, thinking that the last time I saw him, *I kissed him,* and it was a really, *really* good kiss, and . . .

And I've missed him. I have.

Maybe not the way he doesn't actually talk *to* me, but his insights on the show, and the kind of conversation we shared through the bathroom door at the party, and . . . and his arm around me, like he was looking out for me, and the *kiss* . . .

I drag my eyes back up to his, and my whole body feels simultaneously on fire and like jelly—like pins and needles prickling all over my skin, and a mushy mess inside. I should say something, I know I should, but what do you say to a boy you kissed once and haven't seen or spoken to since?

Before I can manage something very casual and ordinary—maybe *hi,* or *why didn't you text me?*—Jake has turned around.

Relief floods his face and he hugs me, looking so honestly, earnestly happy to see me, like the same old Jake and like nothing's ever changed or gone wrong between us. I'm too stunned to react properly. I half-hug him back, and keep staring at Max, who keeps staring at me.

Jake finally draws away, but doesn't quite let go of me.

"Oh man, I've missed you like crazy. Can we not do this again, please? I know I've been a jerk to you, but—"

"No, it's—you—I should have . . ."

Get it together, Cerys, come on! This is your big MOMENT. This is it! Remember? And for God's sake, stop staring at Max!

Right. Yes. The New and Improved Fangirl Project.

Jake.

Not Max.

I finally wrench my gaze away from Max, looking somewhere down at Jake's feet, and then manage to look at the neck of his T-shirt, which is somewhat better, and I take a deep breath.

"I understand," I tell Jake. "I do, really. And I'm sorry. I guess I should've been more upfront with you, and—"

"No, no, Cer, this is my fault. I'm the one who—"

"But it was just—it wasn't . . . I mean . . ." *A mistake, reckless, stupid, just a kiss,* but I can't say any of those things, not with Max right there, and not when I'm trying so hard to be honest right now.

I regret losing Jake; I do not regret that kiss.

But I can't put aside the past few months and everything that's changed and grown between me and Jake over the Discord for a single kiss.

For Max.

Jake's holding on to my elbows, and he falls quiet to let me speak.

"I was scared that I might lose you as a friend, but now I'm understanding how ridiculous that is, and I thought it was all just some one-sided crush, but it's *not.* Is it? Because we—I mean, we are friends, aren't we, but it's more than that, isn't it? That's what all this has been about, right?" I gesture between us, my heart racing. My smile is nervous, but I can't help letting it spread across my face, and my voice sounds a little steadier when I carry on. "The eighty-seven missed messages gushing about a season finale, and staying up till midnight swapping theories and *talking,* properly talking—about our families and school and uni and *everything*. Analyzing why we love certain characters so much because we relate to them a little too hard! And—and being the 'newbie' and the 'rascal,' and I know things have changed between us, and we don't always talk like we used to, but—it's changed for the better, hasn't it? And we—what I mean is—"

Oh God, I'm going to do it, I'm going to actually really finally do it—

"And it's not just a crush anymore," I say, and drag my eyes from Jake's collar to his face as I say, "because I'm falling for you."

But even as the words leave my mouth, my brain registers that something about this is off—and *not* because none of this is like I would've imagined last summer: in a tightly packed board game café surrounded by *Of Wrath and Rune* nerds.

Because Jake's mouth is slack and his hold on my elbows is loose, and it's not that there's a spark of hope in his gaze or a twist of regretful rejection in his eyebrows, it's . . .

The completely, utterly blank look in his eyes.

"Cerys," he says slowly, and my smile falters. "I don't . . . What are you . . . ?"

He's not rejecting me . . .

. . . because he doesn't know what I'm talking about.

There's a small, strangled noise from just behind him, and that's when I notice the wide eyes, flushed cheeks, and speechless, stunned, confused look—on *Max's* face.

And, suddenly, it all falls into place.

Truce? Truce. In the Discord chat. Through the bathroom door.

The way he kept calling me "newbie."

The admissions about being defensive of his fandom.

Mentioning football or school or the sister at uni, and I always *assumed* it was Jake, but—but it wasn't, was it? Because Max shares the same classes, and is on the same football team; he has an older sister at uni too.

Being so *bothered* by how upset I was about Jake and Anissa at the party, like *we* had a connection of our own, enough for him to care about my feelings.

Talking to me about how I was afraid of being judged and liked, like he knew what he was talking about, like I'd told him—because I *had*.

The times he scoffed when I said something about the show or the characters, and I thought he was being disparaging and didn't believe I was genuinely invested, but he was probably just reacting to something he already knew, like it was blatantly obvious already, and went without me saying, and . . .

Oh my God.

It's not Jake.

It was never Jake.

The shock sets in, turning me cold all over. My body doesn't feel like mine; it's leaden and heavy and when I fall back half a step, I see Jake's hands drop back to his sides more than I feel it happen.

I'm not even sure which of them I'm talking to when I say, "You're not Runic Rascal."

Jake says, "Who? Cerys, what's . . . ?"

I force myself to look at Max. *"You are."*

Max gulps. Audibly. His Adam's apple bobs up and down in a hard knot, his jaw clenched so tight now that it strains all the tendons in his neck. He inhales sharply, but again, doesn't manage to say anything.

"Oh my God. Oh, I—I don't . . ." Another step back. Another. I bump into a table, and there's a clatter of some game pieces toppling over. Someone asking if I'm okay.

I don't know *what* I am.

I don't think I know anything at all anymore.

So I do what, apparently, I do best in this sort of situation when faced with a mess of my own making: I get the hell out of there.

"Cerys!"

I'm hyperventilating. I don't even know who's shouting my name. I stumble out onto the damp cobblestone street, lungs clawing down thin scraps of cold air through the vise locked around them, and I keel forward, hands on my thighs, trying to make the world stop spinning, or falling apart, or whatever it's doing.

It's not Jake. It wasn't Jake.

The kiss—that kiss—*Max* . . .

And Anissa, mentioning Runic, and I assumed she meant Jake because *they* were always talking and hanging out, and why shouldn't it be Jake?

I'm mentally scrolling back through months' worth of conversations in the Discord, all the things we talked about—*Max and I*—and suddenly so much else starts to make sense. Why "Jake" didn't invite me over to watch the season finale, why he ghosted me after I asked him to forget about the kiss because—God, no, I asked *Max* to forget about the kiss, not Jake, I said, *"Friends?"* with a goddamn *smiley face*—no wonder he didn't want to talk to me after that!

I have been the *most* colossal idiot.

I haul down another sharp breath, the cold slicing through me, blade-sharp, and straighten up. People are looking, staring, but for once, I don't care.

"Cerys," says the voice again, and when I turn, it's Jake.

His hair is damp, and there's rain spotted on his glasses. It patters down around us; my own face is wet with it, too. I hadn't even noticed.

It's exactly as it should be. A movie-worthy scene.

"I thought it was you," I say, not sure how to explain, how much to explain, what's going on. "You sent me a link to the Discord, and I joined, and you started messaging me—or—or Max did, and I thought . . . All this time, I thought I was talking to you, and when you wouldn't text me back, we were still talking there, so . . . and . . ."

There's just one huge, vital missing puzzle piece I don't understand.

My face crumples, and my voice is thick through the lump in my throat. "Where did you go, Jake? You've been acting weird with me since school started. I thought the Worlds Beyond con, all the *OWAR* stuff—I thought that'd get us back on track. And then after the party—after . . . you just disappeared on me. You're my best friend, and you *vanished*. I thought you'd forgiven me, and we were okay when we were talking again in the Discord after New Year's, but—it wasn't you, and . . . Maybe we aren't okay? I don't *understand*."

Jake's chest heaves, and his mouth twists into a thin line.

"You were so upset when you caught me kissing Max at the party," I press. "You said, 'How could you?' and I thought . . . I'd had this unrequited crush on you for ages, and then I assumed from your reaction that maybe it *wasn't* so one-sided but that I'd ruined my chance. I thought I broke your heart, or something, which was ridiculous when I thought I was falling in love with you, too, and—"

"I didn't have a crush on you, Cerys."

"Well—well, that's fine, that's—" Actually *not* the soul-destroying blow it should be, but I don't have time to think about that right now. "But then I don't understand why—"

"I didn't have a crush on *you*, Cerys," he says again, but this time, I hear it.

Oh.

Oh.

"But—but you—you . . ." I blink; the rain is making my mascara run, and my eyelashes are sticking together.

And a few more things slot into place. Jake never showing much interest in dating anybody, not being obsessed with kissing a girl he liked at a party the way some of the other guys we were friends with were. I just thought he *generally* wasn't bothered, or—or was being mature, or something. *How could you?* he'd said at the party. *You don't even like him.*

But Jake did. Jake liked Max.

"You never told me," I say, because it's all I can say. "I thought I was your best friend, I—did I . . ." *Did I do something, to make you think you couldn't tell me?* But that's not fair, I can't make this about me. This isn't like Chloe revealing to Daphne that she's secretly a semi-successful Twitch streamer and *Pokémon* aficionado.

"I didn't know," he says. He shrugs one shoulder, then sways awkwardly, and holds a hand over his eyes to shield them from the drizzle. It's getting heavier. "I mean, you know, I thought . . . I thought everyone else looked at people—at guys—and were like, 'He looks really good' or 'That's kind of hot.' I didn't think it *meant* anything. But then I got to know Max, we started hanging out a lot, and . . . I just wanted to see him all the time. I thought about him all the time. And you've had me watch enough rom-coms over the years that I just realized one day, *shit,* I've got a crush on my friend."

"That's why you were so upset at the party, why you didn't want to talk to me, after. That's . . . But—even before that, you weren't talking to me. You only saw me—" To watch *OWAR.* When it involved hanging out with Max.

Was *I* the third wheel? Or was Jake, in Max's eyes?

I shake my head. "Jake, I wish you'd just *talked* to me. We could've avoided this—this whole . . ." I wave my hand around in a vague, all-encompassing gesture, and a smile quirks the corner of his mouth up on one side.

It drops away again when he says, "I couldn't, though. Because then it would've . . . been *A Thing.* I'd have been, you know, *coming out,* and you're my best friend, so that would've felt . . . I don't know, final? Like a rubber stamp on it, or something? And I didn't even know for sure *what* I was coming out as. Bi? Pan? Gay? I didn't . . . want to choose the wrong thing, and then it not feel right." He takes a deep, shuddering breath, dragging one hand through his hair and gesturing agitatedly with the other. "It just felt like *pressure* to tell you—or any of the guys from soccer or school, or even Thomas and Ginny. I actually ended up talking to Anissa about it all. She's been a really great sounding board and it just felt sort of low stakes, because we didn't know each other all that well in the first place—and . . . and all I've wanted to do was talk to you, Cer, but I didn't know how."

He looks so lost, so *tired* right then, that I fling myself at him, giving him the big, warm hug he usually doles out so freely. He grabs me back, tight, and I hear him sniffle.

"Oh, Jake. You *gumball*."

"You . . . what?"

I laugh, making a mental note to tell Evie how annoyingly catchy that word is. "Long story," I say. "Are we friends again, though?"

His face is squashed next to mine. "Yeah. Best friends, Cer. Until the end."

"Until the end," I repeat, and it mends some of the cracks in my heart.

Jake and I hang outside for a little while longer, taking refuge from the rain underneath an awning. We talk about how this whole realization left Jake feeling confused and overwhelmed the past few months, and I joke that he should've watched *Heartstopper* with me; he might relate to Nick Nelson. But mostly we catch up on things we've missed in each other's lives—things I thought we'd talked about on Discord, but apparently not.

We stand shoulder to shoulder looking out at the rain, talking about anything and everything, and it feels like I've finally got my best friend back.

He has a great laugh at my expense about the revelation that I had a crush on him, but I can't stay too mad at him. It feels . . . *distant*, somehow, now. I attached so many of my feelings to my chats with @runicrascal that the screen name makes it unnervingly easy to separate those feelings from *Jake.*

Although that may also be helped by the mind-blowing kiss I shared with Max . . .

"So wait, wait," Jake says, gasping for breath, hugging a stitch in his side, undeterred by the way I'm currently glowering at him. "You got into *OWAR* and the conventions and stuff *just* to impress me?"

"So we could spend time together!"

"So I'd *fall for you*."

"I swear to God, Jake—"

He snorts, but tips his head back against the brick wall behind us and sighs. "So . . . you and Max, then?"

"I . . . I don't know." I squirm, twisting to face him better. "I don't want to get in the way of—"

"Of what—*my* massive unrequited crush on my friend?" He raises his eyebrows, and his smile is self-deprecating. "I don't think Max is even a blip on the Kinsey scale. And if he is, I'm not his type."

"The what scale?"

"Ah, my heteronormative friend, so much still to learn." He nudges me with his shoulder, though, smiling, and tells me, "I only just found out about it the other week, don't worry. Anyway, *point is*, he's definitely not into me. I've been spending months trying to untangle whether I'm gay or bi or what, *and* get over a crush so it doesn't ruin my friendship—"

"Mood."

"So you're not getting in the way. I mean, it's weird, yeah, and I don't have to feel *good* about it, but . . . you're my friends. I care about both of you. *I* don't want to get in the way, either."

I groan, leaning to rest my head on his shoulder. "Is this

growing up, Jake? Being all messy and mature? I don't like it, take it back."

He laughs, shifting to sling an arm around my shoulders and tuck me into his side in a way that says *tell me about it.*

And I take a deep breath and tell him, "Love ya, Jake."

"Love ya, too, Cer," he says softly, sincerely, and it's not at all like how I pictured it being.

It's better.

Eventually, though, we're interrupted by Anissa, popping out to eye us both awkwardly. "Er, are you guys . . . ?"

She leaves it dangling: *okay, coming back in, all sorted now?*

She looks at Jake, first, and seems to read something in his expression. "Did you tell her?"

"Yeah!"

Anissa breathes out, smiling, and he lets go of me to let her give him a quick, fierce hug. I hear her whisper, "I'm so proud of you," and it's a very real reminder of how close they've gotten since November.

It doesn't feel so much like someone stealing my best friend, though, more . . . like an expansion. Widening, to include all of us.

And then she turns to me, and she's cringing, nose scrunched up and thick eyebrows twisted at odd angles, mouth in a grimace. "So . . . you were *not* talking about Max earlier."

"I . . ." I was? I just . . . didn't know it? Or I wasn't at all? I don't have an answer, so I settle for an exasperated "You should've told me!"

"I thought you knew! I mean the two of you talk *all* the bloody time, and I was new to the Discord, but *I* knew who he was! Why would *you* not know? I got used to thinking of him as Runic whenever I mentioned him in conversation, and we were obviously talking about the same person . . . And you kissed him! You had this whole thing and then you kissed his face off and then said you just wanted to be friends! I don't know!"

"Apparently I didn't know," I say, and Anissa clicks her tongue, rolling her eyes at me.

"If I'd said something, maybe this whole . . ." She gestures at the two of us. At *me*. "Maybe you wouldn't have told the wrong guy you were falling for him."

"Oh, you're *squarely* at fault here, this is one hundred percent on you," I joke, but then it hits me—what she said, what I did. Max. *Max.* I told him after the kiss I just wanted to be friends, and then I stood in front of him telling *Jake* I had feelings for him—was *falling* for him—and . . .

"I have to talk to Max."

Jake and Anissa raise their eyebrows at each other.

Anissa says, "He already left."

"But I have to—"

"Cerys," she says, "come inside. Everyone's here. Text him, tell him to come back."

"What if he doesn't? What if he never wants to see me again? What if—?"

"He'll come," she tells me, and sounds so certain I can't find it in me to argue. I have to remember that it's not only Jake she's built a friendship with in the past few months; it's @runicrascal, too. Max. "Come on. We're just about to start a game of Settlers of Catan. I'll show you how it works."

Private chat with @runicrascal

@mythicwitch
Max, please come back to the board game cafe. We need to talk

(Oh God, that sounds really breakuppy, doesn't it? I promise it's not)

I know you've given me a lot of chances already, and I'm sorry I've squandered them, but it's because I didn't realize it was you I was talking to. Please, please give me one last chance

Well, I'll be at the cafe till closing, if you can make it, if you want to talk. Until the end x

(*Until eight o'clock—I don't want to miss the last train home. Bloody Sunday schedules)

Anissa was right to make me come back in; even with no reply from @runicrascal, aka *Max,* I'm suitably distracted by all the rules that come with playing Catan, trying my best to keep up with Anissa, Andreas, Jake, and Heather in this nerdier, more strategic version of Monopoly. Luckily, not too many people overheard the details of my entire heartfelt confession to Jake, but they caught enough so that now everybody knows I have, essentially, *You've Got Mail*—ed myself.

"Classic miscommunication trope," Heather trills. "I love it."

"Yeah, I'd love it a lot more if I hadn't made such an idiot of myself. You don't see them confessing all to the wrong man in the movies, do you? Meg Ryan never had to go through this."

From the next table over, Sam tells me, "Meg Ryan picked the guy who put her mom's bookstore out of business, kid, let's not pretend she made only good decisions in that movie."

Heather and I burst out laughing, while Jake asks Anissa what we're talking about and who Meg Ryan is; she shrugs, none the wiser.

For the next hour, I manage to if not *forget* about Max, at least not let him occupy my every thought. I throw myself into the meetup, getting to know my Discord friends better, and even when I give up on Catan and swap to an even more complicated game about bird-watching, I'm having a great time.

Heartfelt confessions and world-changing realizations aside, it *is* a perfect day. It's low stakes, no pressure, just as much in person as it always has been online, and it's a refreshing change to not feel like I have to do or say the right thing, wear the right outfit, or play a part. I've been doing that less at school around the girls, but with them it's more like unlearning a habit, disentangling myself from it; here, it's something I relax into right from the start. I don't worry about who they expect me to be, who I'm supposed to be.

I'm just . . . myself.

Wholly, unashamedly.

I play a blue counter, and pick up a new card, punching the air with a whoop. I slap it down on the board. "Yes! Take that, Theresa, look who's in the lead now!"

"You can't play that!"

"She can," Fiona says, picking up the rule book. "Look, if you . . ."

She trails off though, and while Theresa starts badgering her for an answer, Fiona nudges me, and I realize half the room has gone quiet—that someone's just come in.

I stand, disrupting the game board. "Max."

"What's she waiting for?" Heather hisses from across the room, a little too loudly.

Fiona scoots her chair out of my way as I scramble from my seat in the corner, and there are *way* too many eyes on us. Max looks at the others, then at me, and says, "Shall we . . . ?" while jerking his head over his shoulder. I nod, and follow him outside.

I'm not running away this time, though.

The drizzle has finally let up. The pavement shines with puddles and the sky is a dreary, grubby shade of gray. It's hardly the picture-perfect scene, but I think I'm starting to finally accept that real life doesn't always work out that way.

For a moment, we face each other in silence, and it's as tense and difficult as ever to find something, anything, to talk about.

But I have so much to say now, I'm not floundering around for something to break the silence; it's only *how* to say it, what to say first, and I take a breath—

Max beats me to it.

"I'm sorry," he blurts. "I never meant to lie to you, Cerys. I wasn't trying to . . . I thought you knew it was me. I'd said at the Worlds Beyond con about adding you to the Discord. If I'd realized, I would've—"

"No, it's not . . . It was my fault, I just . . . saw what I wanted to see. I didn't think."

"And I get it," he says, his voice solid and firm, his eyes fixed on mine. "It makes sense now why you were so upset about Jake at the party, and why you just wanted us to be friends and forget—forget about . . . what happened. I know you guys are close, so I don't want to—"

"Max," I interrupt, before he can say the same thing as Jake and I did earlier about not "getting in the way." I really can see why he and Jake became such fast friends; they *are* very similar in a lot of ways. "Max, I said I wanted to forget about the kiss and go back to being friends when I thought I was talking to *Jake*. I—if I'd known . . ."

If I'd known, I honestly don't know what I would've said.

If Max had messaged me away from the Discord and I'd known it was him, I would've handled it differently. I think I would've wanted the chance to get to know him better, maybe without a bathroom door in the way.

"I thought you didn't like me," I tell him. "You'd barely look at me, like it was *such* a hardship to talk to me any time we were in a position to have a real-life conversation—"

Max gives a wry chuckle and drags a hand back through his hair, shaking his head before looking at me again. "Yeah, because I *liked* you, Cerys. And I'm . . . I'm not like you. I'm not cool and—and put-together. I'm the weird cosplay guy who's too into this stupid fantasy series. I don't *do* this. I'm the guy whose name people don't know, remember? I know that I'm . . . well, I'm not . . . *Jake*. Of course you'd pick him. And I don't exactly have a lot of experience when it comes to . . . flirting with a girl I like."

He's so rattled, the usual aloof expression long gone, it reminds me of after Brayden Brown left the group at Comic Con—the realization that Max plays it cool a lot of the time. Like maybe it's something he's taught himself to do, some . . . defense mechanism. He drags his hand through his hair again, and I reach up to catch it, pulling it back to his side, my fingers slotting through his.

"Look, Max, *forget* about Jake. After the party, I was focused on fixing things with Jake because I missed my friend—not because he broke my heart. I kept waiting, thinking *you'd* reach out, though—I wanted you to. I just didn't realize you *had*. And I thought that what we'd built in the Discord wasn't worth losing for a kiss, not realizing that . . ."

I exhale, biting my lip at my own foolishness getting me into this whole mess. Max is watching me so closely, like he can't bear to miss a single word I say, but the way his gaze flickers down to my mouth is a *little* distracting.

"I'm not choosing Jake," I tell him. "He's not the one who . . . Well, he's not *you*. And you're . . . you're the weird cosplay guy who's too into a stupid fantasy series and—Max, that's exactly what I admire about you. I actually really *like* that about you."

Max lets out a ragged breath, staring at our interlocked hands hanging between us. His hand is big enough to engulf mine almost completely, but it trembles. I think mine does, too. The way he looks at me, his eyes searching mine, desperate, a furrow in his brow—it's like he isn't sure if he can let himself believe me.

I'm not sure I can believe it, either. That it's him. That it was always him.

"It's not Jake I've got feelings for. That whole speech I gave earlier . . . that was meant for Runic Rascal. It was meant for *you*. You're the one I want to talk to about my day, about this show, about anything and everything."

His expression softens, a smile quirking at the edge of his mouth. His fingers thread more solidly through mine.

I keep reading fanfics where the characters loose a breath they didn't know they were holding, romances where they feel some sense of homecoming; this feels like that. It makes sense now.

I say softly, "People don't always remember my name, either, you know. My friend Daphne thought I was called Carys at first."

He huffs another laugh.

"And I don't have a whole lot of experience flirting with a guy I like, either. Obviously, or I might've noticed sooner . . ." I roll my eyes. "Can we . . . maybe rewind, a bit?"

"What, start again? Blank slate?"

"No, just . . . go back a little way. Like . . . maybe to the part where I was blabbering on about eighty-seven unread messages, making up stupid nicknames, and staying up all night to talk, and realizing I was falling for *that* guy. For you."

And it's not the scary, world-stopping revelation like it seems in the movies.

It's just . . . a fact.

We've moved closer, somehow, at some point, our bodies almost flush. Now Max's free hand comes up to cradle my cheek and my breath hitches in my throat—he seems a lot more like the confident guy who strode around Comic Con in a wig and bandolier when he tilts my head up toward his.

"D'you mean that?" he murmurs.

"Would you prefer it spelled out in a Discord message? Translated into a fanfic?" I grin. "*Yes,* I mean it."

He lowers his head, not quite all the way, just close enough for the tip of his nose to graze down the end of mine, and my eyes flutter shut. My hands grip his shoulders and even if he hasn't kissed me yet, my foot is ready to pop, my knees are weak, I'll shatter if he lets me go, I'm every cliché in the book.

"Good," he says. "Because I've fallen for you, too. And I'd really like to take you on a proper date, Cerys."

My chat at New Year's with the girls swims to the front of my mind, and I blurt, half teasing, half meaning it, "Are you going to wear the elf ears?"

He laughs, and his lips are still curved into a smile when they finally meet mine, and I melt into his kiss.

epilogue

The July heat is sweltering, and I'm worried that I'm already sweating through my dress. The subway car rocks to a stop and Jake, as the tallest, is responsible for navigating our way through London, and so he cranes his neck over the people packed in like sardines with us then shakes his head.

"West Brompton," he tells us. "Next one!"

The car jolts as it leaves the station, and Jake lets out an "Oof!" when one of the prongs on Anissa's elaborate antlers pokes him in the cheek. She cringes. "Sorry! Sorry!"

She's come as Téiglin, using my art coursework sculpture as part of her costume rather than letting it gather dust in the classroom. Jake's new Daxys wings, made with Max's help, are held carefully, cautiously, in front of him—both to protect them on the journey and to protect other people from being smacked by them. The wingspan is impressive, if canon-accurately wonky.

The motion of the train makes me stumble too, and a hand slides firmly onto the small of my back, keeping me balanced and upright. When I look up to Max with a grateful smile, he teases, "Not that you need saving, my lady."

"I don't mind a bit of chivalry now and then," I respond, and go up on my tiptoes, planting a light kiss on his lips. He pulls me in deeper with the hand on my back, and obviously, I'm only holding on to his shoulders for balance, not to lean into the kiss.

What a ridiculous idea, honestly.

We're both smiling as we pull away, and by then the train is coming to another stop, the automated announcement telling us to *mind the gap* as what seems like half the car piles out into Earl's Court. There's a stormtrooper without his helmet, a couple of hobbits distinguishable by their waistcoats and very large, thick, fake feet. A Deadpool half-falls onto the platform, nimbly catching himself as he trips over someone's suitcase, and runs ahead to catch up to a female Captain America and Loki.

Once we're out of the train station and onto the main road, we find a quiet patch of pavement to fix ourselves up. Max and Jake wrestle with his wings, fixing them into place and checking that they weren't damaged in transit, and Anissa fusses with her antlers, which have gotten a little lopsided since she first put them on in the hotel room we're sharing.

I run my hands over my green dress, pressing out the creases and subtly checking that yes, phew, I have not ended up with huge, hideous sweat patches. My belt is tied neatly in place with a fake foam dagger at my hip, and I pat down my wig, feeling the intricate braids sitting exactly as they should be.

Perfect.

Jake fixes a tiny bend in one of his wings and claps his hands together, his fingerless leather gloves muting the sound. "Sorted! Brayden Brown, here I come. Do you think he'll remember me?" He's blushing; it turns out that Daxys isn't just Jake's favorite character, but he has a raging crush on the actor—which, in hindsight, totally checks out.

"How could he forget?" Max says, grinning. He straightens his bandolier and waves both hands at himself. "You're with *the* best Moonwalker cosplay he's ever seen."

"Well, he hasn't seen my Téiglin yet," Anissa says archly, a smile stretched across her face.

"Guys! Come on! What's the holdup?"

Just across the street, hopping on the corner, Chloe—wearing a cute pair of shorts and a tee from her merch store (she has a *merch store,* how cool is that?!)—is waving us on impatiently, looking agitatedly in the direction of the convention center and the crowds pouring in.

"I don't want to miss the Zelda panel!" she shouts to us. She has her day here planned to the minute: meet ups with other Twitch streamers, some panels, a few exhibitor booths she wants to stop by. Jake's got a similar schedule, actually. Max, Anissa, and I are more than happy to let him take the lead, and go with the flow.

"Be there now in a minute!" I call back, and then look at the others, a bubble of excitement rising in my chest, and a grin on my face. "All right, you rascals. Let's go to Comic Con!"

acknowledgments

As a resident "weird kid" since my school days and a big fandom nerd, I took such joy in writing this book. And as someone who spent a long time feeling like they had to justify their interest in things (including and *especially* writing!) as a teen, I loved exploring this through Cerys's lens—and I hope you all enjoyed reading it.

This is my fifteenth published book, a total milestone considering I turn thirty this year and my writing journey started in earnest when I was fifteen years old . . . (Lovely round numbers and symmetry there, I know.) So to my fellow weird kids and fandom nerds, whatever your dream is, chase it. It's so worth it.

Huge, huge, huge thanks as always to Lauren and Iny, who get a shedload of rambling voice notes of reminders to myself about a scene I want to write, or as I try to work out a plot point during edits—and who both truly understand my level of love for fanfic! Thanks to the whole rest of the Cluster of Nerds (love y'all! Nerds unite), to Aimee (OG fangirl, throwback to our spoof videos of *Merlin* and *Doctor Who* episodes!), to the Physics gang and Amy (if anyone can get on board with a lengthy debrief of *Game of Thrones* or *Lord of the Rings*, it's you lot) and to The hivE (née Gobble Gals, née Cactus Updates—here's to the *Twilight* marathons!).

No acknowledgments section is complete without a big

thank-you to my family! Thanks for always being so supportive (even if you don't "get" the shows, books, and media I'm so into!) and especially for supporting my writing. I literally (and legally, in the case of my first contract!) could not have done it without you.

And, last but by no means least, THANK YOU to all the team behind the scenes! My epic agents Clare and Becca, my editors Katie and Kelsey, along with Shreeta, Jess, and the rest of the PRH UK team, and my wonderful US team, including Emma, Tamar, Colleen, Megan, Ray, Jennifer, and Wendy! Here's to book number fifteen, and many more yet to come!

about the author

Beth Reekles is the author of the Kissing Booth series, which inspired the Netflix films. She first published *The Kissing Booth* on Wattpad in 2010, at age fifteen, and it accumulated almost twenty million reads before it was published in 2012 by Random House Children's Books. A self-confessed nerd and rom-com fan, she is now a full-time author living in South Wales and shares movie reviews on her Instagram.

authorbethreekles.com
@authorbethreekles 📷
@bethreekles ♪

Read on for a sneak peek of *LOVE & LATTES*,
a sizzling story about an overachieving girl who
unknowingly kisses the *one* guy she shouldn't the
night before her new internship begins.

Love & Lattes excerpt text copyright © 2023 by Beth Reekles. Cover art copyright © 2024 by Art of Nora. Published by Delacorte Romance, an imprint of Random House Children's Books, a division of Penguin Random House LLC, New York. Originally published in the United Kingdom as *Sincerely Yours, Anna Sherwood* by Penguin Books, a division of Penguin Random House UK, London, in 2023.

1

The club flashes blue, acid green, lilac, and back to electric blue. The bass thrums through my chest, my bones, and all the way to my fingertips, lifting me onto the balls of my feet with my arms in the air. Everyone's swaying, shimmying, and singing at the top of their lungs to a Harry Styles song that slides seamlessly into a remix of Olivia Rodrigo's "good 4 u."

For an icebreaker evening, this isn't half bad.

And this place is definitely a lot better than the Pizza Express where we spent an awkward, stilted two hours earlier this evening, swapping details of our A levels and college courses and our preferred pizza toppings. (A necessary evil, given that the restaurant was booked for us by our new employer so we could all "get to know" each other ahead of working together on the Arrowmile internship program this summer.)

Tonight is about anything *but* the impending internship.

Which is really saying a lot, because it's taken over my life for *months*, between the application process and the agony of waiting to hear if, out of five thousand applicants, I would be one of the fifteen who made it.

As of today, I am officially one of those fifteen. Tonight, we enjoy a taste of freedom and excitement before Monday, when we start one of the most coveted, prestigious internship programs in London.

Tonight, I let my hair down for once.

For me, that involves some rum and Coke, half a glass of prosecco, and dancing on the sticky floor of a too-loud club with fourteen relative strangers. Four of whom have double-barreled names, and three of whom are students at Cambridge. All of whom seemed pretty okay at Pizza Express, and right now feel like my new favorite people in the whole world.

There are hands on my hips, the brush of a body behind mine. Broad, masculine. One of my new roommates and fellow Arrow-mile intern for the summer, Elaine, a tall, bony girl with long blond hair, catches my eye and waggles her eyebrows, apparently in approval of my new dancing partner. I glance over my shoulder, staring for a moment in the flashing lights before deciding I don't recognize him; he's not part of our group.

I turn back to Elaine and shrug, not minding the attention until I'm grabbed by one of the interns, who, laughing, pulls me away from my dance partner and into a ramshackle conga line back to the bar. By the time I'm jostled to the front of the group, someone's bought a round of tequila shots and Elaine is pressing one into my hand, a lime wedge balanced on top of the glass. Someone else holds out a salt shaker to me. I follow their lead and lick the back of my hand holding the shot, spill some salt there, and pass it on to the next person.

Across the room at the other end of the bar, there's a guy.

And, God, but he's a *cute* guy. Dark, curly hair and chiseled cheekbones accented by a light scruff of stubble, and full lips. He's sitting on one of the few barstools, his elbows on the counter (which, in that light-blue shirt and in a place like this, is a risky move) and hands clasped around a drink.

In spite of all the people packed in here tonight, it's like he can tell I'm looking at him, because he lifts his head and turns in the direction of our group.

Not our group.

Me. *My direction.* He's looking at *me*.

That Feeling When

COVER REVEAL SOON!

A new romantic comedy about an avid fangirl who finds herself working on the set of her favorite fantasy show with a dreamy prince who is nothing what she expected behind the scenes . . . but could it lead her to real love?